The Rose and Her Knight

Minstrel Knights
Book 2

Cara Hogarth

ARE YOU SIGNED UP FOR DRAGONBLADE'S BLOG?

You'll get the latest news and information on exclusive giveaways, exclusive excerpts, coming releases, sales, free books, cover reveals and more.

Check out our complete list of authors, too!

No spam, no junk. That's a promise!

Sign Up Here

www.dragonbladepublishing.com

Dearest Reader;

Thank you for your support of a small press. At Dragonblade Publishing, we strive to bring you the highest quality Historical Romance from some of the best authors in the business. Without your support, there is no 'us', so we sincerely hope you adore these stories and find some new favorite authors along the way.

Happy Reading!

CEO, Dragonblade Publishing

Additional Dragonblade books by
Author Cara Hogarth

The Minstrel Knights Series
The Minstrel and Her Knight (Book 1)
The Rose and Her Knight (Book 2)

Historical Note

The Rose and Her Knight is set in Southern France, 1367, during the Hundred Years' War between the English and French. English kings had held the southwest corner of France ever since Eleanor of Aquitaine married Henry II in 1154. My fictional village and chateau of Vesian-la-Roque is at the disputed eastern edge of this English-held territory. In 1367, however, the war had temporarily moved south into Spain, where the English were helping King Pedro "the Cruel" regain control of Castile. Many French took the side of Pedro's usurping half-brother. This created a lull in war in Southern France. Rafèu, the hero of *The Rose and Her Knight*, has fought the English, even capturing and holding an English lord for ransom, but is now sick of bloodshed and remains in France.

Instead of war, Raf chooses to make music. Southern France was famous in centuries past for its troubadours—composers and performers of songs in Southern French, the *langue d'oc*. These songs were often concerned with courtly love, a concept my hero has taken very much to heart. Medieval tales of courtly love often feature chivalrous knights falling in love at first sight, worshiping the adored one from afar, and performing quests to prove their love. The *hortus conclusus*, or enclosed garden, is a frequent setting for scenes of courtly love. For example, the famous medieval French poem *The Romance of the Rose* begins with the lover-hero entering a walled garden to pluck a rose.

The medieval ballads of Robin Hood, however, were much less noble and cultured. They would never have sullied a troubadour's mouth, but they might have been uttered by a lowly minstrel. The term "troubadour" has noble, high-culture associations. Indeed, the first known troubadour was Duke William IX of Aquitaine, Eleanor's grandfather. But by 1367, troubadours were largely a thing of the past; minstrels of various kinds still existed, but were often considered disreputable wanderers with low morals. Thus Vicomte Rafèu takes a status dive from nobility to riffraff in order to pluck his elusive rose.

While the Robin Hood verse quoted in this novel is derived from original medieval poetry, the troubadour lyrics are my own.

Chapter One

Southern France, 1367

RAFÈU, VICOMTE BRUNIQUEL, was in love—deeply, insanely in love, and he had been for years. True, he had never so much as spoken to the woman of his dreams, but what did that signify? For all his efforts to date, she had proven as elusive as a shard of rainbow, no more graspable than light.

Until now.

Rafèu slipped off his horse to dirty his crakows on the cobbles of the village square. Not the most practical shoes, crakows. The long, pointed tips tangled with the stirrups and, now he was back in contact with the ground, they rather offset his balance. Raf certainly did not wish to get more intimately acquainted with the unmentionables that decorated said cobbles. But crakows were part of the costume. They were non-negotiable, as was the elegantly assembled motley of colors and fabrics that constituted his surcoat, hose, and cloak.

He padded across the *place de La Roque*, scruffy mount in tow. Yes, the nag was an embarrassment, but that was the point. A minstrel did not gad about the French countryside aboard a destrier or even a half-passable courser. Why, even this excuse for a horse might tempt the brigands that littered the hills hereabouts. Besides, a minstrel was not a wealthy man. A wandering player might count himself lucky he had a horse at all.

Raf paused in his progress to assess the inn. Not that there was a choice of accommodations in this undersized village. This was La Roque's only inn, he had been informed. But it was a sturdy-looking building, built of the local golden stone rather than slapped together out of sticks and muck. In truth, he'd settle for a pallet on the taproom floor so long as the place allowed him to practice his minstrelsy…and engage in choice gossip with the locals.

For, even more than bed or song, Rafèu craved information.

He ducked under the inn-yard arch and bequeathed his nag to a stable boy—or was it a stable girl? Hard to tell beneath all that dirt. Then Raf drew a long, slow breath and entered the inn.

Rafèu, Vicomte Bruniquel, was used to the range of reactions his presence provoked when encountered for the first time. There was always an initial stutter, a kind of startled hesitation. Rafèu wasn't sure what prompted it, nor did he really care. The hesitation was then followed by a small selection of responses, chief among which were bashful confusion, doe-eyed glances, and bravado marked by an element of forced swagger.

It seemed the responses to Minstrel Rafèu followed much the same format. The innkeeper's wife—or perhaps she was the innkeeper herself—was definitely of the doe-eyed camp. Conversely, the fellow heaving barrels about behind the wine-soaked counter treated Raf to a hard look and began to heave his barrels with rather more swagger than before.

"God's greetings, honored madam," Raf began, punctuating his address with a small bow. "This humble minstrel craves the joy of filling your worthy establishment with song. In swap for a place to lay my head and a little something to fill my stomach, naturally."

The fellow behind the counter snorted but refrained from comment. Or perhaps a snort was the limit of his vocabulary. Honored madam, however, promptly proceeded to dissolve. Eyelashes were batted. A bosom was heaved. His proposal was accepted, but Raf began to fear that the required place to lay his head would be next to her own.

He was saved from having to reject his hostess outright by the arrival of a party of travelers demanding madam's attention in no uncertain terms. Raf was able to retire to a corner of the long, dim room that constituted the lower floor of the inn, ostensibly to tune up his lute but more pertinently to survey the human contents of the taproom.

He needed locals, not blow-in strangers. This was his last stop before the chateau. He needed inside information.

But first Raf played. He was a minstrel, after all. He must act the part. So, he settled his beloved lute on his lap, melded himself to its voluptuously curved body, and entered a world of courtly love.

Canzos, the love songs of the troubadours, flowed from his fingers and lingered rich as honey on his tongue. Oh, Raf knew he was no virtuoso on the lute, not like that boy-minstrel who had turned out to be a girl. She had employed the fingers of her right hand like individual plectrums upon the strings, coaxing a waterfall of sound in their wake. Rafèu was a mere twiddler by comparison. But he didn't care. He was one with the music, the soaring, inspiring lyrics, and he sang only for her. Not the minstrel-girl Azalais, but his own elusive lady. Eglantine. His wild rose, and about as accessible as a bloom amid thorns.

I love a rare flower
Who clings to steep stone,
Caged by briar and barb
Lovely and alone.

But eventually, the song-spell had to break. His honored hostess saw fit to break it by means of a full-to-overflowing beaker of wine and a similarly filled bodice. He wasn't sure which she wanted him to engage his lips upon first. Luckily, Raf had no such dilemma.

He raised the clay mug to her in gratitude.

"My thanks, madam. My throat is in dire need of lubrication." *That, and no other part of my body.* "If you will permit, I will rest my fingers for a spell."

The contents of the bodice rose and fell in his direct line of sight. Truly, it was rather hard to peer around that mountain range to the landscape of the taproom that lay beyond, but Raf did his best.

Perhaps her tired troubadour would like to withdraw to a quiet chamber for a period? Why, the hostess was even willing to open her own quarters for his convenience. He could drink his wine there undisturbed, with only his dear hostess for company.

Raf summoned up a charmingly apologetic smile.

"My undying gratitude, madam. Forgive me, but I have a need to mingle. A minstrel deals in information as well as music, does he not? There can be no rest for this hard-used throat. I must gather what I may."

The dreadful thought occurred that madam would propose to soothe his throat by means of her own tongue, but she made do with running a wine-red finger down the column of his neck. His skin felt a mite sticky in the aftermath.

Praise God, the exigencies of the taproom dragged her away and Raf was free to mingle as his heart desired. Unaccompanied.

"Her up the hill?" A grubby thumb was crooked in the direction of the cliffs of La Roque.

Raf nodded, plastering an expression of what he hoped was but mild interest across his face. "Yes, the Lady of La Roque. I hear mixed reports of her. You look like an intelligent fellow." Perhaps a slight exaggeration. "Pray tell me what you know."

Raf beckoned the hostess over for a top-up of his new friend's beaker and settled back to hear the praises of his love.

"Word is she drove her husband to his death," was the opening comment.

It took a moment for the words to sink in. But before Raf could react, his friend was warming to his topic.

"Oh, I don't say she killed him. Not *directement*. No dagger or poison. But she drove him to it, if you take my meaning."

Raf raised what he hoped was a nonchalant eyebrow. "I'm not sure I do."

"Bah, she wasn't a proper wife to him, was she? Cold. Damned chilly Englishwoman. So, he had to take his pleasures elsewhere, didn't he? What's a man to do?"

His peasant friend took a slurp of wine. The contents of the beaker diminished by half. Rafèu regarded the fellow.

"So, the Lord of La Roque caught his death between another woman's thighs? Dangerous territory, evidently. Perhaps he should have kept his cock at home."

His peasant-informant guffawed. Unfortunately, he did it while his mouth was still on his mug. Raf surreptitiously wiped his hands on his motley. The wine stains would just add to the decoration.

"Wasn't the woman that killed him." Another guffaw. "*Mon dieu*, what a way to go. No, Ferrand of La Roque got himself ambushed on the way home, courtesy of a crew of brigands. Now, if his lady had been a mite warmer between the sheets, he'd never have had to venture abroad."

Rafèu considered inquiring into this peasant's knowledge of the intimate relations of his lord and lady, but the thought curdled the wine in his gut. One thing was certain—this particular anecdote had *not* featured in the Seigneur of La Roque's funeral eulogies.

Raf thanked the fellow for his time and his invaluable information and looked about for a more sympathetic source of information.

He found it.

The serving maid required some coaxing. She favored the

bashful-confusion reaction to Minstrel Rafèu, to the degree that her replies were almost incomprehensible.

"The Lady Eglantine is an angel."

Ah, this was more like it.

"How so?" Raf asked.

"When my *père* fell off the roof and broke his leg and couldn't work, she waived the rent, didn't she? She even came to visit him. Her, in our little house!"

There wasn't much else to be extracted from her. Mine hostess bustled the serving maid away moments after. Raf suspected madam of wishing to monopolize his attention, so far as female company was concerned.

"Reckon she's maimed or scarred or the like," the village blacksmith declared of the Lady of La Roque.

Raf schooled his features. Lady Eglantine had not appeared maimed on her wedding day, but then, perhaps something had happened afterward to change that? Not her husband, pray God.

"What makes you say that, my friend?"

The blacksmith leaned a pair of forearms the size of Raf's thighs upon the trestle. The leathery skin was crisscrossed with scars and burns, a hazard of the trade. The fellow's face was no vision of beauty either.

"Why else would she wrap herself up so? She wimples herself like an old widow. A woman like that with money, land, only one child—youngish, too—ought to be fishing for a new man."

The blacksmith scratched his beard. It grew in patches, evidently disinclined to grow on fire-scarred skin.

"I had heard the lady is beautiful," Raf said.

"*Mais oui*, the bits you can *see* are." The fellow lifted an eyebrow. Only half of it sported hair.

Was that why her husband had found other women's beds warmer? Because his wife was hideously maimed? Raf refrained from voicing the thought. He would prefer to refrain from thinking it, too. It was time to find a fresh source of information on the Lady of La Roque.

He bought the blacksmith a drink and moved on.

"Oh, she's a fine mistress, for all she's a woman."

Rafèu had located a castle retainer. He was English, a man-at-arms at the chateau—one of a total of three, it turned out.

"Well, she'd have trouble being a fine mistress if she were a man," Raf couldn't resist pointing out.

But the subtleties of gender were beyond the man-at-arms. "Three of us. Three, do you hear? That's all the men-at-arms the chateau's got. Aye, the place is perched on a cliff edge and impregnable to all but ravens, but don't she know the land's at war? Who knows what bastard'll turn up and cause her trouble? A man'd never make that mistake."

"I'd have thought she'd be aware of the war. She is English, after all."

"True, and none too keen on the French, neither. What's the woman doing here, for God's sake? An Englishwoman in a French chateau without a man to help her keep it?"

"Yet you say she's a good mistress?"

"Oh aye, can't argue with that. She never leaves La Roque. No swanning about other people's chateaux wearing velvet and lace for her. She stays at home and takes advice from them as knows how to give it. Reckon she knows every rock in the place. And God knows, there's no shortage of rock."

Well, Raf knew that already. Not the quantity of rock, though one glance at the cliffs and its resident chateau was enough to convince him of that. No, the Vicomte of Bruniquel knew all too well that the Lady Eglantine did not swan about other people's chateaux. More specifically, she had consistently refused to swan into Bruniquel, despite every incentive or temptation Raf had thought to offer. But it wasn't just Raf's chateau she had snubbed. After some inquiry, Raf had discovered the Lady Eglantine simply did not leave her own lands. No neighboring chateau was ever honored with her presence.

Well, if the mountain would not come to Rafèu, then Rafèu would have to go to the mountain. Not the most complimentary of analogies, perhaps.

Raf wandered on. It wouldn't do to pester the man-at-arms with too many questions. He might decide Rafèu was one of the feared bastards destined to cause his mistress trouble.

Before he settled for a second round of *canzos*, Minstrel Rafèu was also informed that Lady Eglantine was under a vow to remain faithful to her deceased husband unto death, that said widow never smiled, and that she never, ever laughed.

Raf sat down in his corner somewhat heavily. He cradled his lute and stared up at the cobwebbed roof beams. Rafèu was in love. That much was incontrovertible and unchangeable. He had loved the lady from afar ever since the day he first saw her. That was how love worked. True *fin'amor*, that was. The love *canzos* crooned of and courtly romances immortalized. Raf might engage in passing lusts with willing women, but that was nothing. A mere itch scratched. No one could alter his soul's yearning for the Lady of La Roque.

Not even the lady herself.

Chapter Two

THE CHATEAU WAS built into the side of a veritable cliff. It gave Raf a crick in the neck just to look up at it, so he focused on plodding up the never-ending path that zigzagged from the village to the chateau above. He had taken pity on his nag and was leading the beast rather than expecting it to carry him up the slope. Best not to kill one's mount so far from home.

By the time he finally reached the gatehouse, he understood why the Lady of La Roque felt so secure in her fortress. Any attacker who made it this far would have to take a nap before he had the energy to assault the walls.

But today the gate was open. Raf had no need to assault his lady's defenses. At least not those of stone or wood.

Getting past the gate guard, though, was another matter. The man practically gargled his English, his accent was so strong.

"Minstrel, troubadour—nay, we don't like music here. Don't sing, don't dance. Fun, what's that, for Christ's sake?"

The guard grinned at him and waited for a reaction.

"I deal not in fun, good sir, but in art," Raf said with a depreciative smile. "The art of beauty and love, no less. *Fin'amor.* The fine seduction of the senses."

"Oh, we don't hold with that sort of thing here. You want seduction, I recommend you get acquainted with your hand." The fellow's grin broadened. He'd lost some teeth along the way, probably when previous visitors lost patience and exercised their fists as a means of persuasion.

Raf summoned up what he hoped were reserves of charm and diplomacy. "Pray bear a message to your lady, good sir. A wandering minstrel begs the honor of filling this noble chateau with song and story for however long it please its mistress."

"Don't reckon it'll please her at all, come to that. Oh, aye, hold on to your horse. I'll go, I'll go. But sit yourself down and catch your breath a moment. Reckon you'll be wandering back down that hill soon as I return."

The gatehouse guard whistled up a temporary replacement, commanded Raf not to move, and plodded off, in no evident hurry to petition his mistress.

Rafèu had no choice but to settle himself on a non-too-comfortable rock and let his nag trim the nearby weeds. And wait.

His lady was an impregnable castle. It seemed she did not move beyond her walls, and entering those same walls required a downright devious strategy. No, an inspired strategy.

William and Azalais had inspired him with the romance of their minstrel disguise, their music, and their love. No matter that they'd ransomed Azalais's father for a fraction of what the nobleman was worth. They had given Vicomte Rafèu so much more than money.

They'd shown him how to storm the castle.

But first, Minstrel Rafèu had to get inside the gate.

EGLANTINE OF LA ROQUE was scratching numbers onto parchment and blotching her fingers with oak gall in the process when Osbert interrupted. Eglantine had no objection to lifting her eyes from the ledgers. Osbert was English, and he'd accompanied her to La Roque. Besides, even an eccentric man-at-arms was a welcome distraction from bookkeeping.

"We got a visitor at the gate, m'lady. Wants to come in, he does."

Eglantine's gaze dropped back to her ledgers. Osbert's presence was not so welcome anymore.

"Who is he? What does he want?"

"Didn't ask his name. Sorry, m'lady. Probably not important, though. He's just a minstrel."

"A minstrel," she echoed. "A *minstrel*? Is that what he called himself? Not a troubadour or a jongleur?"

Osbert shrugged. "Reckon he said minstrel, for all he's a Frenchy."

"A Frenchman who calls himself a minstrel? How strange." Maybe he modeled himself in the English style. French musicians did not refer to themselves as minstrels.

She lifted her gaze to Osbert again. He wasn't the most imposing of gate guards, although that was only one of the duties he took on. He was middle-aged, shortish, and about as broad as he was tall. An unlikely choice for keeping undesirables out. He also had strange notions of politeness toward visitors.

"I take it this minstrel wishes to entertain us," she added.

"Oh, not *entertain*, m'lady. He says he don't deal in fun. His words, those. Takes himself a mite seriously, I reckon. He talked about art, for God's sake."

The expression on Osbert's face set Eglantine's lips to twitching. But his words sparked a thought.

"What does he look like, this minstrel? A vagabond? A low opportunist?"

Osbert squinted. "Low? No, he were taller than me. A fair bit taller than me, come to think of it."

She sighed. "No, I mean does he look disreputable?"

"Ah." Osbert nodded, then shook his head. "No, he's got a horse and a lute, and I never saw a single rip on his clothes. Got an air about him, too. Bit above your average vagabond, I'd say."

Eglantine frowned. *An air about him.* That didn't sound promising. She propped her chin on her hand and stared at the stone wall opposite.

Then, as if her thoughts had summoned him, Con burst into the solar. It seemed the clouds had parted and sunshine streamed into the room.

"*Maman*, can I go with you to the hayfields? Can I ride Bayard?"

"Not *maman*. Speak in English, Con," Eglantine said absently. It was an old refrain, but now it was fresh fuel to her thoughts.

"Yes, *Mother*. So can I go to the hayfields?"

"Maybe," she said, still distracted.

Not the desired answer. Con scrabbled up into her lap, regardless of oak-gall ink and curling parchment, and wrapped his arms about her. "I'll be good. Please, Mother. See, I'm speaking English."

Eglantine laid her cheek on his tousled blond hair and breathed in his small-boy smell. Slowly, she slipped her arms about him. "Yes, you're a good boy. You can come with me when I'm ready. But first, Con, you must stay here and meet someone."

"Someone?" Con straightened and looked into her face. "Who?"

"Someone you don't know. Just wait and see." Then, suddenly conscious Osbert was still in the room, Eglantine dropped her arms.

She removed her son from her lap and addressed the gatekeeper. "Pat the man down, Osbert. Remove his weapons and bring him here. I will see this above-average minstrel for myself."

THE GUARD WAS taking his sweet time. Rafèu was beginning to wonder whether this gate-man with a sense of humor had exercised it at Raf's expense and would never return. He crossed his legs for the fifteenth time and surveyed the rather magnificent view spread out before him. It didn't work. All he could see was the lady as he'd seen her last, a white-faced widow at her husband's funeral.

Of course, she hadn't killed him.

"M'lady says I get to pat you down."

The guard was standing in the open doorway, a grin plastered over his face.

Raf rose to his feet with unconcern. He had taken measures.

"I take it I am invited into the Lady Eglantine's presence?" Raf unbuckled an item from his belt and handed the guard a dagger, still sheathed. "Be assured this is the only edged iron you will find on my person."

It wasn't strictly a lie.

"Still…" The guard waggled his brows. "Never pass up the chance to check for a hidden ballock, I say. Ballock-*dagger*, of course."

Upon which, both Raf and his excuse for a horse were checked. Praise God, his ballocks were not. Nor was his lute. Then both were led under the gate arch, and it was official— Minstrel Rafèu had breached the castle.

But it was only the first step. Raf found he was barely breathing as he paced behind the stumpy little guard. He passed unseeing into the keep, simply following up twisting stairs, lute in hand. If he gripped its wooden neck any tighter, he'd likely sabotage his mission entirely. What good was a minstrel with a splintered lute?

Then the guard stepped through a door and announced, "The minstrel, m'lady. Here he is, all patted down."

"Thank you, Osbert," came a cool voice.

Even in those three words, Raf could hear the accent. Elegant English. The hairs on his nape prickled.

"Stay with us, Osbert," the cool voice continued. "Well, minstrel, come forward."

Raf was standing just outside the doorway. The undersized guard was blocking his view.

This was the moment. He was about to come face to face with a dream, with longing incarnate, and Rafèu could not move. She had been his angel, his hope, his *lady* for so many years. Now that the time had come to step forward and gaze upon her face, Raf was struck by a paralysis that had never before unmanned him, not even during the siege of Combret.

Especially not during that siege. After all, it was she who had sustained him through it—her image and his true and undying love.

Now his lady was waiting for him. Would she recognize him? More importantly, would her heart?

It was too much to contemplate.

As much to escape his thoughts as in obedience to his lady's command, Raf made himself step forward. He passed under the doorway, strode to the center of the chamber, and sank to his knee in a deep obeisance, head bowed.

There was a moment of silence.

Then: "*Maman*, why is he doing that?"

"MOTHER," SHE CORRECTED Con automatically, but Eglantine wasn't looking at her son. Her gaze was resting on the figure before her. She could see little enough of the fellow so far, save the elaborate motley of his clothing and the flow of straight black hair that currently hid his face. Quite long hair for a man, she mused. Not that she was interested in his hair, of course. It was his abilities as a minstrel that mattered.

As a minstrel, not as a mere troubadour.

"I am not the King of France, nor even his queen," she said in English. "Stand, Sir Minstrel. What is your name?"

The figure rose. He did so slowly and with the grace of a dancer. Then he lifted his head and looked her straight in the eyes.

"I am known only as Raf, O Lady of La Roque. I am named for the archangel Raphael, but to call myself such smacks of pride. So, I am merely Raf, a wandering minstrel, and thus of no place in particular."

Eglantine barely heard the words returned in French-accented English. The appearance of the man before her drove them from her head, as did the expression on his face. It was a striking face, not classically handsome as her late husband's had been, but somehow more than handsome. Long black hair framed a face full of angles, high cheekbones, a slanting jaw, and an aquiline nose. And those eyes, as deeply black as his hair. They were full of an expression of...what? Eglantine could not tell, save for its undeniable intensity.

As for the rest of him, this archangel had height, evident grace, and an air of subtle power and sensuality. A darkly fallen angel. Eglantine's fingers curled.

If he wasn't a minstrel, she would throw him out of La Roque immediately.

Perhaps she still would.

Beside her, Con stirred. Then the boy stood, squared his small shoulders, and declared, "Welcome to La Roque, Minstrel Raf. I am Constantine, heir to these lands, and this is my mother, the Lady Eglantine."

Eglantine shook herself mentally. She had just been shown up by a six-year-old. A flush of pride followed. Her son. Somehow, he knew the courtesies due to a visitor to his demesne. When his mother failed to deliver, Con had stepped in.

She reached out and squeezed his small hand.

Then the minstrel smiled and swept a bow to Con. Eglantine's stomach tightened. That smile. Dark sunshine. It warmed the entirety of Raf's face, and it reeked of danger. It was time to intervene.

"Minstrel, my man-at-arms informs me you wish to entertain the inhabitants of my chateau. Is that so?"

The archangel inclined his head.

"My household has no such need for entertainment. La Roque holds no great feasts. The chateau is small, and even for its size it is underoccupied."

Some emotion flashed in the minstrel's eyes.

"Mother, can we hear him play?" The small, warm hand tugged on hers.

She hesitated. Her original idea returned, tentative.

This Raf was too striking, too French, too…well, too much altogether. But he was at least a minstrel, not a troubadour.

"Play, then," she said. "But you must sing in English, not French."

Chapter Three

S*ING IN ENGLISH?*

Had it been anyone other than his lady, Raf would have laughed. It wouldn't have been a very nice laugh, either. English was no fit language for song, especially not here. This was the land of the troubadours. Everyone knew the finest music was sung in Southern French, in the *langue d'oc*.

Besides, Minstrel Rafèu knew no English songs. He could only speak the language passably because he had entertained an English captive for the best part of two years.

Perhaps he should have simply called himself a troubadour, and then he would never have been expected to sing in such a barbaric tongue. But Raf had been set on this path by Azalais and Guilhem. They had called themselves minstrels, and it had worked for them, hadn't it? Besides, deep down, Raf suspected he didn't deserve the title of troubadour. He was a competent player, but he wasn't a divine one. An English minstrel was a lesser being.

Unfortunately, the title also implied he knew the odd English ditty.

But she was waiting, his lady in a wimple and all-too-concealing brownish gown. He had never seen her at close quarters before, and it was doing most peculiar things to his composure. Oh, she was beautiful—her wimple framed pale, creamy skin, a delicately pointed chin, an enticing arch of a mouth. And her eyes, wide, thickly lashed eyes of an indescribable green, lingered on him, ethereal, questioning, and distinctly reserved.

But her beauty was not what floored him. Raf had dallied with beautiful women before. Why, they sought him out, more often than not. But this lady would not seek him out. She was not of this world. She was untouchable, and she had dwelt in his soul for years.

Now she was warm and living flesh before him, and she was acting in most unaccountable ways. She was asking him to sing in English, a language not of love but of war.

"Well?" she prompted, and there was a hint of impatience in her voice.

It looked like it was sing in English or give up his plan. And all hope of his lady.

But what song? If he'd sung at all in his English captive's presence, it had been in French. Now Raf's mind was a blank. Without thinking, he sank onto the nearest bench. He unwrapped his lute and settled it absently on his lap, then plucked a few strings to check the tuning.

A pattering of feet registered in the muddle of his mind. Raf glanced up to see the boy before him. Constantine. The child was watching Raf with bright-eyed anticipation. He had his mother's eyes.

"What will you play, sir?"

A damn good question.

"What sort of music do you like?" Raf returned, stalling.

The boy jigged. "I like songs that tell stories. You know, adventures. Interesting stuff. Can you sing songs like that?"

An even better question. Could he? It wasn't Raf's usual fare, and nor was it what he'd intended singing to the Lady Eglantine. But the boy's words had stirred a murky corner of his mind.

An English tale of adventure in song. It was barely worthy of an English minstrel, but right now it was all Raf could think of.

Oh well, what did he have to lose? He would likely get kicked out anyway.

So, Minstrel Rafèu strummed a martial chord or two, and began:

Hearken, good yeomen,
Comely, courteous, and good,
One of the best that ever bore bow,
His name was Robin Hood.

It was a tale of a disreputable English outlaw who fancied his skill with the longbow. He wandered around some godforsaken forest and accosted monks. Hell, what was Raf thinking? There wasn't even any elegance to the verses. His lady would throw him out on his ear.

But Minstrel Rafèu sang on. At least the outlaw ballad had plenty of action to it. The boy had begun jigging again, too, bouncing on the balls of his feet roughly in time to Raf's beat.

Raf prayed that meant the small lord was enjoying himself and not in imminent need of the garderobe.

Finally—*finally*—Minstrel Rafèu got to the last verse. A few strums more, and the torture was over. His tongue felt defiled. He'd probably have to clean his lute. He bowed his head and waited for the axe to fall.

EGLANTINE OBSERVED THE minstrel. She had alternated between watching the tall, dark man and her son throughout the performance. Eglantine had heard songs of Robin Hood when she was a child in England. She'd even heard this one before, but Con had not, for he was growing up in France. And Con needed to. Well, he didn't necessarily need to hear tales of outlaws, but he needed English stories and songs.

Even better, her son evidently adored what he'd just heard.

He was bouncing more than ever now the strumming had finished. He was also bombarding the minstrel with questions. Was Robin Hood real? Why didn't the fellow use a sword instead of a bow? What's a yeoman?

And the questions were all in English. Con was speaking English without being prompted to do so, and the minstrel was scrabbling for replies in his accented English.

She still didn't want this dark archangel in her chateau. She was already tensing against the tug of fascination mingled with…what, repulsion? No, outright fear.

But just look at her son. *Hear* him. The child needed to learn of his homeland. Her son wasn't French; he was English. He must not grow up as a mirror image of his father.

She steeled herself to consider the minstrel again. Praise God, the Frenchman was not looking at her. His black-velvet gaze was fastened upon Con. Every time he smiled at her son, little creases appeared on either side of his mouth. Little crinkles at the corner of his eyes, too.

Oh God, this was ridiculous. Madness even to consider it. She wanted those eyes to crinkle for her.

But he was only a minstrel. A wanderer who would soon be on his way. Someone of absolutely no consequence.

A tingle scattered itself over her skin at the thought. He didn't matter. Perhaps, then, she could…

"Minstrel," she said.

He looked up. The smile he had been directing at Con slipped from his eyes.

"My son seems to like you," she said.

"Yes! Yes, Mother!"

"Shh." She put a finger to her lips. "I am not talking to you, Con." She swallowed a smile at his continued use of English, and addressed the minstrel. "You wish to stay at the Chateau La Roque for some days?"

"I do, my lady."

"A few days only?"

"However long you wish, my lady. I am at your command."

Ha! As if any man was ever truly at her command.

"Your stay is dependent on conditions, minstrel."

"Speak your will, my lady."

She narrowed her eyes at him. "My will is this—it is my son who enjoys your song and stories. It is for his sake that I will allow you to stay. For a time."

Eglantine drew an overdue breath. Her instincts were at war. She wanted him here. She wanted him a hundred leagues away. She also wanted Con to learn the songs and stories of England.

"You may sing in the hall during meals, as is customary with traveling players. But you shall sleep in the hayloft, not in the hall or any part of the keep. Osbert will show you where to go."

A glance at her man-at-arms, silent and watchful in the background. He would not let any harm come to his mistress.

"And most importantly, minstrel, your songs and stories will be in English."

The dark eyes widened. Dear God, it was hard to hold his gaze. Some treacherous part of Eglantine just wanted to smile at him. Thank heaven for her wimple. She willed her features to remain as bland and constrained as the fabric that framed them.

"You wish me to sing solely in English, my lady?"

"Oh, you may sing the odd French song during meals," she found herself saying. It came from that part of her that wanted to keep him here. She was afraid this Frenchman would reject her demands entirely if she didn't bend a little. It was a stupid, stupid reason.

She straightened. She had changed her mind. No, her mind was all over the place. "I give you a day's probation, minstrel. Tonight you shall perform in English in the hall." A pause. "And a little French, if you wish it."

Then, because her eyes needed some respite, she directed her gaze at Con.

"Would you like more songs like the one you just heard?" His blond hair tousled further in a bout of nodding. Eglantine allowed herself to smile. She felt her face relax and warm. "Well then, you can keep company with this minstrel during the day, *if* I decide he can stay. He will give you stories about England."

Then she lifted her gaze to the minstrel. "In English, do you understand?"

⇥⟫⟪⇤

WELL, THE GOSSIPS were wrong about one thing, at least. His lady *could* smile.

Rafèu trailed the man-at-arms toward the stables in a daze. He was to sleep in the hayloft above the horses for the duration of his stay, and it could be a very short stay indeed. His lady demanded English of him. *More* English songs. God in heaven, did the English sing at all? Raf had just exhausted his entire repertoire, and he knew beyond doubt that if he couldn't manufacture more, he was evicted.

But that wasn't the prime reason for Raf's daze.

She had been smiling the first time he laid eyes on her, all those years ago. Back then, her face had been radiant with joy. She had been about to be married, and Raf had fallen in love, instantly and irrevocably.

Today her smile had been different. It was softer, deeper, directed at her little boy, but some remnants had lingered when she turned to Raf. Now he understood why the Romans had blamed love on an irresponsible godling with a bow. Her smile had pierced him like an arrow to the heart.

"Right, minstrel man. This is where you sleep."

Osbert had come to a standstill at one end of the stables and now jabbed his thumb at the mezzanine roof above. A ladder of dubious workmanship connected the upper level to the stable floor. Raf only prayed he would not drop his lute on the way up.

"May I keep my mount in the stable?"

"Nag, more like. Did its mother dally with a goat?" Osbert

grinned at him, but Raf forbore to react. "Aye, keep your goat in the stable if you like. I've heard what you players get up to. Can't keep your drumsticks in your hose."

"Perhaps you did not notice, I do not play a drum, good man," Raf said mildly.

The grin vanished. "Well, whatever you keep in your hose, mind you keep it there," Osbert growled. "Or cozy up to your goat instead. La Roque is a decent place. You get familiar with the maidservants, and I'll make you sing like a choirboy the rest of your life."

Raf swept a small bow in reply. Better that than declare he had no designs on any maidservant…only on the Lady Eglantine herself.

Osbert stumped out, leaving Raf to negotiate the ladder in peace. Predictably, his crakows made ascending the ladder more interesting than necessary, but, once safely at mezzanine level, Raf discovered an expanse of sweet-smelling hay and absolutely no evidence that anyone else slept up here. Unless they possessed four feet and a brown, furry coat. Quite a pleasant bedchamber, all in all.

His lute stowed, Raf went to fetch his poor, maligned nag. It was still nibbling weeds outside the gate but was happy enough to swap weeds for a warm stable and hay. He was about to return to the loft to ponder the problem of English music when visitors arrived. Two of them.

"There you are!"

The voice was high and light and spoke in English. His fate was already upon him, and he still hadn't recalled a single English song. Maybe he could improvise on the theme of Robin Hood? It wouldn't take a great poet to echo the ballad he'd sung earlier.

"Margie, this is the minstrel. He's going to tell me stories."

Con entered the stables towing a young woman by the hand. Not *his* lady. This specimen of womanhood was not wearing a wimple. Her blonde curls were barely contained by a fillet, and her eyes were blue rather than the ethereal green of his lady's.

Still, she was quite pretty as maidservants went.

Then it struck him. *Stories.* Con had said stories rather than songs. His mother had mentioned the word, too. Raf breathed out. That he could do. Oh, he'd ensure they were English stories, spoken in the very best English he could manage, but stories were so much more manageable than song. After all, King Arthur was from Britain, was he not? Raf knew a whole trove of tales of the round table. He'd just have to wrangle them into English.

"What's your name, minstrel?"

Margie the maid was treating him to a coquettish smile. Raf recalled Osbert's dire warnings of singing like a choirboy. Hellfire.

Raf made her a small bow. "I am Raf, mademoiselle. And you?"

Her smile grew. "Mistress says you've got to speak English, so you must call me Margery, not make like I'm some Frenchy mademoiselle."

"Ah." Raf made a rueful face. "You are English too, Maid Margery?"

"Aye. I came with my lady when she was first wed. I was with her in England, too. Now I look out for this young master more than I fuss with my lady's hair or clothes."

"Mother wants me to speak English just as well as French," Con broke in. He screwed up his small face. "Why? I am a French lord. This is my chateau; these are my people. My father was French."

Margery leaned close to Raf to murmur, "What he means is I get to play nursemaid 'cause my lady wants the little lord to speak English."

The maid did not lean away noticeably once she'd finished. It gave Raf an idea.

"So, are you here for stories now, Lord Constantine?"

The boy blinked. "That sounds funny. Lord Constantine. Make me sound like a...like—"

"Like a Roman emperor? Your Imperial Mightiness." Raf swept an obeisance so deep that it could have doubled for a stable broom.

The small lord cackled.

"Constantine was made emperor when he was in England," Raf said, digging into his history. "Maybe I should tell you that story, Your Grace."

"Yes! Yes! Oh—" The small face fell. "But not now. I am to ride out with Mother now." The grin returned. "We're going to the hayfields. I shall ride my own horse, you know."

Thank heaven for small mercies.

"Does Margery go with you?"

"Oh no. *She* doesn't like horses. Says they're nasty things that kick and bite, don't you, Margie?"

Raf turned his smile upon the maidservant, and watched the color dawn in her cheeks. "Perhaps, then, Margery could assist me while you are busy galloping across the fields, Your Mightiness."

"Yes, Margie. You stay and help Raf." Con puffed himself up into an imperial pose. "Help Raf. It is my Roman-emperor command."

Chapter Four

RAF WATCHED THE boy disappear out of the stable door, presumably in search of his mother and the promised fields.

"What do you need me to help you with?"

The question was cast in a decidedly breathy tone. It came from right beside him. Hmm, this was going to be tricky. He couldn't just ask outright.

"Will I be keeping you from your duties, Maid Margery?"

"Oh no. Now, has Osbert shown you where to sleep? Con said you were to sleep in the hayloft. Have you got some bedding? Did Osbert show you the well and the garderobes and the midden?" She pulled a face. "That Osbert, I wouldn't trust him to wipe his own arse. Oops." A hand clapped over her mouth. "I do gabble on. So, what about dining? Do you know where to sit? You're to play at the evening *repas*, I think."

Well, he was getting plenty of practice in English, anyway. But only of the spoken variety.

Raf smiled. "Pray show me the sights of the chateau, fair maiden. Do not neglect the stately garderobe or the mountainous midden. I see you understand a minstrel's needs well."

Oh dear, Margery looked set to dissolve. Perhaps he was laying it on too thick. Best get to the point.

"Do tell me also of your lady's English background. What music does she like? What music do *you* like? I am a minstrel, fair

Margery. I crave new songs. Pray sing me some of yours. I care not for meals when I can dine on song."

EVERYTHING WAS AS it ought to be at the hayfields, so far as Eglantine could see. The peasants were scything and raking and heaping; there was gold dust in the air and mice scampering and hawks hovering overhead. Even better, Con had neither fallen off his pony nor sent it careering through the hay workers. Admittedly, she had turned her back for a moment only to find Con burrowing joyfully through a pile of hay. His hair and clothes were a mass of itchy shards. Now it was imperative to find Margery to assist in the stripping and bathing of one tired and itchy boy.

But the maidservant was proving elusive.

"Stop scratching, Con. You'll only make it worse."

The boy was grumpy and wouldn't listen. Eglantine sincerely hoped it was simply an infestation of hay shards.

"Oh, for heaven's sake, where's Margery?" She spoke to the great hall in general. She and Con had combed what seemed the entirety of the chateau.

"That minstrel wanted her help," her son saw fit to mention now. There was a brief cessation of scratching. "I gave her my imperial command."

Eglantine felt her brows shoot up. "Your imperial command? I had no idea I had given birth to royalty."

But Con wasn't listening. He'd found a new itch.

She took hold of his small shoulders. "Go to our chamber and take off your clothes, Con. All of them. I'll be there just as soon as I've found Margery."

And she set off for the stables.

SHE HEARD THE music before she entered. The rippling notes of a lute. *He* was playing. The hairs on her arms prickled. She stood still before the stable doors.

But the voice was not that of her dark minstrel. Not unless he'd learned to sing in a decidedly higher pitch than she'd heard earlier.

She peeped around the doorframe.

It took a moment for her eyes to adjust to the light. Out here, it was a bright summer's day, a perfect day for haymaking. Inside the stables, there were numerous wooden partitions, stacked equipment, horse feed, and, of course, horses. A song drew her eyes upward to the hayloft.

There, cushioned on a throne of hay, sat the Minstrel Raf, fingers busy on his lute and eyes entirely occupied with Margery. Her maidservant was singing, her face full of joy.

Eglantine just stood there and watched.

Really, the minstrel was quite lovely to look at. No, lovely was an insufficient word. There was too much dark power and grace in him for that, too much glittering intent in his eyes. She didn't want to look away. The slip of his straight, dark hair over one shoulder, the intensity of his gaze, the predator-like focus of the man. Oh, she could see why Margery's cheeks were pink.

He was a minstrel, through and through. Admittedly, she hadn't much direct experience of wandering players. In the year since her husband had died, she had avoided inviting strangers into La Roque. Why, she wasn't even keen on inviting people she *did* know into the chateau. And while Ferrand had lived, he had not been inclined to open his doors to music makers. The only exception was for great feasts, when the Lord of La Roque felt the need to entertain his guests with more than meat and wine.

Eglantine wondered now whether her husband had feared the seductive reputation of the wandering player. It was all very well for the seigneur to slip his hand up whatever skirt took his fancy, but his lady?

Eglantine ceased to prop up the doorpost. She stepped

through the stable door.

The movement evidently caught the minstrel's eye. His gaze flashed to hers, and the plectrum slipped from his fingers. Margery sang on a few words, but then she, too, stuttered to a halt. But Eglantine wasn't interested in her maid's reactions.

The minstrel looked mortified. Those high cheekbones lost all color, and he just stared at her, speechless.

Eglantine permitted herself a small smile. "Have you finished with my maid, minstrel?" Silly question, for Margery still had all her clothes on. "I regret I have need of her."

But Margery was already brushing down her skirts and hurrying toward the loft ladder.

Brushing down her skirts? Perhaps the hay had already been used for more than a musician's seat.

She gave Raf a nod. "I will see you at the evening meal, minstrel. I am looking forward to further entertainment."

RAFÈU REMAINED A hermit in his hayloft until the sun began to sink. He needed to practice the songs the English maid had taught him. He played until his voice grew rough and his fingers prickled. Oh, he knew it was unwise to wear himself out before his debut performance in the great hall, but there was no help for it. He'd had a damned good shot at burning his bridges already, and he was not going to risk another incendiary event. He needed to practice his new English repertoire and remain an evidently celibate musician.

Worse, the boy had not returned. Con had wanted to, Raf knew, and Con was his key to remaining within La Roque. The only possible reason the boy had not come back was that his mother had forbidden it. The Minstrel Rafèu had shown himself to have immoral tendencies. He was no fit companion for a small lord.

But now it was growing dim. The ladder would not be any easier to navigate in darkness, not if he wanted a whole lute. Besides, it was the hour of the evening *repas*. Raf had a hall and a seat to locate, and a lady to impress.

He had some catching up to do.

So Raf descended the ladder, checked his nag was content, then strolled across the dusky courtyard between the stable and the central keep of the chateau. He glanced up at the gray-golden tower as he approached, all five looming stories of it. Where was her chamber?

Not that he had any nefarious designs on her boudoir. The Vicomte Rafèu's love for his lady was pure. It was not founded on base passions.

Now for stairs, and a good quantity of them, too. Naturally, the great hall was on the third level of the keep. A castle's ground floor was always reserved for storage, the next up was usually the kitchen. Then came the hall, the center of all chateau activity. Raf had taken no note of the hall on his first entry to the keep, but now he took a moment to observe. He lingered just inside the door and scanned the space with purpose.

After all, it might contain his lady.

It wasn't an enormous room, but then, La Roque wasn't an enormous chateau. It couldn't be. The whole complex was wedged into a ledge on a cliff. So, unlike his own Bruniquel, this hall boasted only one long trestle table rather than trestles along three sides of the hall. Nor were there people enough to fill three such tables. Perhaps there were only a dozen seated on the benches before him.

Not, of course, counting Lady Eglantine and her son. She sat at the table's head, Con beside her.

She was looking directly at him, with just the suggestion of a raised eyebrow. An angel in a wimple and modest, unadorned gown. But she didn't need adorning. She was already perfection. There was a poise about her, self-possession, a little distance even. But it was her eyes that drew him in and cast an unearthly spell over his senses.

Raf bowed. Lute outstretched, he swept a deep obeisance in the doorway. Then, when he'd got a grip on more than his lute, he strolled down the hall toward his lady.

He never got there. A familiar fellow rose from the table and blocked his way.

"Osbert, captain to the Lady Eglantine and La Roque, and sometime gatekeeper," he introduced himself, as if Raf had never laid eyes on him before. Well, he hadn't, not with Osbert in the capacity of captain or in the possession of a name, for that matter. *Captain?* This undersized jester? No wonder the man-at-arms down in the village grumbled.

The so-called captain did not wait for a reply. He jerked a thumb. "Your place is over there, minstrel. Get to it."

A stool had been placed midway down the hall. It looked like a milking stool. Said milking stool was located near enough to the head of the table that Raf's music would be heard, but too distant to speak to his lady without yelling.

Well, the Minstrel Rafèu knew his place. Apparently, it was upon a milking stool. One more bow to the hall in general, and he placed his posterior on the seat.

What now? Did he just start strumming unannounced, or must he await his lady's command? He thought back to similar situations in Bruniquel, to the musicians he had hosted, most recently Guilhem and Alain, or Sir William and Lady Azalais, as it had turned out. He couldn't remember. In Raf's experience, musicians just materialized and then the music happened.

Raf glanced around. A dozen pairs of eyes looked back, but his lady's was not among them. She was speaking to her captain, the undersized English boulder. She was probably discussing Raf's imminent eviction. But Con was looking at him. The boy was jigging on his cushioned chair. Just as well he wasn't seated on a bench, for every other unfortunate sharing the plank would be vibrating in time. But the jigging and the expression in the child's eyes confirmed it—Con wanted a song. He wanted a tale of adventure set to music.

Well, let the music happen.

Raf smiled at the boy and rippled his plectrum over an opening chord. Something a bit more dignified than Robin Hood.

Would King Arthur do?

DEAR GOD, THAT voice. Smooth and rich as honey, but with the slightest rough edge. Like honey crystalized. She couldn't look at him, no matter how that voice begged her to. Instead, Eglantine watched her son.

Con was a fidgeter. He couldn't stay still. But now look at him perched on the edge of his lordly chair like a statue, gaze fixed upon a certain minstrel.

It probably helped that Con had taken an unaccustomed nap that afternoon. After his bath and the de-prickling operation, he had actually dozed off. Now he was more alert than ever.

The minstrel stumbled. That honeyed voice tangled over an English phrase, and his fingers barely maintained the accompaniment. English wasn't his first language, that much was obvious. He was a Frenchman by birth.

Eglantine's stomach tightened, and she shoved her trencher aside. Why had she invited yet another damned Frenchman inside her chateau? Had she learned nothing?

Yet Con was still mimicking a gargoyle, mouth open and perched on the edge of his chair. He didn't care about stumbles and mispronunciation. He just wanted the story.

Eglantine glanced down the table. Margery also seemed inclined to turn into a gargoyle, although her expression had a distinctly different cast to Con's. She looked like she wanted to eat the musician.

A smile tweaked the corner of Eglantine's mouth. She had thought the whispers about wandering players were mere rumors and exaggeration. Now, though, she was starting to believe otherwise.

His next song was in the *langue d'oc*. One of those *canzos*, a love song, no less. She refused to look at the singer, so Eglantine again anchored her gaze upon Con. It only took a verse before he changed back into a flesh-and-blood boy, and one who almost certainly had ants in his braies. Oh, the minstrel sang his love song beautifully. No stumbles this time, and an aching depth of longing in his tone. But Con was no longer enchanted. He began to prod at his food.

Not so Margery. That particular statue was melting like butter in the sun, and Eglantine didn't bother to hide her grin.

"What are you laughing at, *Maman*?"

"Mother," she corrected him. "Nothing—the music is making me happy."

"Yes! Yes!" Then Con paused. "But only when he sings in English, you mean."

No, be it English or French or the language of the heathen east, she rather thought she'd like anything cast in that tone of rough velvet from those lips. Damned minstrel charmer.

"Yes, only when he sings in English, Con."

"So, can he stay a bit longer?" He bounced in his chair. "He calls me Your Imperial Mightiness. He's going to tell me the tale of Emperor Constantine. He never got to tell it today. You made me have a bath. So, can he stay? Only if he doesn't sing songs like that, of course." A derisive flap of his hand.

"Your Mightiness? So, the man's a sycophant, too," she murmured.

She glanced toward the singer. It was a mistake. He was looking at her. His eyes, their expression, hit her like a visceral jolt. She flicked her gaze away. For heaven's sake, did all women react to him in this way? Men, too, probably.

"Sicko-what?" piped up Con.

It was the contrast—Eglantine laughed. It was quite an audible laugh. People turned on their benches...and the minstrel's shoulders stiffened. Her laugh faded. The Lady Eglantine didn't cackle aloud.

She looked at her son. "A sycophant is a flatterer, Con. He says nice things he doesn't really mean."

A bit harsh, but there it was.

Con's forehead developed wrinkles. "I don't think he was being nice. I think he was having fun."

"Maybe," she murmured.

"Can he stay longer? Just a few days? We never have minstrels. Why do we never have minstrels, Mother?"

Because they're...what? Immoral, disreputable wanderers you can't trust. That was the usual understanding of the breed. But that also made them strangely desirable and wickedly attractive.

Eglantine had never thought about it before. It had just been simpler to bar La Roque to all comers, entertainers included. So why should she make an exception for this one?

She murmured a noncommittal answer to Con, and then, before he could argue some more, she rose from her chair.

"Stay here," she told her son. "I must talk to the sycophant."

Chapter Five

R AF HAD BEEN dealt a wound.

He was familiar with the experience—the situation at Combret had been particularly fruitful in that regard—but he couldn't recall a besieger's rock or an opponent's sword that caused him such piercing pain.

To combat the pain, Rafèu bent his head to his lute and sang one of the English ditties the maid had taught him earlier. Not that all the English songs in the world would do him much good now.

His lady had laughed at him. She'd caught him singing love songs with her maidservant earlier, and now he was worthy only of her laughter.

Raf sank into the world of the silly little English song and focused only on pronouncing its barbarous words correctly. Better that than focus on the wound piercing of his heart.

So when the Lady Eglantine materialized before him, it was like a buffet with a mailed gauntlet.

"Pray do not stop on my account, minstrel."

But the song had already withered on his lips. His throat was too dry to croak another note. He kept his head bent, awaiting the final blow. This was the very closest he'd ever been to his lady. If he just tilted his chin, he would bathe in the radiance of her beauty. But he could not look up. She was regarding him with anything but love.

"I simply came to inform you that you do not have to leave at dawn. Unless you wish to, of course."

Raf remained quite still for a few heartbeats, juggling the words to see if he'd misunderstood. Then he lifted his gaze to hers.

Green eyes regarded him, calm, guarded as a castle keep. He wished his were as guarded. It was likely his lady could read his every last naked emotion at will. And what she read would not be the sentiments proper to a minstrel.

But if she did so, the Lady Eglantine gave no sign.

"I thank you, my lady," he said, his voice huskier than any minstrel's ought to be. "I am all eagerness to fill the young lord's ears with English song and story. And to delight his lady mother's senses in whatever degree I may."

A strange expression entered her eyes then, an expression so slight and fleeting that Raf had no hope of parsing it. He might have thought he'd pushed his minstrel pleasantries too far, except for the words that followed.

"Oh, you please his lady mother's senses well enough, minstrel. See that you continue to do so."

A small wave of the hand toward his lute, or was it to his person in general? Then she glided away.

Raf suddenly found himself able to play again. That was all it took, the merest breath of hope. Perhaps the Lady Eglantine was not entirely unaffected by him.

ROSES. THEY WERE the first things she had planted at La Roque all those years ago when she came here as a bride. The one she tended now had been among them, a pale English rose transplanted into French soil. And it had thrived. She had made sure of it. She had watered it with her own hands in the baking heat of summer, squashed the sap suckers with her own fingers, and trained it up these harsh stone walls. Now Eglantine was nipping off every dead bloom she could reach, trying to focus solely on the clambering, prickly plant.

Her focus kept slipping.

It would have been better if Con were here. He was the only other being allowed in her garden, her sanctuary. Con would have kept her attention solely focused on him. But her son was not here. He was off with that minstrel, draining him of every song and story the man knew, just as he had been for the last handful of days.

She jagged her thumb on a thorn. *That* drew her attention. She whipped her hand away from the stem and gazed at the bead of blood. Yet even that could not hold her focus for long. Her thoughts slipped back to Con. Absently, she put her thumb to her mouth and sucked at the wound. Just like Con would.

Was she jealous of her son? Con could spend all the time he liked in the minstrel's company. Not so his mother.

No, of course she wasn't. If anything, she was jealous of the minstrel—a piece of flotsam who had floated in her chateau door and was now absorbing all Con's spare moments. Eglantine didn't have to order her son to go to Raf for his English lessons. The problem was restraining him long enough in the morning to dress the child and see that he had some morsel to eat. Even so, she wondered whether Con ever found Raf still abed.

At which thought, an image of the dark minstrel, sleep-tousled and in need of a shave, materialized so clearly in her mind that he may as well be standing before her. No, *lounging* before her on his bed of hay, his eyes heavy-lidded and inviting.

Dear God in heaven. Eglantine jerked her thumb from her lips. Suddenly, the action seemed far too intimate. She returned to snipping at spent roses with a vengeance.

It was no good. She could not snip away this feeling. It rose, hot and fierce as the French sun in her stomach. She *wanted* the minstrel. She wanted to shake her hair free of its wimple, rid herself of this too-modest clothing, and feel those dark, brilliant eyes linger on her. She wanted him to want her.

Snip, snip…and then there were no more dead rose blooms. She looked about the walled garden. What now? She must have something to do with her hands or she might find herself doing something most unwise. Immodest.

Eglantine tucked the scissors into her apron, took a deep breath, and faced the truth.

It had been too long. That was all. She had been a virtuous widow since Ferrand was discovered dead, returning from one of his many lady loves. Long before that, she had been a virtuous wife, a practically celibate wife. Yet even when Ferrand was alive, even in the first month of their marriage, she had not felt like this.

Oh, she had loved Ferrand, but the physical proceedings between them… Well, she had done her wifely duty, but that was all. Ferrand's attentions had not inspired her to want more. So why now this strange longing?

Eglantine brushed her hands down on her gardening apron, and then she did the deed—she tugged her wimple loose. It took some doing, for when Margery bound the linen around her head each morning, she ensured it perfectly concealed every tendril of hair and that it would not budge until the evening toilette. Eglantine required it so, despite Margery's suggestions that Eglantine need not be so strict. *You have such pretty hair, mistress.* But Eglantine knew Margery's golden curls far outshone her own. Not that that was the point.

Except perhaps where minstrel tastes were concerned.

Her wimple was off. The linen hung from her fingers like a discarded shroud. She lifted the ghostly thing and hung it from a thorn. Then Eglantine was free to trail her fingers through her hair, unbinding it, wondering how it would feel to have another's hands in its length.

It was just as well the garden was a true *hortus conclusus*. No window but her own overlooked it; no person but Eglantine herself and Con were permitted inside it, unless she ordered it.

No one could see the Lady Eglantine trail her fingers though her hair with impossible yearning.

Even Ferrand had avoided her garden. He declared his wife degraded herself by grubbing in the dirt—that was what servants were for—and he had left her to her strange English ways. But the moment she stepped out of the *hortus conclusus*, Eglantine would have to dress appropriately again. She didn't know why she'd bothered to tug the wimple off in the first place.

She might crave the touch of a dark minstrel who would soon wander off again, never to threaten her heart or her home, but she would never be so bold as to solicit his attention. Even if she did, he would likely reject her in favor of a prettier and more accessible maid.

Eglantine tucked her hair behind her ears and lodged a wide straw hat on her head. Heaven forbid she burn her English-pale cheeks with French sun. Then she located a spade. She would attack this stony French soil and soften it with compost, exhausting herself in a most unladylike manner in the process. If she couldn't achieve sweet exhaustion in Raf's arms, she'd simply dig herself into a stupor.

Unless she could dig up sufficient boldness to proposition a minstrel.

HE HAD BEEN here four days now. Four days of acting the respectful but charming minstrel, and where had it got him? Within sight of his lady. Rafèu might even occasionally exchange words with her, but it was not enough. Yet he did not know how to advance any further, and he lived in dread of outliving his use so far as Con went.

Noises drifted in from outside the stable block. Small-boy chatter, interspersed with feminine replies. Ah, they were here.

Raf brushed the hay from his motley, slung his lute over his back, and slithered down the hayloft ladder.

"Raf!"

He looked up and grinned at the small figure in the stable door.

"Lord Constantine." An extravagant bow.

Then his gaze flicked of its own accord to the silhouette beside the boy. His heart seized for one moment, and then it resumed its normal beat.

"Maid Margery," he murmured, treating her to a small bow.

It was only courtesy, any minstrel would do as much, but the maid's cheeks turned pink.

"Good morrow, minstrel. Did you sleep well all by yourself in the hay?"

"How could I do otherwise, good maid? I am lulled to sleep by the farting of horses, the screeching of owls, and the scuttling of rats. I want for no sweeter lullaby."

Which was a blatant lie, of course, but he didn't want her offering to sing him to sleep. He did not need English songs that badly.

A giggle. "Is that where you get your songs from? Perhaps I could come and listen, too."

"Margie, haven't you got work to do?" Con interrupted in a tone an emperor would approve of. "Mother is in the garden, and she said you were to do some mending while I'm with Raf."

Margery sighed gustily and bobbed a mocking curtsey. "Yes, your lordship. Mistress has a pressing need for me to darn your hose." Then a smile lit her admittedly pretty face. "Maybe I could bring the mending down here. Plenty of light in the courtyard. Then I could listen to stories, too."

Oh God, no.

"No, Margie. Mother said you must mend *in the solar*. There's lots of light there. Now go away. This is men's business."

An imperious gesture, Margie was dismissed, and Raf could breathe again. This minstrel disguise came with unexpected hazards. Evidently, he was too convincing.

"Men's business?" Raf raised an eyebrow.

"I just wanted her to go away. She acts funny around you. Besides, Mother did say she was to mend in the solar."

Interesting.

Or maybe not. Probably the lady was simply keeping her innocent maid out of the depraved minstrel's reach.

But then, why entrust her only son to his care?

No time for further pondering. Con was demanding stories. They went to a secluded corner of the courtyard, retrieved the two wooden swords they'd stowed behind the fig tree there, and then began the lesson in English culture.

It was the tale of Culhwch and Olwen today. Again. Yes, it was a barbarous Welsh tale full of unpronounceable names, but Culhwch was King Arthur's own nephew and, by heaven, he got up to some fun. Raf had begun to tell the tale yesterday in the approved fashion, accompanied by the odd strum of the lute, but Con had become enthused, grabbed a stick, and taken Culhwch's role to heart. Now the lute was superfluous, and Raf was required to take up a stick, too. They had a fearsome boar to hunt so Culhwch could win the hand of the fair Olwen.

Raf conducted a running commentary in the required language while he and Con set about the action. And it wasn't just a boar they had to hunt, but a wily salmon, and then, naturally, the Black Witch in the Valley of Grief, located in the uplands of hell. Finally, Con—Culhwch—confronted Olwen's own father.

"Hast thou had thy shave now, man?" Con bellowed. Raf had coached him in the words.

Raf rubbed his jaw, squinting most evilly as he did so. Olwen's giant father had required a most convoluted shave, courtesy of a magical boar's tusk. Just as well Raf had managed to run a blade over his cheeks at the well this morning. He didn't know his lady's tastes in facial hair, but the story required a very thorough shave.

"I have," he said.

"And is thy daughter mine now?" yelled Con, waving his

sword.

If only it were so simple. Hunt a fierce boar, drain a witch's blood, and shave a giant to win the lady. Raf pulled a leer. He was a reluctant father-in-law, and a monstrous one at that.

Actually, according to the story, that was all it took. The giant grumbled but handed over the girl. Then some bastard chopped off his head. Didn't seem quite fair.

So Raf tweaked the ending. Couldn't have the little lord learning dubious morals, could he?

"No!" Raf growled in his best giant's voice. "You'll never have my Olwen, you runt of a knight. You think a shave is all it takes?"

And he shook his sword most threateningly, but well away from said runt of a knight.

Con understood what a true knight was to do. He gave a wild yell, whirled his stick, and took to battle.

It was actually quite tricky to defend himself with a stick without causing any damage to his attacker. Of course, Culhwch must win, and the giant's head must be severed. Con knew how the story ended. The problem was, Con evidently had some training in swordsmanship. His thrusts weren't entirely wild.

The other problem was that Raf didn't actually want to die.

Worse still, in the process of yelling and clattering sticks, they'd acquired an audience. First, there was the stable lad. Then a passing servant or three. Then Osbert, the sometime captain of the La Roque.

Finally, and Raf nearly dropped his staff when a sideways glance informed him of this, the Lady of La Roque herself.

Chapter Six

OSBERT HAD SENT a servant for her. The man tugged on a string, and a small bell had tinkled in the garden. That was how she knew to abandon the watering bucket and exit her green haven of peace. Servants did not enter the *hortus conclusus* unless ordered to, and that order could only come from Eglantine.

She found the fellow shifting from foot to foot on the other side of the door.

"Yes, Jacques?"

"Osbert sent me, m'lady. He said to come quickly. He said Lord Con's fair in mortal danger."

"*Where?*"

"In the courtyard, near the stables, m'—"

But Eglantine was already running. She only slowed to a more dignified pace before descending the steps from keep to the courtyard. Best not to trip on her skirts and kill herself by tumbling down the steep stone before she'd saved her son.

Once on the courtyard cobbles, she followed the sound of clattering and shouting and rounded the corner of the stable block to see…what? She paused, heart hammering. Slowly, the circle of watchers drew aside for their lady.

Eglantine saw two men fighting with wooden staves. No, it was a man and a boy. *Her* boy. Eglantine gasped and flung out a hand.

Then she paused.

Why hadn't Osbert already stopped the fight? Her captain was right there, standing, sword in hand and a glower most thunderous on his face, observing the battle minutely. Surely Con would listen to her captain if he commanded the boy to desist? Surely even his attacker would obey an order from Osbert?

Or perhaps it was simply too dangerous to shout out. It would distract her son in the heat of battle.

Fingers clenched, she lowered her hand and stared at the dreadful scene. And things began to make sense.

Actually, Con was just fine. It was his opponent who was in mortal danger, and that opponent was the minstrel, Raf.

Her son had acquired a stout length of wood and was jabbing and swiping and generally pounding at his opponent. Any one of those blows could crack a man's head open. The minstrel held a staff, too, but he was only using it to defend himself. No matter the flurry of blows Con directed at him, Raf only blocked them, catching them on the broadside of his staff and deftly casting them aside. And he did it so effortlessly, with such lithe grace, that Eglantine could almost forget the danger he was in.

This wasn't a fight. It was more like a mummers' play or an acrobat's performance.

Then Eglantine ceased to think. She just watched.

This was the man she'd entrusted to sing her son stories, but he wasn't wielding a lute now. It seemed he had other talents.

Con chose that moment to yell out, "Die, giant!" He followed it up with a wild overhead swing of his staff that would surely knock Raf senseless.

She flung out a hand involuntarily, then controlled herself.

Raf had twisted neatly aside, and now called out in the court-liest tone imaginable, "You'll never have her, Culhwch, by my oath! No, not if you shave every hair upon my body." Then he slipped his stick under Con's descending blow and sent it glancing to one side.

They were both grinning, and the sight took her breath away.

And Raf, his dark hair flying, his long frame gracefully evading every blow, evidently knew what he was doing. It was like a dance, a deadly, beautiful dance, and she could watch it forever.

Until the minstrel shot a startled glance at her and fumbled his next block.

Eglantine cried out. She wasn't sure what she said, and no one paid any attention. For with an almighty *thunk*, Con landed a solid blow to Raf's shoulder and chest, and the minstrel was falling.

Her son gave a bloodcurdling yell and leaped upon his fallen opponent. He scrabbled astride the minstrel's torso and laid his stick across Raf's throat. Eglantine's innards lurched like a ship in a storm, but now was not the moment to pay attention to her stomach. She sprang forward.

"Give me your daughter, giant!" bellowed Con.

There was a moment of silence. Then the minstrel's laughing gaze slipped to her. Eglantine was now standing a mere pace away from the two.

Not that Con was paying her any heed. But the minstrel was. The man was flat on his back, his hair splayed out on the dirt. And he was gazing at her with eyes as dark and shining as jet.

He answered Con, but he looked at her.

"I'd rather have your mother, Culhwch."

OH GOD, NOW he'd ruined it.

She'd been standing so close, her eyes alight with a more complex blend of emotions than he could ever decipher, and she'd been looking at *him*, not at her son. As if she gave a damn. Just a small one.

He shouldn't have said the words, especially not in Con's hearing, but he couldn't help it. He'd barely mouthed the phrase. It was a mere whisper, and he might have doubted he'd even spoken aloud, save for her expression.

Immediate blankness, as if a gate was slammed shut. What-ever mix of expressions had been evident an instant before were locked away. The Lady Eglantine straightened and surveyed the onlookers.

"The performance is over," she said, then cast a cool glance at Raf's midriff. "Or it will be as soon as my son has released his prisoner."

She raised an eyebrow at the boy. Con jigged in response. Unfortunately, he did so on Raf's stomach.

"I am Culhwch, knight of Arthur's round table, and this is my foe," Con declared, but then the thoughtful lad spared a glance for his seat. "Yet the giant has fought valiantly. I suppose I can let him go."

"I thank you, Lord Culhwch. I am all gratitude that I get to keep my head," Raf managed, although it was tricky to vocalize with a staff across one's throat. Then he dared a glance at his lady. "By rights, you see, he should chop it off."

What was he hoping for, that she should smile, or even come to his defense? No, the gate remained closed. That pale and perfect face might have been cast in marble.

Con scrabbled off him. Ah, he could breathe again, for all the good it would do him. Then the small gentleman offered his foe a hand up. Raf's audience of assorted servants and the lady of his heart watched in silence as he rose and dusted himself down. Well, what need did a minstrel have of dignity?

Then his lady spoke in a tone as chill as a winter dawn.

"Con, I see your swordplay is in need of refinement. Master Osbert, you were watching keenly, I believe. Pray take my son aside and offer him some instruction."

The Lady of La Roque turned back to Rafèu. Still with no discernible expression, she uttered his doom:

"Minstrel, you will come with me."

And without waiting for a reaction, she turned and walked with perfect poise back toward the chateau.

EGLANTINE TURNED HER back on him, on all of them, and walked with as much steadiness as she could muster back up the steps. She must assume Raf was following, but she would not look back to make certain. She was quivering too much inside.

Did she hear footfalls behind her on the circling steps? It was like a story, like Orpheus leading his Eurydice out of the Underworld—she could not turn and look, except the minstrel Orpheus was following her this time. She hoped.

She shouldn't hope.

The staircase spiraled up and up within the walls of the keep, past the kitchen, past the hall, and then to the solar. Eglantine paused in the doorway of her private domain, seeing the chamber as if looking through the minstrel's eyes.

Light flooded in through a southern-facing window that boasted the only glass panes in La Roque. Expensive, luxurious glass. The light illuminated heavy wooden chests, rich tapestries, silk cushions, a table on which she wrote up her accounts, and Margery, obediently mending hose.

The maid glanced up, and her eyes widened.

They were not widening at her mistress.

There were no more footfalls behind her, but Eglantine could feel the man's presence as a tangible thing. The skin on the backs of her arms tingled.

She tried for a calm and authoritative tone. "Margery, you have sewn enough. I commend your diligence—now go down to the courtyard and take the air. Con is there. When my son is finished with Osbert, you may mind him." A deep breath. "Now go. I must talk to the minstrel, alone."

Margery's eyes flicked to the man who was undoubtedly standing behind Eglantine, then back to her mistress. The maid was not one to conceal her feelings. There were all sorts of questions and sentiments bubbling just under the surface, foremost among which was, undoubtedly, *Why in God's name does the mistress want to be alone with that man?*

Eglantine ignored the unspoken questions and stepped into the solar. Yes, Raf had followed her. He strolled in behind her and filled the room with his dark velvet presence. Not that she looked at him.

Margery rose and tidied away the mending with more wiggling than seemed strictly necessary. She also managed to brush up against Raf in her exit from the chamber—quite the feat, considering the minstrel had moved well away from the door arch.

Eglantine walked to her parchment-littered desk and leafed through the fine leather for want of something to do with her fingers. For heaven's sake, she was just as bad as Margery, although she prayed she wasn't quite so obvious. What idiocy was this?

The door closed softly, and there was silence.

What now? Where did she start?

As it happened, she didn't have to.

Steps approached, crunching softly on the rushes. More rustling. Eglantine's fingers clenched parchment. She must look at him now. She knew she couldn't control her features if she did, but there was no avoiding the necessity.

She turned to him, and her breathing stopped. The minstrel was kneeling before her. Again. The light played over the sharp angles of his face, and his eyes were as soft and fathomless as night.

"My lady, I most humbly beg your pardon. I was presumptuous. I—" He shook his head.

Her minstrel, lost for words? Something stirred within her, some unsuspected seed of boldness.

Eglantine reached out a hand and laid it upon the man's shoulder. Her hand was none too steady. Ah, he was real, solid, and warm. She had broken some kind of barrier between them. She, the reclusive Lady Eglantine, had determined never to touch a man in intimacy again. Especially not a French one.

But this man barely counted as such. He was only a wandering player.

"Rise, Minstrel Raf. I admit I was concerned when I saw such swinging of sticks in the vicinity of my son, but no harm is done." A small squeeze of his shoulder. "Except perhaps to you. Are you damaged, minstrel?"

Do you need the tender ministrations of the lady of the house? Perhaps you should remove your tunic, and I will tend to your bruises.

She nearly said the words, but no, that was far too bold. She removed her hand.

"No. But I meant…" He didn't finish the sentence. He obeyed her command and rose instead.

Oh, she'd known what he meant. Those words. *I'd rather have your mother, Culhwch,* he'd said. Whoever Culhwch was.

He wanted her. She chose to believe it was so. Had she mistaken that look, that soft tone? She did not want his apology. She wanted something else entirely.

But how?

"We were enacting the tale of Culhwch and Olwen, my lady. Culhwch was one of Arthur's knights. It is an English story."

She smiled. "Don't let a Welshman hear you say so, minstrel. I trust you didn't tell the tale in Welsh?"

An echoing smile lit his face. Dear heaven, those deep, dark eyes softened to melting point and little lines appeared at their outer edges. It entirely scrambled Eglantine's thoughts.

"Welsh? No, God forbid. I perfected my English on a captive Englishman. He was a gentleman and a knight. I know no gentle Welshmen. I only tend to see them at the other end of a longbow."

Then those beautiful lips tightened. The smile vanished. Something he had said? But Eglantine had barely registered the words. She had let his tones wash over her, felt the caressing timbre.

"Minstrel, I…"

Eglantine turned abruptly, twisting her hands. How did one begin? She was a novice in this field. *He* was the expert. He should take the lead. It was all part of a minstrel's daily round. But he was not helping.

Evidently, he hadn't registered what she wanted, otherwise, he'd be getting on with it, wouldn't he?

Well, if it was bluntness he was after…

She squared her shoulders and turned back to him. Raf was watching her, an unreadable expression on his face.

"You have entertained my son well."

Greatly daring, she reached out to run a light hand over Raf's shoulder and chest where Con had landed his blow. Did a shiver run through the man beneath?

"It seems you have skills beyond the lute and song, minstrel." A tiny frown flickered over his face. She hurried on. "I would explore those skills further. I would have you entertain me." She could barely hear herself for the thundering of her heart. She hurried the words out: "I would have you entertain me here, alone, in the privacy of my chamber."

Those depthless eyes still watched her. No movement, no word. For God's sake, did she have to spell it out?

Eglantine lifted her chin. "I would reward you well for your services, minstrel."

Chapter Seven

R AF STOOD QUITE still. The lady evidently didn't recall the full story of Culhwch and Olwen. Culhwch had won the hand of the fair Olwen. He was a knight. He had wed his love honorably, admittedly after removing her father's head. That was what the Vicomte Rafèu had meant when he uttered those fateful words.

His lady had understood them quite differently, and who could blame her? She did not see an honorable vicomte before her, but a low minstrel.

One paid a minstrel for his services, and now she was offering to pay him. Christ, the lady of his heart wished to turn him into a man-whore.

The thought sent a wave of warmth through his body, most unwelcome warmth.

This was, most indubitably, not the plan.

But her little pointed chin was lifted and her lips were white where she pressed them together. She looked very vulnerable right now. And he knew if he didn't say something or act soon, she would seal that vulnerability up within her walls and never open her heart to him again.

Not that it was her heart she was offering.

He had to do something, however much it went against the grain.

So Raf lifted one finger and reached for his lady. He was a

little surprised that it did not tremble.

He touched her. He laid his finger on her brow just where her wimple ended, and he brushed it softly over her skin. She shivered beneath his touch. Raf slipped his finger down, tracing the perfection of her face, over a high, pale cheekbone, then down to her jaw, to finish at her chin.

The walls were still down, and those glorious, soft green eyes were full of expression, emotion *he* had evoked.

Dear God, the feelings they stirred in him were beyond comprehension or control. What was he to do with this wave of tenderness, yearning, and—heaven forgive him—molten desire that washed over him?

He could not do as she asked. He could not be mere entertainment to her, however well paid. He was a vicomte, damn it, not a base, wandering player. Perhaps he should say as much right now. Raf had always intended to reveal his true identity when he deemed the moment was right, when he'd won her love and respect.

But that moment was not now. He knew it. She didn't respect or love him—she just wanted a minstrel's touch. And if that minstrel suddenly transformed into a French vicomte, Raf was almost certain he'd be thrown out. Politely, maybe, but the gate would be barred to him. Permanently.

Rumor declared that the Lady Eglantine did not wish to wed again. Rumor had even whispered that she despised French noblemen. The latter was impossible, of course, but perhaps she distrusted them. On the other hand, it seemed she didn't mind French minstrels.

He employed his finger to angle her chin up a little, the better to gaze into her face. Wordlessly, she allowed it.

Her eyes did all the speaking. They spoke too much. They begged him to continue, whispered of aching bliss and delights beyond imagining.

He was teetering on the edge. Raf had to glance away, even if it was only to shift his attention to her lips. They were slightly parted, like a rosebud on the verge of blooming. He brushed the pad of his thumb over that beautiful mouth, reverently. Felt her breath feather his skin, fast and uneven.

There could be no harm in it, surely? So far, nothing he had done constituted a breach of honor, and this was France—kisses were so commonplace as to be invisible. Men kissed each other in greeting, friends kissed each other, knights even greeted noble ladies with an entirely proper and respectful kiss. She wanted more of him than a mere wandering fingertip. Perhaps a kiss would suffice.

On the basis of such eminently sensible reasoning, Rafèu bent to touch his lips to hers.

In hindsight, it was easy to identify where his plan had gone wrong—her lips had been ajar. Worse, as he bent to brush a chaste kiss over the rosebud mouth, it opened just a fraction more. So, when he finally touched his lips to hers, what could a courteous knight do but match his lady? It would not do to keep his lips sealed tight when hers were so softly open.

That was his downfall. Her mouth opened to his, and the next thing he knew, his arms were about her, drawing her to him, and she had lifted her arms to twine about his neck and in his hair. His tongue slipped between her lips, and she gasped and melted against him. And years—goddamn *years*—of pent-up longing took control of his body and demanded that this kiss should never end.

Unless, of course, it ended in his trailing passionate kisses over every inch of her pale, creamy, completely edible skin.

Sweet heaven, what was he doing? His manhood was a lump of solid rock, and she couldn't help but know it, for his arms held her to him so closely. But there were so many layers of clothing between them. Too many. His fingers were already tugging at that starched white wimple. She had her hands in his hair, and he wanted the same. She was too wrapped about in modest defenses, and the wimple was the outer bulwark. It had to go.

But the hair covering was stubborn. It resisted his efforts. It demanded just a fraction more attention than Raf was willing to give it, and that was what finally did it.

A sliver of sanity trickled through.

He was acting the lascivious minstrel. This was no way to treat his lady. And she'd declared she would pay him for his services, services he was all too willing to render in his current heated state.

It couldn't be. It *mustn't* be.

"My lady," he managed, and the words came out rough-edged. "I am overwhelmed. I am not sure I have the skills you seek. My *forte* is music and story, not…"

He knew better than to complete that sentence. Besides, it would have verged on falsehood. He was no great musician, he knew, but he had had plenty of practice in playing upon the instrument that was a woman's body. Of recent years, he'd taken to imagining any woman he touched to be Eglantine. But to touch the real thing…it was no lie to say he was overwhelmed.

"I find your skills suit me well enough, minstrel. So far." Her voice was husky. "I do not require a virtuoso performance."

Hell and damnation, how was he to wriggle out of this without offending the lady or getting his own hide thrown out?

"I…I am most sincerely honored, my lady. This is not a situation that has occurred to me before."

Her eyebrows lifted. Her hands were still upon his shoulders, a little tense now.

"Perhaps you normally confine your attentions to maidservants," she suggested.

"My lady, you are as the sun. Your beauty eclipses all others. I could not look at another woman."

"Phrases worthy of a song, minstrel. Is that a direct quote?"

Rafèu let his arms drop from about her. He took a small step back. "It is not, but perhaps I need to try my hand at composition."

"Perhaps," she said absently. Then she drew herself up straight. Dignified and reserved. "The proposal still stands, minstrel. Give it some thought, but do not think too long."

A flick of her hand. He was dismissed, and she turned from him and walked to where a heavy tapestry divided the room in two. She slipped between its folds and was gone.

EGLANTINE RETREATED INTO the portion of the solar where she slept—she, Con, and Margery. She sank onto the canopied bed, unsure her legs would continue to hold her up, and listened. There was the faintest trace of footfalls, the opening of a door, and he was gone. The dark presence had left the solar.

She was trembling. She couldn't think straight. What had she done?

But Eglantine could not remain sitting. This shivering energy must be channeled somehow. She sprang to her feet and paced to the window—not the grand, glassed solar window, but the smaller, shuttered one that opened from her bedchamber to overlook the secluded garden. She flung the shutters open and leaned out.

Why hadn't the minstrel simply complied with her wishes? Oh, he'd understood them well enough. Her knees nearly buckled at the memory of his lips, his hands, and that yearning solidity she'd felt when his thighs pressed against her. He'd understood what she wanted, and he seemed all too willing to follow orders. Then what?

She gripped the stone windowsill and stared down at the greenery below, unseeing.

Dear God, she wanted him. It was far worse now she knew how he felt, what his touch did to her. That combination of gentleness and barely contained passion. Surely he wanted her, too? He couldn't manufacture that delicious solidity, could he? And those kisses had *felt* real. But maybe performers could call up these emotions at will. After all, their livelihoods depended on it.

Perhaps she had just made a pitiful fool of herself. She was a widow so deprived of a man's touch that she'd pay a wandering player to relieve her loneliness.

It was too much. Eglantine jerked upright and slammed the shutters back into place. No more thinking—she had to *do* something. So, she fled to her garden and attacked weeds with a ferocious and single-minded energy.

She delved and dirtied her hands until the light slipped from the sky, her garden turned to shadow, and Eglantine was forced to return to the real world of the chateau, to enter the evening hall and face Raf again.

⟫⟩⟩⟩⟨⟨⟨⟪

RAF SANG ONLY the most mild and respectful love songs that night. Nothing in the least bit bawdy or suggestive. And he wasn't even sure his lady was listening. She was reading a book.

Still, just in case, Raf threw heart and soul into one last *canzo*:

O my adored one,

I'll never sully your pristine bloom,

You shine as the sun,

Without you, I dwell in gloom.

At least Con was listening. The boy had wandered over to observe Raf once he finished poking his food at the head of the table. He waited until Raf had finished the *canzo*, then:

"Do you know any songs of Culhwch? Boar-hunting songs, maybe?" Con gave a small bounce. "Songs about giants?"

"Can't say I do. The Welsh are said to be obsessed with song, but I for one can't get my tongue around their language."

"Tell us a story, then."

"I ought to ask your lady mother first, my emperor. She seems distracted. Tell me, Your Imperial Highness, is she feeling low?"

Con wrinkled his brow. "Don't know. She hasn't said much. She's just reading—sometimes she does that."

"Reading?" Raf chuckled at Con's expression. What lady strained her eyes to read by candlelight? Actually, what lady could read in the first place? "What is she reading? Does it have giants in it? Maybe she can read it to you."

The boy made a face. "No giants, just plants. She calls it a herbal. But it does have pictures." Con grabbed his hand. "Come and look. Then you can ask her about stories, too."

Raf hesitated. Con tugged. Raf gave in.

He craved her presence. He wanted her to look up at him with those clear, forest-stream eyes. But the power she held over him... He wasn't sure that if she commanded him to her chamber, he wouldn't simply obey.

It seemed unlikely she would do so. She was currently finding a collection of scraped calf hide more engrossing than him. Or was her book yet another carefully erected defense in her castle wall?

So, he let Con lead him to the Lady Eglantine. Raf bowed. She placed a finger in her book and lifted her head slowly, as if reluctant to be dragged away from the crabbed Latin.

Her gaze met Raf's briefly, then flicked away. She looked at Con.

"Yes?"

"Mother, Raf wants to know if you're feeling low."

Raf closed his eyes briefly. He should have known better.

She did not look at him but seemed to consider the question. "A little low, I thank you," she said to Con. "But nothing that the blessed peace of my garden cannot cure."

"Your garden, my lady?" Raf glanced at the volume on the trestle before her. He could see bright images of leaves and flowers on the open page. "Do you study which plants may effect the greatest cure?"

She took a sharp breath, but made no answer.

"Mother, I want Raf to tell some stories. Love songs are boring. Can he tell some stories instead, please? Of course he'll tell them in English."

"Yes, anything but more mournful songs of unrequited love," murmured the lady, still not looking at him. "I quite agree, Con. Love songs *are* boring, at least they are when they simply wallow in sentiment. Love is an illusion, a fleeting trap to catch the unwary. Be warned, my son."

Chapter Eight

ON DID NOT appear in the stables the next morning. Instead of one small boy eager for stories and all the clanging of sticks that went with them, the Minstrel Rafèu was presented with Margery. He did not want to consider what she was eager for.

"The little lord needs more practice in horse riding," the maid announced. "That's what my lady says. What do I know about horses? Maybe she's right. Anyway, the little lord'll ride out with Osbert 'cause Osbert speaks English, too. And English horse riding's got to be better than French horse riding, hasn't it?"

Raf most certainly didn't want to encourage Margery, but he had to know.

"Does your mistress have a particular dislike of Frenchness?" The notion was beginning to worry him.

The maid's smile grew confidential. Hell, he *had* encouraged her.

"Don't you know, minstrel man?" The maid leaned in to nudge him on the arm. "It was her husband, the late lord. He was French." A shake of the head. "Saints preserve us, *was* he French."

Raf set his teeth. "Of course he was. He was born here. This was his patrimony." A sweep of his hand to encompass the chateau and its surrounds.

"That's not what I mean. You wouldn't understand, what

with you being French, too." A lift of the eyebrows. "He *acted* French. English men don't speak so sweet and charming. Just look at Osbert, for heaven's sake. Lord Ferrand loved to sweet-talk women, *all* women, just so as they were pretty. Aye, and he didn't just stop at talking. Christ, he even tried it on me."

"Not all French men are like that," was the obvious reply.

Margery shrugged. "S'pose so. Maybe just the handsome ones 'cause they can get away with it." She smiled. "And he was passing handsome, our Lord Ferrand. Reckon the mistress fell madly in love with him, what with all his sweet-talking ways."

Yes, she had. Raf knew it for a certainty. On the day he had first seen Eglantine—on the day of her marriage—she had been radiant. She outshone the sun. Happiness and love lit her face to a pitch of perfection that was difficult to look at. Yet once seen, it was far more difficult to look away. Her hair had been arrayed in loose golden-brown curls, crowned with roses. There had been no constraining wimple, no constraint at all.

And Raf, too, had fallen in love. She was not for him. She had eyes only for her handsome husband-to-be, but that did not matter. She was perfection, an unattainable ideal of the kind immortalized in song. He had carried that vision of beauty and love in his heart ever since. Indeed, it had probably saved his life.

"She loved him, and she was heartbroken at his death," Raf murmured. He knew that for a certainty, too, for he had been at Ferrand's funeral. He had seen her bleak, closed-off expression then. The end of love.

Margery laughed. "She might have loved him for a bit, all of about two weeks, but by the time he got skewered by a brigand, she was more than happy to be rid of him."

"What?"

"All right, maybe three weeks, then. But he was a right das-tard, that one. Nice to look at, nice sounding, too, just so long as he got what he wanted, but he never cared for Lady Eglantine. The only thing he loved about her was her dowry. He got her with child, and then he went off and did his damnedest to get a pile of other women with child, too."

Raf found his arms were rigid. "Not all French men are like that," he managed to repeat between his teeth.

"Oh, it's all right when they're minstrels." Margery was standing far too close now. "No one expects a wandering player to settle down and act responsible."

It was definitely time to steer her away from matters amorous.

"But that doesn't explain why your mistress wants her son to speak English more than French, or to hear English stories and song."

Margery shrugged. "She's funny that way. She don't like it here much. She says her flowers don't like it neither. Reckon she'd go back to England if she could."

"Her flowers?"

"I reckon if the mistress is in love, it's with her garden, minstrel man." Margery shot him a teasing look under her lashes. Evidently, she preferred men to flowers. "She thinks of herself as a plant, and one that don't care much for French soil. Her name means 'wild rose,' did you know?" A shake of her blonde curls. "Some people take their names too seriously."

"So, what am I to do?"

He hadn't meant to say the words aloud. Thank heaven Margery understood the question to address a different topic entirely.

"You've got the morning off, minstrel man. You can lounge in the hay all morning if you fancy." Her smile suggested he wouldn't have to lounge alone. "You know what, I've remembered some more English songs for you. I can teach you right now if you fancy. I've got plenty of time."

Maid Margery, a nail in his coffin. And Con's sudden need for riding lessons—more nails hammered in. Raf was dispensable. Indeed, his lady would dispense with him entirely if he did not act soon. And acting did *not* include disporting himself in the hay with a certain friendly maid.

"Where is your mistress?" Raf asked hurriedly.

"Oh, don't worry about her. She'll spend the morning in her precious garden. She told me so. And she's given me no extra tasks, so…" Margery smiled sweetly up at him. "My songs are all yours, minstrel."

Rafèu managed a smile in return. He feared it wasn't very sweet. "I regret I have…tasks to attend to, Maid Margery." He kissed her hand by way of an apology—probably a mistake—and hurried to his nag's stable, where he proceeded to give it the most thorough grooming of its scruffy life. In the process he wrestled with concepts of gardens and French men and feminine reactions to the same.

It was midway through tugging knots out of the beast's mane that the idea came to him.

Rafèu promptly abandoned the comb, scrubbed his horsey hands at the well, and gave his own mane a combing for good measure. Then he glanced down at his motley, rubbed some dirt off his crakows, and gave his minstrel attire a crooked smile. Please heaven he wouldn't have to wear it for much longer.

THE MORNING SUN slanted down into the enclosed garden and baked her plants. The only solution was endless buckets of water. If she didn't water them in the morning when the summer sun was only mildly sizzling, they would be but dry sticks in the afternoon glare.

The spring water gathered in a deep, stone-bordered pond in the center of the garden, having got there by trickling down a runnel from the cliff. The pond was the perfect garden feature— decorative, deliciously soothing, and cool, and it provided Eglantine a practical place to refill her buckets. She could even sit on the stone rim when she needed a respite from lugging water, as now.

She sat beneath the weeping tamarisk. Not an English plant,

but a pretty one, and quite tough enough to withstand the heat that blasted the center of the courtyard in midsummer. Eglantine herself was not tough enough for such heat, hence the tamarisk shade. Her broad-brimmed hat offered insufficient shadow.

The tamarisk wept pink flowers into the water, and Eglantine tugged off a glove to stir the cool, pink-speckled surface. Then she used her dampened hand to cool her brow. She surveyed her green sanctuary. The more delicate, English plants clustered in profusion against the walls and the cliff face. The symmetrical beds toward the center of the courtyard mostly contained tough French herbs at this time of year—thyme, oregano, rosemary. The English flowers that had bloomed there in spring were all withered now.

If she stayed in this chateau, in France, long enough, she would wither too. She was already wilting inside. Was she so unworthy of a man's interest? Love she could do without—she had Con. That was all the love she needed. But in these last few days, a feeling had been growing like a weed in spring—she craved human touch.

No, not merely human. A man's appreciative, even hungry touch.

Not just any man's, either.

But he didn't want her, and so she drooped like an unwatered plant.

Her fingers swept the water restlessly. The little rippling sounds mingled with the desultory birdsong and the underlying notes of a lute.

Her hand stilled. The sounds of water subsided. The rippling lute notes did not.

Eglantine frowned. Was the minstrel playing in the hall? Or in the courtyard, perhaps? He certainly wasn't in the hayloft. The notes sounded far too close at hand for that.

It was rather nice, actually—soft lute notes filtering through her garden, with no accompanying lyrics of love to disturb her. She leaned against the tamarisk tree and closed her eyes, just listening. Her hand drooped in the water. She let the music flow over her. It seeped into her, easing her tensions, reviving her wilted spirit. Just a little.

Then—curse it—the man had to add words to the music.

I bare my soul for you, O lady of my heart,
Name the dread deed, and it is done.
Though wild beasts of the forest tear me apart,
I strive till all obstacles are overcome.

Eglantine set her teeth. Her eyelids flicked open. There was something amiss. She stood up abruptly. There was the slightest hiccup in the music. She scooped up a trowel and began a slow round of her garden—looking for weeds.

She found a particularly heinous weed on a stone bench tucked between a wildly rambling rose and a plum tree. He stopped playing the moment she ducked beneath the plum tree. The detestable words died on his lips.

"What are you doing here, minstrel?"

He laid his lute aside and stood. The rambling rose clawed at his dark hair. She would have liked to have done the same.

"My lady, I came to find you."

The velvet of his tone stroked her senses. It threatened to melt her. His eyes were worse. The way he gazed at her, holding nothing back—it was terrifying.

"You should not be here. No one is permitted entry to my garden unless I give them permission. *You* do not have it."

The intensity of his gaze slipped, thank goodness. "I did not know. Pray forgive the intrusion." A brief hesitation. Then: "I came because I had to, my lady. I must speak to you, in private."

"You had every chance of speaking to me yesterday, minstrel. And more. Pray, what is it you neglected to say then?"

He startled her then—he took a step forward and dropped onto one knee before her. Never a good idea in the shadow of a rosebush. A small, savage part of her hoped he'd settled on a particularly spiky thorn.

But only a part of her. Most of her being was absorbed by him, this beautiful, dark man who had touched her, then withdrew, and was now gazing up at her with unchecked passion in his eyes. Dear God, what now?

"My lady, I am not what I seem. I have deceived you for too long. It is not right. I beg you, hear me out."

Something tightened within her.

"Are you or are you not a minstrel?" she said, a little surprised to hear how cool her voice sounded. Downright chilly.

"I play the lute and I sing, my lady. But I need not do so for a living."

Which meant he need not perform any other unwanted services for a living either, doubtless.

"If you are not a minstrel, what are you?" She was gripping her trowel like a weapon. By God, she had some weeding to do.

"I am the man who loves you, my lady. Without reserve. Without hope. I traveled to La Roque solely for that purpose—to lay my heart at your feet."

"You mock me, false minstrel. Speak the truth—who are you? *What* are you?"

It was so hard to keep gazing into his eyes, beautiful, bottomless black eyes that seemed so very sincere. But he admitted it himself: he had deceived her. Who knew where the truth lay? Doubtless he was deceiving her still.

Or if he was speaking the truth, he deceived himself.

"I am Rafèu, Vicomte of Bruniquel, my lady. And I come to claim you as my wife."

He caught her hand as he spoke—the one without the trowel—and she did not know whether the shock that rippled through her was due to his words or his touch. The ground was unsteady beneath her feet.

"No!" The word was a gasp. She snatched her hand away and stumbled back a step or two. "No, you bastard, you have deceived me." She flicked her hand as if to rid it of any trace of him.

He rose slowly to his feet. "Not a bastard. Unfortunately, it seems. If I were a bastard minstrel, you'd want more to do with me." He gazed at her with disconcerting directness. "But I speak no word of a lie when I say I love you, Lady Eglantine, and that I wish you to be my wife."

"No, you *do* lie. And you deceive yourself, vicomte. Whatever you are. You *do not* love me. You barely know me. You mistake a moment's lust for something deeper. And why would I wish to marry you? If I were going to marry, it would be to an honest Englishman, not some playacting French lord who has inveigled himself into my chateau. Get out!"

Eglantine was shaking. It was all too evident in the arm she flung toward the garden door. The trowel in her hand only emphasized the quivering.

He was simply looking at her, his mouth slightly parted—as if he would say more. Oh, she remembered those lips on hers so very well—the blaze they lit in her, the passion, the possession.

Yes, the possession. That was it. He wanted to possess her, just as Ferrand had possessed her. He was a man cut from the same mold—a French nobleman who thought he could own her. A man who had no idea what love was, and was probably incapable of ever knowing.

She had thought she'd loved Ferrand too. Ugh. The very notion left bitterness in her mouth. It was a lesson learned. A mistake she'd never make again.

She could not trust her desires. They were fleeting flames that would soon burn themselves out. But first she had to get rid of what fueled them.

"Get out," she repeated in a voice of iron. She jabbed her trowel in the direction of the door. "You will leave La Roque immediately. I do not want to see you again, vicomte or minstrel or whatever you are."

Chapter Nine

H E LEFT. RAF exited the garden and sleepwalked back to the stables. He threw himself in the hay and stared at the beams of the stable roof.

He had played this all wrong. He should not have hurried into revealing his true identity and purpose. He should have won her heart first, then declared himself. But he had been afraid she had no more use for Minstrel Rafèu and that his eviction was imminent, so he hurried. He had blundered into her private sanctuary and thrown his heart at her feet.

She had kicked it away.

Raf clenched handfuls of hay. The dry stems splintered into his palms. He had been so cursedly clumsy. Margery had told him about Ferrand of La Roque, his philandering ways, and Raf had not used that knowledge. At very least, he should have told Eglantine outright that he, Rafèu of Bruniquel, was *not* like her late husband. Nothing like him.

Now what was he to do? Raf stared at the roof. The pain, the tension in him was so all-encompassing that he could do nothing but lie there and endure it, teeth gritted. *Think*, for God's sake. He could not leave, could he? He would never see her again.

But she had ordered him to go. He, a vicomte, was ordered out of the chateau as roughly as a vagrant. If he did not do so of his own accord, Raf did not doubt that Eglantine would summon her men-at-arms to escort him. Osbert in particular would be delighted to oblige.

That gave him an idea. It wasn't hope, exactly, just a dusty ray of light. Osbert was out with Con, riding. Raf suspected that his lady would summon Osbert the moment the captain returned and have him scour the chateau for any unwanted minstrels. Or vicomtes.

But Osbert wasn't here yet. That gave Raf time.

He still lay on his back and stared at the roof, but this time he began to see it for what it was—sturdy. And not overly steep.

Raf sat up. He made short work of gathering his meagre minstrel belongings. Then he slithered down the loft ladder and went to his horse. He rubbed its soft nose and patted its flank. Moments later, he was leading the creature out of the stable and through the chateau gate. He farewelled the gate guard conspicuously—it wasn't Osbert, of course—turned his back on the castle, and descended the precipitous path to the village.

GARDENING WAS NOT producing its normal soothing effect. Eglantine stabbed at the dirt with a vicious trowel, but it wasn't earth she saw beneath the descending steel. It was warm human skin. Not that she had ever seen much of his—matters had never progressed so far.

Damn him to hell, why couldn't he just be a wandering minstrel? She *wanted* his skin, warm against hers.

But she was getting far too hot and bothered, stabbing soil in a summer garden. She stood up and scanned her green haven for something else to attend to—and heard the bell ring.

Ah, that was the proper way to gain her attention. She set aside her trowel and went to the garden door.

Osbert. Precisely the man she most wanted to see. Eglantine smiled at her captain. He did not smile back. In fact, there was a strange tension about his jaw and brow.

"M'lady, can I have a word?"

The smile slipped from her face. "Con! Has anything happened? Is my son…"

She couldn't complete the sentence. Osbert had just been out riding with her son. What else could make him look so grave?

"The little lord is just fine, m'lady. I left him with Margie."

But the grave look was still there.

"What, then?" Eglantine demanded.

The man-at-arms gestured at the door and the hatch through which they were conversing. "Reckon the matter requires some chewing over, m'lady. Can we go to the solar?"

Eglantine flung aside her gardening apron and hat and hurried for the stairs. If it wasn't Con that Osbert felt a pressing need to discuss, then there was only one other option. And Eglantine did not want to air the problem of Rafèu, Vicomte Bruniquel, where anyone might overhear.

"THERE ARE MEN in the village."

Eglantine eyed Osbert. "Yes, there usually are," she answered.

The man-at-arms shook his head. "No, m'lady. Strange men. Lots of them. They weren't there when the little lord and I rode out, but by the time we ambled back…"

Eglantine also shook her head, more to clear it than in negation. Her mind was full of a certain false minstrel, and more recently worries about her son. It had no room in it for a strange horde of men.

"I've ordered the gates closed," Osbert went on.

"What?"

"Precaution, m'lady. Them down the hill didn't look like merchants or minstrels to me. They're a bleeding great lot of soldiers. All got the same tabard on."

Eglantine rubbed her forehead. She was catching up, if slowly. "But the war is in Spain now. Du Guesclin went to Castile, and Prince Edward followed him. Between the two of them they drained Southern France of most of its swords. Only brigands remain."

"Brigands don't doll themselves up in tabards. This lot is a company. Reckon the war in Spain is over."

"You fear it has come back here," Eglantine whispered.

"Fear so."

It was all too much for one morning. Eglantine took a turn around the room, finishing at the great glassed window. She peered between the panes but saw nothing to enlighten her. She could not see the village from here. A defensible castle did not present breakable windows to the world. But below in the main courtyard, there seemed more activity than normal.

Osbert seemed to read her thoughts. "I told all them that I saw outside the walls to get inside. Just in case."

"And now the gate is closed," Eglantine murmured.

"Aye, my lady."

She turned to him with sudden energy. "I have one small task for you regarding that gate, my captain. I have asked the minstrel, Raf, to leave La Roque. Make sure that he's gone, if you please, and that he stays out."

For the first time since he'd entered, a grin spread over Osbert's mouth. "A pleasure, my lady."

RAFÈU WATCHED THE activity in the courtyard below. He could see the gate from his vantage point, too. It was shut and bolted. Occasionally, the gateman would conduct a conversation with someone standing invisibly outside and that person would be admitted to the courtyard. The gate was then re-bolted.

Raf knew full well the reason for this activity. He had been in the village of La Roque that morning. He had seen the men. He had observed Osbert's return and the flurry of orders issued in his wake.

None of it changed his plans. It simply solidified them.

Now the sun was high in the sky, Rafèu was slowly baking on the stable roof, and the guard was conducting a lengthy discussion through the chateau gate. Then the guard turned and sent a messenger scuttling off, to return with none other than Osbert, ill-mannered captain of La Roque. Evidently, this was no ordinary request for admission.

Raf had had enough. He couldn't hear a word of what was being said, he was broiling inside his new outfit, and he would shrivel up from thirst should he stay here much longer. While all eyes were—hopefully—fixed upon Osbert, Raf slipped back down into the hayloft, then out of the stables and into the chateau keep itself. His motley was a thing of the past. His crakows were stowed in the stable. Pity, as he'd enjoyed the flamboyant costume—when it wasn't tripping him up. Now Raf the minstrel was transformed into a quite ordinary and invisible serving man. He could only pray that was what others saw.

He found his lady in the ground-floor storerooms, praise God. It was the best possible location she could have chosen for his purposes—a single great room supported with innumerable sturdy stone vaults and littered with barrels and bales and casks. Raf was spoilt for places to hide. It was also blessedly cool.

Lady Eglantine was assessing supplies with a couple of servants.

"And this year's wine—have the grapes been pressed yet?" she asked. She was speaking in French for once. Most of La Roque's occupants were locals.

"Some, my lady. The main harvest's yet to come, but we've got the early stuff here. Wouldn't want to drink it yet, though."

"So we have the remainder of last year's press, and the beginnings of this one. Which means our wine stocks are low, yes?"

"Not low precisely, my lady. We've got plenty of wine to see us through to the main pick...lest we can't get to the grapes."

A weighted silence followed.

"Well then, let's hope nothing prevents us stamping on grapes to our heart's content," said his lady briskly.

Raf's lips twitched. That was a sight he'd like to see—the demure Lady Eglantine with her skirt around her knees and her legs purple with grape juice. Perhaps he'd offer to lick them clean.

In the most respectful way possible, of course.

The vision was dissipated by the arrival of Osbert. Raf shrank back behind a vault.

"M'lady, it's happened. The leader of them down in the village wants a meeting with you. The leader of the company, I mean. English, he is, and a sir."

With infinite caution, Raf maneuvered himself until he'd acquired a view of the speakers. His lady's face seemed pale and set in the dimly lit storeroom. If only she had accepted Raf's offer of marriage. He could ease this burden from her shoulders. This exquisitely made woman should not have to make these decisions alone, or at all.

"Who is he? Do you know of him?"

"He sent a couple of fellows to the gate. Didn't come himself but, aye, the fellows gave his name—and, oh aye, I've heard of him."

"Well, then?"

"He's Sir Garit of the Ruin. He's an English knight fresh back from Spain."

"Garit of the Ruin?" Eglantine echoed. "A ruin, for God's sake? Doesn't the man have a proper name?"

Osbert shrugged. "That's what they call him, m'lady. It's how his men spoke of him. Reckon it refers not to his lands but to the ruin he leaves in his ungodly wake."

Eglantine curled her fingers. "I do not like the sound of that. What is this man's reputation, Osbert? What you know of him?"

"His messenger's still dancing on the doorstep, m'lady."

Her chin rose. "Let him dance. I will know all I can of the wolf before I meet him in the flesh. *If* I decide to do so."

Raf smiled in the dark. *Well said, my lady.* A surprisingly strong decision.

Osbert grinned. It seemed he was of a mind with his mistress. "The fellow's from England. Southern parts, they say. He's got himself quite the reputation, see? French don't like him, not one little bit. His company's not big, but it knows what it's about. Reckon they carved a swath through Spain and got back here in sunny France afore most anyone else did."

In gist, it was what the Vicomte of Bruniquel had heard too. Unfortunately. He may have avoided war to the best of his ability for the past two years, but even Rafèu had heard of this ruinous knight. He hadn't heard much, but it had been enough. The conclusion was obvious: Garit of the Ruin was a man best unmet.

He only hoped his lady came to the same decision.

"And the man himself?" Lady Eglantine inquired.

There was no particular intonation in her voice, but Raf's skin still prickled. The Lady Eglantine didn't like French nobles, but what about those of an English variety?

"He's not got much to his name back home, but he's been walloping the poor devils in France for near-on twenty year now. Reckon he hasn't done so badly out of it either. Riches, reputation. Don't s'pose he's got where he has by being nice, m'lady."

Eglantine sighed. "You warned me for years it might come to this. I listened. I am not unprepared." She indicated the piles of stores about her. Raf's brow wrinkled, but his lady spoke on: "Well, what do you advise now, my captain? Should I meet this fellow, or do I simply order him off my land? You know as well as I that we haven't the strength to compel him."

Osbert stared at his feet for some moments. Then: "Damn him to hell, m'lady, but I reckon you're better off having a word with him. Maybe he's just passing through. Maybe he'll have a nice, polite word with you and then bugger off on his way. Dunno till we ask."

Raf was sorely tempted to step from behind his buttress and declare a resounding *no*. He had no idea what this Garit wanted, but he did *not* want the man in the same room as Eglantine. Raf thoroughly approved of Osbert's slamming the chateau gates shut. They should remain that way until this troop of strangers had found another village to harass.

He restrained himself with difficulty, and strained to hear his lady's reply.

"I pray you're right, my captain."

Eglantine firmed her lips. Indeed, Raf suspected she was giving her lower lip a chew. His own mouth tingled at the thought. He could kiss all her cares away. If he were her husband, he would...what? Face down this Garit in her stead? Single-handedly drive every last English soldier from of La Roque? He knew not. But he would support her, guide her, love her. She should not be so alone.

"All right, then. I agree," Lady Eglantine said. "I will speak to Sir Garit. I grant him an audience in my solar within the hour. But he must enter the chateau alone. I promise him safe conduct, but I will *not* open La Roque to a swarm of soldiers. You must remove his weapons and accompany him through the chateau, Osbert—and you shall remain with me to hear whatever has to say."

The solar. It was a pity she couldn't just meet this Garit fellow down here in the storeroom where Raf could remain conveniently hidden. But no, the solar was the proper place to meet a noble guest. A storeroom was for servants. By rights, the lady shouldn't be down here even now.

Osbert departed. Eglantine turned back to the waiting servants and resumed her discussion of wine, and salt cod, and flour, and malting barley, and...

Raf only waited long enough to ensure his lady's attention was firmly elsewhere. He ceased to prop up the vaulting and instead made his quiet and cautious way toward the corner staircase. If he made it to the solar before Eglantine, there was a chance he could hide himself sufficiently to overhear her interview with the English war leader.

Despite appearances, her man Osbert seemed competent enough, but one stumpy man-at-arms was too little protection against a man of Sir Garit's reputation, even if Garit were stripped of his weapons; even—dammit—if the man were bound and held at knifepoint.

For the first time, Raf missed his sword and other knightly accoutrements. They were in Bruniquel still. He'd not thought he'd need them in La Roque. All he had now was a short dagger. Even that he'd had to smuggle in under cover, bound to his lute neck. But, by God, it would be enough. If necessary, Rafèu would give his life for his lady—she would *not* fall into the grasp of this ruinous knight.

Chapter Ten

"SIR GARIT OF the Ruin, m'lady."

Osbert ushered the man into the solar. Eglantine rose to meet her unwelcome guest, all dignity and calm reserve. Or that was the intended effect. Margery had fussed with her mistress's wimple and gown and ensured that all was in place, neat and confined. It was Eglantine's armor. Only her hands and face were exposed.

Margery had wanted to dust her cheeks with color too, and to darken her eyelids with some other arcane powder, but Eglantine had refused.

"I am a modest widow and the chatelaine of a castle. That is all. I do not need to appear attractive. I do not wish this knight to perceive anything beyond the proprietor of a chateau."

And now he was here, perceiving whatever he wished to perceive.

Eglantine sketched a curtsey. "Welcome, Sir Garit. I am Eglantine, widow of Ferrand of La Roque and mother to his heir. Pray, be seated."

She spoke in English to emphasize their common homeland. They should not be enemies.

The man who had entered the solar bowed, then glanced around at the proffered seating—cushions, a padded window seat, the stool at her desk-of-business.

"Thank you, my lady. I prefer to stand. I trust my business with you will not take long."

A Southern English accent. It was music to her ears.

Eglantine surveyed the visitor. His face and person should have had an equally pleasing effect on her eyes. The man was undeniably handsome, at least if one favored men that were carven blocks of muscle and featured sun-bleached blond hair and vivid blue eyes. It was the tanned skin that made his eyes seem so startling by contrast, she decided. This was a man who spent a lot of time outdoors, probably killing other men. Possibly women, too.

"As it please you, Sir Garit." Eglantine turned and resumed her seat at the desk. Somehow the proximity of so much parchment was reassuring. She folded her hands in her lap. "Do you and your men intend to stay long in the village of La Roque?"

It was a pointed question, but he *had* implied he wished to speak of business and speak it quickly.

"That depends on you, my lady." The man's gaze seemed to take in the entire room, its glass window, its solid stone walls, and its mere female owner, sitting motionless on a stool.

"How so, Sir Garit?"

Osbert quietly moved to her side. He took up a position just behind her, a solid, silent presence.

"Lady Eglantine, my men and I have just returned from Spain. We are among the first to do so. Prince Edward lingers there too long. He has won the battle but he has lost the cause. Pedro of Castile is tardy in repaying his English saviors, and while the prince waits for money, his forces are dying, not of war but of disease. So I returned."

Garit paused a moment and regarded her.

"You wonder what this has to do with you and my presence in your village? Let me explain. My men and I have returned to France earlier than most, but be assured the remainder of Edward's army will not be far behind. English soldiers will soon flood Southern France."

Eglantine did not shiver, but it was an effort not to. Unemployed warriors without a war to busy themselves with. Fighters lacking funds. It was a phenomenon France had known before. This was why she had stocked her storerooms so liberally. Why couldn't the bastards all just stay in Spain? Or go home to England. Why couldn't *she* go home to England?

"I thank you for the forewarning, sir. I appreciate your consideration of a fellow countrywoman."

And she prayed that was all that brought this blond lump of muscle to her gates.

A fool's prayer.

"I come to offer my protection, Lady Eglantine. You are a woman alone and your chateau is undermanned. You need a male protector."

Eglantine stiffened. She glanced at Osbert, and Garit interpreted the look all too easily.

"I mean no disrespect to your captain, lady, but that is not what I mean. You need a man to guide and protect you, not simply take your orders. You need a husband. You are a widow in a land at war. Marry me, and I will protect you and your son. This I swear."

Eglantine did not gape, but she was certain her eyes widened and her cheeks turned to chalk.

The fellow didn't even bother to get down on one knee. He hadn't praised her beauty or extolled her virtues. He hadn't even seen her son. And his face had not softened one iota. It was a bleak contrast to her previous proposal. When had it been—only hours before?

For God's sake, *this* was why strange men were not admitted to La Roque, and especially not noblemen. They automatically assumed that an unwed woman was in want of a man, and that that man was necessarily them. Heaven help her, did she have to lock herself up as an anchoress?

But at least he is English, a voice whispered in her head. *At least he is honest and forthright. He doesn't pretend to love you. He would not break your heart because he doesn't want your heart.*

It was not enough.

"I thank you for your offer, Sir Garit," she lied through her teeth, quite literally. "But you are mistaken. I do not need a husband. Perhaps you have noticed that La Roque is built into a cliff. A good position, is it not? It is the sort of castle that may be defended by a mere handful. I have all the men I need. I do not need to marry to protect myself."

She thought she heard a sigh at that—a heartfelt exhalation. It had not come from Osbert. She narrowed her eyes at Sir Garit. The man wore no more expression than he had upon first entering. It was a calm, capable expression that said, *I will deal with whatever the world throws at me, and I will conquer.*

Eglantine's hands tightened upon each other. She was eternally grateful for Osbert's presence behind her.

If only Raf were still here, a stupid little voice whispered in her head. She would like him to stand behind her too.

But no, she had sent her first suitor of the day on his way. Her dark minstrel was gone. Osbert told her he had been seen descending to the village, a man in motley leading his horse. Further investigation showed his belongings were gone from the hayloft. It was as if Rafèu had never been there.

"Let me be blunt, Lady Eglantine," the blond man went on.

"I thought you had already."

Garit's expression did not change. "No castle is invulnerable. Even the most well-fortified and well-stocked chateau will run out of food eventually."

He paused. Evidently he wished to let the words to sink in.

Then, perhaps because his first words had not been blunt enough, Sir Garit hammered his point home further. "My men and I have wealth enough, but we require a stronghold to safeguard it and us. We could take a castle by force, but that would take time and loss of life. This is better. I am unmarried and you are a widow. I will protect you and your son. He will inherit in time, should he live. No son I get on you will have precedence. That I swear. My proposal benefits both of us. What possible reason have you to refuse me?"

What possible reason at all?

Her heart thudded a drumbeat in her ears. She heard the threat in his calm and reasonable words. *We could take a castle by force. No castle is invulnerable.* Marrying her was simply the easiest means of attaining his ends.

She was about to open her mouth and order the bastard out of La Roque—the chateau and the village too. She was about to throw his foul proposal in his tanned and handsome face, when Osbert stepped forward.

"Sir Garit, my mistress thanks you for your proposal and your straight talking, but she needs time to reflect. Reckon she needs to take advice and settle her thoughts a tad. How about you wander back down to the village, sup an ale or two, and await her decision?"

The war leader inclined his head. His expression didn't change. "I prefer wine, but yes, it is only reasonable. I will give you time to consider the matter, Lady Eglantine. A day, no more. In the meantime, be assured my men and I will treat the village with respect. We are not invaders."

Not yet. Not unless you wish us to be.

Then Sir Garit of the Ruin bowed to the Lady Eglantine and departed, Osbert hurrying in his wake.

Leaving a chill in the midsummer air.

RAF REMAINED BEHIND the curtain for a long time after Sir Garit left. It was as well he'd chosen to secrete himself where the room-dividing fabric met solid stone wall. He'd selected this dim corner of her bedchamber for greatest invisibility, but now he was simply grateful he had a stone wall to lean against.

Sir Garit—a distinctly presentable and *English* knight—wanted to wed his lady. That was bad enough. It might have been catastrophic had his lovely lady not declined, coolly and definitely. No, what was infinitely worse was what would happen next. Either Eglantine would change her mind, urged perhaps by Osbert, or Sir Garit of the Ruin would resort to other means of persuasion.

A coldness washed over Rafèu. He leaned against the stony wall and saw nothing…but the past. The walls of the chamber were closing in on him.

"Has he gone?" His lady's voice wafted through Raf's reverie.

"Aye, mistress. He gave me no trouble. Gave him his sword back and showed him the gate. Out he went." Osbert coughed. "But I didn't like the way he looked about him on the way. Like he was seeing everything round him and making an inventory of what we've got."

"As if he were considering whether La Roque would suit him and his men? Like a buyer before a sale?" Eglantine snapped. "No, more like a looter before he starts pillaging."

Good. She sounded fierce. True, Raf had never imagined his love as a she-wolf. She had been all delicacy and demureness in his mind, a perfect rose that might be bruised by a gust of wind. But Raf found he didn't mind this unladylike quality at all right now. So long as it was directed at the English knight.

"No. Reckon he was assessing La Roque's strengths and weaknesses, m'lady. Like a would-be bastard besieger."

For the sake of all that is holy, don't say that word. It must not come to that.

"Siege?" His lady calmly countered Raf's prayer. "He doesn't want a siege. He said so himself. He said it would take too much time and loss of men. He just wants a convenient castle for him and his men, and a wife to warm his bed."

A little of the tension drained from Raf. She was right. His fierce lady had a point. Garit had definitely said that he preferred to avoid the loss of time and men involved in besieging a castle. He needed a stronghold, and he needed it now.

Unfortunately, Osbert was not on Raf's side.

"Sir Garit said he didn't fancy the loss of time and life, m'lady. He didn't say he weren't up for it. Oh, make no mistake—I saw it in his eye. The whole lot was a damned threat. Why would he take his men off and find another castle to besiege if you refuse him this one? He reckons La Roque is vulnerable because it is held by a woman and a boy."

"It is not vulnerable," Eglantine snapped. "La Roque is built into a cliff face. It is reputed one of the most impregnable chateaux in the region. Garit must know this. He would be a fool to try to take it by force. He may be a churl and a boor, but he didn't strike me as a fool."

"No castle is invulnerable," Osbert muttered. Garit's own words.

"For heaven's sake, Osbert! What would you have me do? Curtesy and say sweetly—*Yes, Sir Garit. Of course I will be your wife. Here, let me give you all La Roque and entrust my son's life and inheritance to your hands.* Well? What else is there?"

"If he reduces La Roque, he will take all anyway. Do you know the laws of siege, m'lady? He who takes the castle takes all. Garit won't feel himself obliged to wed you *or* respect the lives of any soul within its walls."

A silence, filled to the brim with Raf's own thoughts. Perhaps Eglantine did not know the laws—or more like the brutal realities—of siege, but Vicomte Rafèu did.

"Counsel me, my captain." The lady's voice was low. Raf thought he detected a tremor in it. "What do I do? This English invader presents me with two options—wed him, or be besieged. I believe we can hold out in the face of his aggression. La Roque can withstand a siege, and Sir Garit cannot stay here forever. He must give up eventually and go away. Am I wrong? What else can I do?"

This was where Vicomte Rafèu ought to part the curtains and present himself. Yes, it was outrageous that he had hidden himself in a noble widow's bedchamber for the purpose of overhearing this most confidential of conversations. Yes, the Minstrel Raf had been thrown out of La Roque, and, upon catching sight of him, Osbert would probably attempt to make theory a reality. But these were minor matters. His lady needed him. She was threatened. She knew not what to do, and her captain was not being particularly helpful.

Yet Raf remained frozen. His head wasn't working. All rational consideration of the situation had been rudely shoved aside. What replaced it was memory—visceral, all-too-vivid memory.

"You got a point, m'lady. We *could* hold out. Maybe Garit will give up and wander away when La Roque don't fall sweetly into his lap. But it's a damned risk. We don't know what siege gear he's got. What if he's lugged a cannon with him? Do you know of gunpowder, m'lady?"

Silence. She was probably shaking her head. Raf would not have shaken his head. He was all too intimate with cannons and their effects.

"Then there's the village, m'lady. The soldiers are already cozied up in it. We can seal up the chateau, but we can't do nothing to protect the village. Dunno how many people have fled already. Them with sense probably have. Then there's your lands."

"My son's lands," Eglantine corrected him.

"Sir Garit will make an ungodly mess of it. I've seen what Englishmen do in France. Helped 'em do it a couple of times, for my sins."

"I don't think so," Eglantine said slowly. "Garit will look to feed his men, but he will not destroy what he wishes to own."

"And the village?"

"He will use it to house his men, will he not? My people will be thrown out of their homes or forced to serve the enemy."

"Likely enough," Osbert said. "Reckon the women of the village will be forced to cater to English appetites too. Begging your ladyship's pardon, but I don't just mean food."

Raf frowned. He could not dispute the captain's words and

the horrible reality behind them, but there was something more going on here.

"They will suffer because I refuse to, you mean?" Eglantine's tone was flat.

The sound of shuffling feet. "You could put it that way, m'lady."

"What else do you think I should consider, Osbert?"

"Begging your pardon, mistress, but you're an unwed lady without a male protector. Your son's got no pa, and his lands are downright vulnerable. You'd do better to marry again, least for his sake. Reckon your best option is to demand a legal document outlining the little lord's right to La Roque, then you marry Sir Garit."

❧❦❧

Chapter Eleven

RAFÈU REMAINED THE rest of the day in the hayloft. As a hiding place, it was a bad choice. Everyone knew he had been sleeping there before he was asked to leave. Perhaps some part of him wanted to be discovered, to have all choice wrested from him the moment he was tossed out on the hillside and the gate clanged shut behind him. But he was not. The inhabitants of La Roque appeared to have more important things on their mind.

So Raf watched the scurrying about of servants and men-at-arms through the chinks in the loft. He couldn't see what was going on in the keep, but he had a fine view of the activities on the battlements. A pulley had been set up over the gatehouse, and servants busied themselves feeding it baskets of rocks. Raf heard clanging, hammering noises from the cliff-face portion of La Roque. The baskets of rocks appeared from that direction. At least the chateau would not run out of stones to drop on enemy heads.

A part of Raf admired the activity, applauded it as sound forward planning, but mostly it was as if someone had deposited their basket of rocks on his chest. It was a particularly well-loaded basket, and it would not budge.

Eglantine had decided to fortify La Roque for a siege.

His lady had declared that she didn't wish to marry *anyone*, let alone a man who demanded it with an army at his back. But then she very reasonably told Osbert that negotiations could be reopened at a later date—should Sir Garit decide to besiege them in the first place. If it turned out that marriage was the best of all possible solutions, well, she would cross that dung heap when she came to it. The tone in which she uttered those last words made Raf wonder.

But attitude to marriage aside, where had a woman acquired such sound siege strategy? Eglantine was acting as a man might do, and with more common sense than many men of Raf's acquaintance.

She had also asked Osbert to send word to the villagers. They had to be warned. It was too late to admit them to the chateau—even if it were possible, it would put too much strain on La Roque's supplies—but there were other ways she could help them.

Eglantine had shouldered the burdens of a man and leader, and all Raf could do was sit in the hayloft and watch. It went entirely against the grain.

On the other hand, he should leave while he could. Once the siege began—pray God it never began—he could not simply open the gates and stroll away. The gates would *not* be opened, for invaders would pour in, and if he tried to descend La Roque's walls, he would be used for target practice by notoriously capable English archers. If he left now, he might still return to Bruniquel with a whole skin.

He *should* leave now, but he couldn't.

He would not abandon his lady. What sort of a worthless knight fled with his tail between his legs when the lady of his heart was threatened? Eglantine may not want him—at least, she had a passing fancy for his person, but didn't want a bar of his soul—but Raf could not leave her. This was the stuff of songs—of hopeless, tragic love songs. Only now did he understand them—the knight who would be faithful to the end, without reward and without hope. She *needed* him now, whether she wanted him or not. She needed every man she could get to defend La Roque.

Even so, every instinct screamed at him to flee while he could.

And when he finally fell into a restless doze that night, Raf's sleep was rent by jagged-edged impressions—of smoke, destruction, screams, and despair.

THE ENEMY WAS at the gate. She had been expecting it all morning, and now here he was. Sir Garit of the Ruin was standing, clad in full war harness, with a wall of men behind him and a gate of wood and iron before him. She could see it all through the arrow slit.

Eglantine was no lover of the French summer sun—except for today. For once, the sun was on her side. She hoped the overmuscled lump had worked up a good sweat trudging up the hill and was now slowly boiling in his steel shell.

For said knight was taking no chances. He had assumed the sealed gate meant his proposal was rejected, and that a flight of steel-tipped arrows might express Eglantine's feelings more clearly. In spite of the white linen flag one of his men was holding.

Garit's visor was flipped up. He stepped a pace nearer.

"Do I address the Lady Eglantine?" he called, scanning the blank stone and wood. Doubtless he could see figures on the battlements above and faces at the arrow slits, but he could not see her.

"You do." She spoke loudly and firmly. Eglantine would not bellow or screech. "You also address Constantine, heir to La Roque, whose lands you occupy against his will. My mind has not changed, and I declare that you are no longer welcome in the village. If you are a true Englishman and a knight, you will not harass an English lady in her home. Leave in peace and with my good will. There is nothing for you here."

There. She was rather proud of that speech. A true knight and fellow countryman would not menace her. She had shown him his duty. His honor would dictate that he leave posthaste.

Beside her, Con was practically bouncing on the spot. "Let me look, Mother. Let me see the soldiers."

"Do you want an arrow in your eye?" she said. "Haven't you heard how good the English are with their bows?"

"You're standing there." He jabbed a finger first at the arrow slit then at her. "You haven't got an arrow in your eye."

"That's because they haven't started shooting yet."

"Well, I'm safe, aren't I? Let me look, Mother. *Please.*"

Sigh. He was the future lord of the castle. She probably owed it to him. "Just a quick peek, then. But as soon as I need to reply, you must move. Understand?"

Con gave a nod and then scrambled into the bow embrasure, the deep indent that allowed an archer to aim through the gap. He practically inserted his face into the arrow slit.

"Don't make yourself so obvious. Back a bit!" she nearly yelped.

Praise heaven, the boy obeyed. Even so, she was so focused on not having an apoplexy on the spot that she nearly missed Sir Garit's next words.

"I am a true Englishman and a knight, Lady Eglantine. In that capacity, I offer you my protection as your husband. You are a woman alone in a land at war. I cannot depart and leave you to the returning armies' mercy, French or English. They will not be so courteous as I."

Eglantine grabbed Con's shoulders and hauled him out of the embrasure. She had words to say, and they would not wait.

"You have a strange notion of courtesy, coming to my gate fully armed and with a small army at your back," she called. "I am *not* a woman alone. I have a loyal household and fine men-at-arms. I need no husband to tell me what to do. Take your courtesy elsewhere. The gates will not be opened to you."

Diplomacy be damned. He was trying to undermine her

before her own people. She didn't need a man to keep them safe. She needed to hold La Roque secure and *on her own* until Con was ready to step into his patrimony. That was her duty, and that was her desire. A man—a husband—would only threaten all she hoped to achieve.

But if Osbert had doubts on the score of her competency *sans* husband, perhaps others in her household did too. The only cure for that was to prove them wrong. She would hold La Roque against all threats. All men.

"I shall remove my men from your gate, Lady Eglantine, if they so offend you. We will, however, remain in the village of La Roque. There is but one way in and out of your chateau, I believe, and that is by the path to the village. We shall guard it for you. No one will traverse the path, on pain of death. You and yours will remain safe within your chateau walls—until you change your mind, which I trust you will do before your supplies run out. I do not wish to wed a skeleton."

All spoken in a clear and carrying voice. No particular expression infused it. Sir Garit was not incensed. He simply stated his point and waited for her to submit to it.

And it took a moment for the truth to filter through. Without saying the word, Garit of the Ruin had just declared he would besiege La Roque. Her chateau was well-nigh impregnable, but that was now precisely the problem. The one steep access path to the castle would be easy to blockade. Garit would not let anyone in or out, *on pain of death.*

Oh, there were ways up the cliff and into the woods above, or down the precipitous slope to the lower meadows and woods, but they were best suited to a squirrel or a mountain goat. Besides, Garit would probably take these into account.

"Does he want to marry you, Mother?" Con was tugging at her sleeve, frowning up at her.

"He only wants to marry me so he can own La Roque," she said. "Don't worry, I won't let him. He wants to steal your home. He won't have it."

Even if she were reduced to a skeleton and she had to watch her son slowly starve?

She clenched her hands to stop them from shaking.

"M'lady, he's waiting. He wants your reply," Osbert said. "It's not too late—"

"Yes it is!" she snapped. "We have plenty of supplies, and he and his men will soon get tired of waiting for a mere woman to capitulate."

She said that last bit nice and loud. Then she set her jaw and leaned into the bow embrasure.

"You are no true knight, Garit of the Ruin. To remain on my son's lands is an act of war. An honorable knight would depart immediately. Go. Restore my good opinion of you. It is not too late."

But it was.

Eglantine retreated from the arrow slit, hoping that her trembling wasn't too evident. Some silly, weak part of her was wishing she hadn't thrown Raf out of the chateau. A larger part of her wished her false minstrel had remained what he'd seemed. A true minstrel would have comforted her now. A true minstrel would not demand anything in return, save a little money. His music would soothe her, and his hands and lips... Well, soothing was not precisely what she wanted.

But no, she was plagued with false men. Eglantine would raise her own son to be true, and in order to do that, she would bar La Roque to all invaders. Would-be damned husbands. It was far too late to restore her good opinion of any man who aspired to own her.

HE HAD OVERHEARD it all.

Raf had listened in, quite still in order to cause not the least rustle of hay, from the convenient vantage of the loft. Now he saw his lady retreat from the gate, her shoulders rigid and her chin held high. Con bounced beside her, peppering her with questions.

She halted in the middle of the courtyard. The greater part of the chateau's inhabitants appeared to be out there too. They were looking at her expectantly. He read fear and surprise on those faces, but a touch of pride in their lady too. Raf gave a rueful smile. If he could see his own face, he'd probably read the same emotions. Fear, definitely—unmanly, unknightly fear. The sort of fear that wound itself tight in your gut and brought the memories flooding back.

But pride, too. For his lady had been magnificent. She *was* magnificent. Eglantine had told Sir Garit exactly what she thought of him. She thought about as highly of the man as of a smear of dung on her shoe. And now she was about to address her people.

His magnificent lady took a deep breath and squared her shoulders. She spoke in French, so everyone present could understand her:

"Listen well, people of La Roque. You are safe here inside the chateau. We are all safe if we work together. Sir Garit will not threaten you unless you leave the protection of these walls. So I ask you all to stay inside the gates—for your own sake. For everyone's sake. If anyone opens the gate, we will all suffer. The invaders will simply enter and take all we own. You will be at their mercy. Do *not* leave the chateau."

A pause, during which the listeners murmured and shuffled. A few looked less than convinced. Then Eglantine went on:

"I have prepared for this. We have plenty of supplies. Sir Garit plans to starve us into submission. He has planned badly. He will fail. The English invader will give up and leave long before our supplies run low. He has not the luxury of waiting. We do."

Raf wanted to believe her, by all the saints he did. What she said made sense, but… His innards tied themselves into a Gordian knot and tugged tight. War was an unpredictable beast. Sieges could end in betrayal from within, or starvation so dire that those besieged looked upon each other as food, or a final attack so brutal that none were left whole. And Raf had stayed here, knowing all this, to expose himself to a state of siege. Again.

Because of her.

She was the woman he had dreamed of for years, the beautiful, unattainable flower of perfect womanhood. Now she was the commander of a castle under siege. It was a role no woman should have to undertake, most especially not his rose.

Eglantine spoke on:

"Should any of you have concerns or need to bring anything to my attention, come directly to me. I want no secrets among us. Speak to me of your worries. Otherwise, continue with the tasks you have been set. I have faith in you, my people. Because of you, La Roque will stand strong."

Raf felt like clapping. Not a good idea in his current position. Even if he wasn't currently secreting himself, she would likely think he mocked her.

It wouldn't be mockery. Her words had flooded him with warmth, a tingling pride quite unconnected to her beauty or any other sublime womanly attribute.

The Lady Eglantine had finished her address. She was returning to the chateau keep, Con beside her and Osbert a blocky shadow in her wake. She was holding herself erect, proud and strong. To Raf's eyes, she moved in a little circle of isolation, despite all the people in the courtyard. So alone.

I want no secrets among us, she had declared. Raf agreed. It only took one disaffected person to betray a whole castle.

It was time to stop being a secret himself. Rafèu had knowingly incarcerated himself in a besieged castle—was he moon-howlingly mad?—and now he must step up and contribute to its defense.

Chapter Twelve

Eglantine was in the kitchen when Con popped up at her side like a rabbit from its hole. She looked down at the boy with a sigh and a raised eyebrow, and then directed that eyebrow at Margery.

"Have you developed a sudden interest in baking as well as smiting?" she asked her son. "I asked you to give me a little space. I have a lot to do. Perhaps you recall we are under siege?"

She was addressing Margery as much as Con. She'd asked the girl to keep Con out from under her feet. The boy was full to bursting with events at the moment. He emanated questions and suggestions, not to mention an exhausting amount of jigging about.

"Sorry, my lady. We *were* staying out of your way, so Con said we'd go to the stables to check on the horses—"

"Yes!" the boy broke in. "They're under siege too. I needed to check the horse food supplies. That's what a responsible lord does."

He seemed to inflate as he said the words, and Eglantine hid a smile. Well, it was only fair. Here was she in the kitchen, discussing human supplies. Con had thought of the nonhuman inhabitants.

"Don't worry, Mother. They've got lots of hay," Con concluded. "I checked. Raf helped me."

"What?"

"Yes, Raf took me up to the hayloft and said there was so much dry grass up there that he could barely carve out a place to curl up. That's what he said."

Oh, maybe the false minstrel had shown Con the hayloft before he left. That made sense. The man had slept up there. He'd played to Margery up there too, the abominable charmer.

"Um, sorry, my lady," said Margery again. "I had no idea. Truly I didn't."

"What are you talking about?"

"We just went into the stables and he was there."

Eglantine's brow crinkled. She was beginning to get a bad feeling about this. "He?"

Margery blushed and ducked her head. "Aye. The minstrel, my lady."

"And you saw him today?"

"Yes! Just now." Con planted himself directly before her. "I missed him, Mother. Why did you say I couldn't see him anymore? Why did you say he was gone?"

Eglantine flexed her fingers. "Because he *was* gone. I ordered him to leave. He shouldn't be here, Con. You shall not see him again."

"I beg your pardon, my lady. I do not wish to make a liar of you."

That voice. Rich as French velvet and abrading her nerves like the roughest hemp. The owner of the voice stepped forward. He had been there all along, she realized—silent in the background. She had been too focused on Con and Margery to notice.

Of course she hadn't seen him—he shouldn't be there.

"You!" She was not happy to see him. Her heart did *not* stutter as she looked up into those dark eyes. A tingle did *not* slither down her arms as she dropped her gaze to his lips. "Beg all you like, false minstrel. My pardon is not granted. You are the liar."

He lifted a dark brow. "My lady, if we may speak alone?"

"No!" She would not allow herself to be alone with him ever

again. Strange things happened in such circumstances. "There is no need for speech, Vicomte Rafèu. You must leave. Margery?" She rounded upon the maid. "Fetch Osbert. Now."

Eglantine only glanced away for a moment, just to ensure Margery really did depart on an Osbert hunt. When she turned back to the false minstrel, her jaw sagged. The fellow had sunk to one knee before her. Again. He had one leg laid upon the kitchen rushes, a surface doubtless decorated with flour, blood, and lard, and much else besides.

"For God's sake, minstrel!"

It was as well she was standing close to a kitchen table. There was a nice, long knife upon it, most recently used for carving up meat, by the looks of things. It was still damply red.

Eglantine grabbed the knife and pointed it at the infinitely offensive vicomte.

He did not flinch. He gazed up at her steadily, his eyes penetrating to her soul.

"My lady, hear me out before you stick me with that thing."

She could not meet his eyes any longer. Her gaze slipped down—and she blinked. Laid across the man's open palms was a dagger, and quite a sizeable one too. She had a knife—he had a knife. If he was proposing marriage again, it was a strange accessory to choose.

"I lay my sword at your service, Lady Eglantine."

"That's not a sword!" piped up Con.

Eglantine's lips twitched. She clamped them tight. She would not smile at any aspect of this situation.

"I regret, Lord Constantine, that I did not bring my sword with me to La Roque," the not-minstrel said. "Minstrels wield lutes, not swords. Besides, worthy Osbert would have stripped me of this dagger too had he discovered it on my person. Thus I can only lay my dagger at your lady mother's service."

Con had the effrontery to grin at the kneeling minstrel. "That's all right. We can lend you a sword."

"No, we cannot," she said through clenched teeth.

"But we've got spare swords in the armory," Con interjected before she could say more. "I've seen them. Osbert says we don't have enough men-at-arms in La Roque. We've got the swords, but we need the men to hold 'em. That's what he says."

"We do not need *this* man to hold them," she said flatly. "He is unwelcome in La Roque. He needs to leave."

"Why?"

A child's default question. What could she say: *This too-beautiful man wants to marry your mother, while she just fancies taking him to her bed? This false minstrel has lied and deceived his way into La Roque, and that he deceives himself even more by thinking himself in love?* Heaven help her, if her wimple wasn't firmly covering it, she might tear her hair out.

"There is no call for questions, Con. This man is a stranger. I asked him to leave, and he is still here. He cannot be trusted. La Roque is under siege. We cannot keep untrustworthy strangers under our roof. We do not need more mouths to feed." She jabbed her bloody knife at the kneeling man, but did not jab too close. Why blunt a perfectly good kitchen knife? "Get up, false minstrel. Your 'sword' is not wanted. *I* do not want you in La Roque. This time you will leave."

She had to hold him at a knife's length, for a stupid, weak part of her was whispering its snake song in her mind. *Why not let him stay?* it said. She wanted him to wrap his arms about her and hold her tight. She wanted to melt into his strength and let his mouth drive away all thoughts of siege.

A throat was cleared with intent close by. She wrenched her gaze away from the minstrel. Osbert was standing in the kitchen, looking reassuringly stolid and practical.

"Don't reckon we can do that, m'lady. Sorry, m'lady. No one can leave. If we open the gate to boot out this piece of…" He clamped his lips shut, evidently recalling a shred of etiquette at the last moment. "If we open the gate to let this lute twiddler out, those English brigands may take advantage and barge in."

"Thank you, good Osbert," Raf murmured, getting to his feet

and brushing his hose free of stray rushes. "There is also the slight matter of my own skin. Unless my ears deceived me, Sir Garit has promised to pepper anyone departing La Roque with English arrows."

"I don't give a hen's fart about your skin, minstrel," Osbert growled. "The Englishman can fill you with more holes than a sieve, for all I care."

Eglantine nearly smiled. So much for etiquette. But it was most definitely not a laughing—or even a smiling—matter. Osbert was right, curse it. She herself had declared that the gates must stay shut.

"*I* think he's trustworthy. I think he should stay, Mother. You're good with a sword, aren't you, Raf? And you won't eat too much, will you?"

"Con, be quiet. There is more at stake than you know."

Eglantine clamped her lips shut. Of all the stupid things she could have said. Now Con was going to pester her until he knew everything. And there were some things she simply wasn't going to explain to her son, at least not for many years yet.

"We could send him out the back way, m'lady."

They all looked at Osbert.

"What back way? Do you mean he should climb the cliffs?" Con uttered the words that Eglantine had only thought.

Osbert nodded. "Climb up 'em or climb down. We could send him over the wall by night. He'd have some chance of keeping his skin whole that way."

"Or of breaking my neck," Raf added. "I prefer to put my sword at your disposal instead, if you don't mind, captain."

"You'd more likely stick your sword through our hearts in the night, minstrel," Osbert growled.

Raf sighed. "My dear Osbert, it seems I must be plain. For all our sakes. I am not a minstrel. I am Rafèu, Vicomte Bruniquel. Perhaps you have heard of the Fortress of Bruniquel? It lies a day's ride to the north. I disguised myself as a lowly minstrel in order to woo your lady. Yesterday I laid my heart at her feet. She does not want it. So be it. I now lay my sword…*dagger* at her feet instead. And know this: I am an honorable knight. I do not stab people in the dark of night—unless they stab at me first. Nor do I have any love for this invading English knight. Let me defend a lady in need as chivalry demands."

It was a lot of words for her captain to digest. By the look of his face, they were going to cause him a stomachache. She had not enlightened Osbert regarding the true identity of the minstrel. Con either. It had seemed unnecessary once he left. Now the two of them—three, if one included Margery—were eyeing the vicomte who'd materialized in their midst with wondering disbelief.

"This fellow asked you to marry him, my lady?" Osbert's face shifted into ominous lines. "He swanned in here as a disreputable—nay, a licentious—minstrel and then made approaches to you?"

Perhaps it was the strain of it all, but Eglantine was sorely tempted to laugh. *Licentious?* Where had Osbert acquired that word? And how would her captain react if she told him *she* was the licentious one?

"That is no way to speak to a vicomte, Osbert. Set your mind at ease. He has acted honorably in all his dealings with me." Too honorably. "His only fault is his disguise."

What, was she defending the accursed fellow now?

"Why don't you want to marry him, Mother?" Con was standing unnaturally still. "I think he's nice."

"No! No more questions, any of you. It's my turn to ask questions. Osbert, as I see it, we have two options. First, we could require the vicomte to clamber the walls in the dark and sneak away into the woods at great risk to his own skin."

"Or my neck," Raf murmured, rubbing the aforementioned body part. Eglantine flexed her fingers.

"Alternatively, we could—with great reluctance—take him up on his offer of aid. We would thereby gain one more sword arm and one more mouth to feed. Do you see that there are any other options open to us?"

Her captain scratched his short beard. It featured more gray hairs than brown these days. Osbert had sported no white bristles when he came with her to La Roque as a mere man-at-arms. The unmannerly fellow been with her all those years, protecting her through her marriage to Ferrand and beyond. She trusted him. Perhaps he was the only man she did trust. Osbert did not deceive her—or himself.

It wasn't Osbert who answered. "Lady Eglantine, are you certain this English knight will not attack directly? From what I overheard, it seems like he intends a passive siege. He threatened no trebuchets or cannon, and your front gates are hardly conducive to a heavy ram. It appears he means to hole you up here and simply wait for you to submit. Is this your understanding, my lady? And yours, good captain?"

"We cannot know what he intends," Eglantine snapped. "I can't read minds. Can you, vicomte?"

"He said he'd only threaten them that stepped outside the gates," Osbert said.

"And we can assume he wants a whole chateau—defensible and weatherproof—not a shattered ruin," Eglantine said.

"Not to mention a wife in one piece," Raf murmured.

Eglantine narrowed her eyes at him. Was *that* why he had stayed? The chivalric and all-too-romantic vicomte had lingered in La Roque to snarl at any other man who sought her hand?

"There you have it, vicomte. We can assume Sir Garit means harm only to our stomachs, but we cannot know it for certain. It is also my hope that he will think better of his plan within the week, once he sees I will not open my gates to him." She gave Raf a hard stare. "And that I have no intention of marrying anyone."

"Why do you ask this, my lord?" Osbert's tone was not quite so hostile now. He was giving Raf a considering look. "Sounds like you know something of sieges."

She turned to Raf just in time to catch his expression. Those dark eyes went blank. They were walled. His lips became an unsmiling line.

He gave a slight shrug. "I simply ask, good Osbert, because there may be a third solution to the dilemma I pose you."

Chapter Thirteen

STRATEGY IN THE kitchen, heaven preserve him. At least his lady had put down her bloody knife. Still, Raf could have wished for a smaller audience—fewer cooks, serving maids, and small boys, for example. One could not trust anyone in time of siege. It only took one person to betray a castle.

Osbert evidently read something in Raf's expression, for he glanced at his mistress and muttered, "Perhaps we should discuss this in greater privacy, m'lady."

Eglantine's chin went up. "As you will. Come. We will retire to the *privacy* of the solar."

She cast Raf a cool look, and then turned and glided to the stairs, neatly sidestepping buckets, casks, and assorted kitchen staff in the process. Along the way, Margery was directed to take Con anywhere *but* the solar. Raf glanced at Osbert and received a look that was only half a glower in return. He'd have preferred it to have been all glower, given the choice. There was a thoughtful cast to the brown eyes that made the hairs on Raf's neck prickle. Still, he obeyed the captain's gesture and followed his lady up the circling stairs—and heard Osbert's stumping footsteps behind him like knells of doom.

They entered the solar, Osbert barred the door with an ominous rasp, and Raf found himself the target of two sharp-edged stares.

Eglantine had seated herself on the plain stool at the parchment-strewn table. She had her back to the parchment and was facing him. That she was seated and Raf was still standing ought to have given him the advantage, but it did not. This was her room, her desk, and her captain behind him—she had not given up any of her power. Besides, Osbert had questions. Inconvenient questions, Raf just knew it.

Thank God, his lady spoke first. "You spoke of a third option, vicomte. Pray, enlighten us."

Something deep within him responded to her voice. It was like a stray finger trailing over lute strings. Or was it heartstrings? It tipped him off balance.

"A third option," he murmured. "Ah, yes." *Pull yourself together, man.* "You mentioned, my lady, that you hope this Garit will remove himself and his men within the week. Once he perceives you are immune to his charms."

She gave a soft snort at that.

"But what if he doesn't, my lady?" Raf went on. "What if, against all common sense or common decency, this English knight entrenches himself in your village and remains there for months, even a year? It is possible. It is possible that, having seen you—and your chateau, of course—he will find the attractions of La Roque too potent to relinquish."

Eglantine opened her mouth, then hesitated. Raf's gaze lingered upon those lips. They were doubtless laden with uncomplimentary phrases for him. But she settled for: "It *is* possible. What then?"

"Then you might consider a third option, my lady—should I remain. You could send me over your walls in the dead of night, and I would do more than leave a lady to her fate. I would bring aid. I would raise a small army to drive these English invaders from your lands."

"Why wait?" growled Osbert. "You could do it now."

"No!" Eglantine broke in. "He will not do it now, nor will he do it later. What sort of obligation would that put me under?

These men, vicomte—they would be yours, I suppose?"

"In part. I might ask aid from other nobles."

"Other *French* nobles, no doubt. You would create a war on my doorstep, and expect me to be grateful for it. Very grateful. By God, I'd do better to just accept Sir Garit's so-charming marital offer and be done."

Raf swayed a little as he stood. It was as if she'd hit him.

"No, my lady," he said softly. "I have no coercion in mind. I do not offer you aid in swap for marriage. I would not force you to my will, however subtly."

Osbert glanced at his mistress and then at Raf. "Well, if he's not off over the wall to get help or to present himself as a target to English bows, does he stay, mistress?"

Eglantine went very still. Her gaze slipped to Rafèu, then slid away. "I suppose so. If he wishes it."

Raf's heart gave a strange lurch.

"Good," said Osbert, causing Raf further heart problems. "Because if I'm not mistaken, m'lady, your sneaky suitor knows a thing or two about sieges. I don't. I've never landed myself in a siege, neither as an attacker or a defender. Nor, so far as I know, has anyone else in La Roque—except this man." The brown eyes settled on Rafèu with disturbing acuity. "Well, my lord vicomte?"

No. I have never been within so much as the scent of a siege. No such stench of suffering or burned flesh has ever entered these minstrel nostrils. I have more respect for my own hide and for others than to place myself in such a position.

That was the response he wanted to give. But he was no longer Raf the minstrel. He was an honorable knight, the Vicomte of Bruniquel. He did not shy from the truth.

"What does it matter?" he heard Eglantine say as if from a great distance. "If he stays, it will only be as another defender. You are my captain, Osbert, and I command in La Roque. Noble or no, I will have no stranger tell us what to do."

"Vicomte?" Osbert spoke nearer now. He was practically at Raf's elbow. "Spill the loot. *Have* you been in a siege?"

It was a direct question. Raf couldn't very well ignore it.

"I have."

The voice that spoke those words was not that of a minstrel's. It was decidedly un-melodious.

"Besieged or besieger?" Osbert's questions were buzzing wasps that would not be batted away.

"Besieged."

There. Just one word. Such an inadequate sound to encompass the reality it described.

"Enough, Osbert."

His lady's voice swiped away the buzzing wasp. Osbert was just opening his mouth to launch more stinging questions into the air. Eglantine's hand lifted in the direction of her captain, but her gaze was directed at Rafèu. Lake-green eyes fringed with soft brown. He would like to sink into that lake, let its waters close over his head and shut the world out.

Something in him registered that Eglantine was looking at him with the oddest expression—curiosity, concern, a touch of empathy, perhaps? Of course not. She knew nothing of his past. She would never know. It was not a fit matter for a lady's ears.

"We have established that our unwelcome guest has prior experience of being besieged, Osbert. That is enough. I remain in command of this chateau, and you remain my second-in-command." It could have been a harsh statement, but it wasn't. Eglantine's tone was firm, but it had gentle edges. "We will, however, listen to any advice our guest sees fit to offer us."

What in hell was he doing here? In a chateau hemmed in by hostile forces—damned *English* forces, for God's sake. Advice? What advice could he, Rafèu, give the lady he'd sworn to love and protect in such a situation? *Marry the English brute*, he should say. *Wed the hideous fellow and spare yourself the experience of siege, my lady.*

But then he looked at the Lady of La Roque. She had the face and form of an angel, all wrapped in the drab garments of a nun. This was the lady he'd worshipped from afar, the untouchable and ethereal subject of his dreams and songs. But that wasn't what struck him now. It was her expression, the swirl of emotion betrayed by eyes, lips, and jaw. She was frightened, she was stubbornly determined, and she saw him. She felt *for* him. For it wasn't desire that lit her eyes now, although he had no particular objection to that emotion. It was understanding of a sort, and yes, empathy.

Raf's innards contracted.

He bowed, more a marionette's jerk than an elegant courtesy. "I thank you, my lady. I am content to remain a mere thrower of rocks or a watcher on the battlements. My sword—once I have one—and my rock arm are at your disposal. I swear on my lute, on the Chateau Bruniquel, on my very honor as a knight, that I will do all in my power to protect you and everything you hold dear. Do with me as you will."

He kept his gaze lowered against that too-watchful gaze, and waited. To be dismissed? To be relegated to the battlements, rock in hand?

After a moment, a long moment, his lady spoke. "Supposing you have some experience of surviving a siege, Vicomte Rafèu— however slight that experience might be—I would hear your thoughts of how best we too may endure such a siege. What would you do were you in my place? What would your priorities be?"

Raf stared at the chamber floor. It was composed of wooden planking, no doubt supported by weighty beams beneath, and softened with intricately woven rugs. He poked the edge of a rug with a crakowed toe. The villager he'd traded with hadn't wanted Raf's impractical shoes.

He didn't allow himself to dwell on specifics, just general principles. "The outer defenses would be my highest priority. I would post watchers on the battlements in shifts, at least two at a time, and give them the means to raise the alarm quickly should anything happen."

Osbert grunted. "Aye. I stuck a couple of bells up there for watchmen to strike."

"Watch-women as well as men," Raf murmured. "Women are as capable of striking a bell as men, and you're a little tight on defenders in general, I guess."

Osbert's beard twisted itself into an odd shape, but he nodded.

"And I would have everyone in the castle trained in bearing weapons," Raf said. "Not only in anticipation of attack and invasion, but to keep those within chateau walls active and in good heart. I would include women as well as men in this. Children too. A long siege drains its defenders. It makes them hopeless—they just want it to end. I would give those in La Roque power and heart. Let even the feeblest know they can take action."

Raf was finding the floor fascinating. He wanted no questions, no penetrating looks.

"What you say makes sense, vicomte," came the lady's soft, English-tinted voice. "I had not considered it. Should this siege drag on, and I pray God it does not, then we will have discontent, even despair within the walls. I take your point and I agree. I will learn to defend myself too. I do not anticipate I will be good at it, but I will set an example."

Raf could not help but glance up at that. Oh, he knew full well what he'd said, but he had never intended the Lady of La Roque to take up arms. But she was looking at him with a slight smile in her eyes.

Her smile touched her mouth, probably in response to his slack-jawed expression. "Your notion of giving the defenders heart gives me other ideas too. Food, for example. I do not want anyone to feel deprived, or that starvation is just around the corner. Oh, we shall be careful with our supplies, but I think we may inject a little interest into our diet. Something special in the kitchen."

She put finger and thumb to her chin. "And my garden. I will plant greens. We must have something fresh in our diet. Herbs and salad leaves. It will take work, but greens do not take long to grow. And you, minstrel…vicomte…whatever you choose to be, I would ask you to continue to entertain us in the evenings."

She was looking at him with a light in her eyes. Oh, she had taken his idea to heart with a vengeance. Raf's lip quirked. By God, La Roque would become a party chateau at this rate. Fancy foods, sword-sports, and music for all. Eglantine's siege would be one long feast.

"Music and dancing?" he said. "A few rousing tales to stir the blood? Yes, I think I can do that, my lady. If I am permitted to draw upon my French repertoire as well as my English."

He half expected her to object to that, but no, she simply lifted her shoulders. "I do not find myself so enamored by all things English at the moment. Yes, you will put heart into us too, Rafèu of Bruniquel." Her gaze lingered on him. He felt it warm him, seeping through the rough weave of his garments, into his skin and into his heart.

Then her brows drew together a fraction.

"What did you do with your clothes?"

For one wild moment, Raf thought he stood naked before her. Skin that had been warm an instant before flared hot. He glanced down. Ah. The ugly peasant clothing he'd taken in swap for his multicolored minstrel wear. He'd sold his horse for a song at the same time, all in order to re-enter the chateau unobserved.

"Doubtless some cowherd is wearing them now. Perhaps he sings to his herd. Do you prefer me in motley, my lady?" Maybe she really did prefer minstrels.

She ignored that. "And your horse? Well, that…thing you rode here?"

"I am insulted on behalf of my mount, lady. My noble charger has vacated your stables. It will no longer gorge itself on your horse bread. I only hope it has carried its peasant owner far from here by now."

"You did this all to stay here? Did you not notice the infestation of soldiers in the village while you were there?"

"A veritable plague of Egypt, my lady."

"And yet you came back. Why? You know I will not wed you. Be clear on this point, Vicomte Rafèu—protect me from this Englishman all you will, but it will not alter my decision. I will not marry you. I cannot be bribed or coerced into wedlock. I will not be trapped again."

Trapped again. The words were a bucket of icy water to the face.

Yes, that was the reality of the matter. He was trapped within stone walls again. She did not wish to be trapped either, but here they were.

He had willingly put himself in this position, for her, and she didn't want him.

Raf set his jaw. He had decided, and now it was too late to turn back. This was the ultimate test. He would do this for Eglantine. He would prove his love to her, even if he had to starve to do it. He would endure the horrors of siege again. For her.

"I bow to my lady's will. I respect her wishes," Raf replied. There was no hint of mockery in his voice now.

He looked at her, ignoring the glowering presence of Osbert, trying to ignore the heavy stone walls pressing in upon him. He just drank in her uptilted face, pale, perfect skin, and vulnerable, kissable mouth. Not that he would ever kiss it, not again. She would remain inaccessible, but Raf could worship from afar.

"I am your true knight," he said softly. "Do with me as you will. Put me to the test in whatever way you see fit. I do not require anything in return."

Chapter Fourteen

T HERE WAS NO attack that day, nor even the next morning. Eglantine did not know whether she'd expected one or not, but no one in La Roque was taking any chances. Especially not her own true knight. He had gone from the solar straight to the battlements and stayed there until the stars blinked ice-white and the moon dipped in the sky. She knew this because Osbert had told her.

Which also meant they had had no music that night. Raf was on the walls waiting for an enemy that did not attack, leaving Eglantine to face a strangely quiet hall filled with tight-lipped retainers. Music would have helped, she was sure.

He would not get away with it tonight. The castle would not fall if Rafèu absented the walls for one evening.

Music would have helped her, at least. Raf's music, and his velvety, deep voice. His songs certainly made her think of other things than sieges. It was only a pity he would not act the minstrel in other ways too. That would provide a welcome distraction indeed.

Eglantine swallowed a smile and led the way to the middens. A couple of menservants trailed behind her, equipped with baskets and unimpressed expressions.

There were shovels and rakes near the midden. Eglantine took a shovel and dug first into one steaming pile and then the next.

"This one," she announced, indicating her preferred heap of decomposing waste to the servants. "It's well rotted and mostly comes from the stables, by the looks. Straw and dung is good, but I don't want anything too wet or smelly. Understand?"

The two menservants looked at each other and then her. They each nodded, and one muttered, "If you say so, m'lady."

"It'll be worth it," she said. "You'll see. About ten baskets should do it. Leave them at the garden door."

"How about we cart the lot in and dig the crap in for you too, m'lady? Begging your ladyship's pardon."

"No," she said sharply. Then more softly, "Thank you, Jacques. I will have no one in my garden but myself."

Two heads bobbed, and Jacques began to roll up his sleeves. Eglantine paused. Here before her stood two strong men, long-term servants at the chateau who did heavy lifting on a daily basis but had likely never held a sword in their lives. They might have to soon.

"When you've finished that, come to the courtyard by the stables. I believe you'll enjoy the task I have for you there more than this one."

She left them shoveling crap in the afternoon sun, and walked toward the stable courtyard.

Osbert was there, laying out weaponry upon a newly erected trestle. Con was assisting—if assisting one could call it—but chiefly bombarding Osbert with questions about each and every weapon he picked up and waved around.

Eglantine hefted a sword. It was carved from a length of wood.

"This won't do an Englishman much damage," she said.

"Aye, that's the point, m'lady. It's for training."

"Remember me and Raf, Mother? That's what we used." Con grabbed a second wooden blade and wildly swished it through the air.

"Yes, I remember." Entirely too well.

Osbert carefully prized the weapon from Con's grip. "We're about ready, little lord. Want to go ring the bell and rustle up some hands to hold these swords?"

Con needed no further prompting, and the courtyard began to fill with would-be swordsmen—and women. Osbert busied himself equipping each with a weapon befitting their size and experience, and Eglantine glanced around at her infant army. La Roque boasted a total of three men-at-arms, Osbert foremost among them. Neither of the other two were present, but that was probably because they already had arms and presumably knew how to use them. This crowd was composed wholly of servants— stable boys, kitchen maids, and the like. The way they were clutching their new weapons suggested that this was a novel experience to most.

Eglantine sank against the stable wall.

Heaven help them, *she* had brought them to this. She had three soldiers, for God's sake. Three experienced men-at-arms to defend an entire castle. Oh, and a stray French vicomte who knew how to wield a wooden sword.

The thought made her scan the crowd anew. Where was he? Suddenly she wanted to see him, needed to rest her eyes on his dark elegance. Silly thought. As if he was in any way the answer to La Roque's problems.

She waylaid Con. He had acquired another wooden weapon. At least it *was* a wooden one, devoid of any cutting edge.

"Where's Raf? Have you seen him?"

Con looked up at her and grinned. "You *do* like him, don't you, Mother? You didn't throw him out after all."

"Whether I like him is not the point. Have you seen him? He should be here."

"He's up there." Con jabbed his sword at the battlements. The gesture came perilously close to a servant's head. She grabbed the sword and tugged it from his hand. "He's been up there for *ages*," Con went on. "Osbert won't let me up there to talk to him. I want to look at the enemy. Can I go up there,

Mother?"

Eglantine sighed. "No, you can't. You're the lord of the cha-teau. It's vital for all of us that you stay safe. Here." She proffered the practice sword. "Pay attention to Osbert. I need you to be the best swordsman you can possibly be. And that includes not whacking innocent bystanders with a wooden blade. Under-stand?"

"Yes, Mother." Con gave her a grin full of small white teeth and sincerity. And far too much excitement to trust for longer than five heartbeats.

She glanced again at the huddle of servants holding weapons as if they'd just picked up snakes, and her stomach contracted. She needed Raf.

Eglantine sought out the nearest stairs, bunched her skirts in one hand, the better to climb, and ascended the same battlements she'd just banned Con from.

The wooden stairs were hot, sheltered as they were by the walls. A trap for the afternoon sun, but as soon as she reached battlement level, a breeze feathered her cheeks. Ah, this was why Raf chose to linger up here all day—a cool breeze and the airy, sweeping view.

Naturally she'd been up on the battlements before. It *was* her chateau, after all. But in recent years, Eglantine had preferred not to gaze out at the all-encompassing Frenchness that surrounded her. She had looked inward, creating a realm of English beauty and safety in her garden instead. But now that she was shut in against her will, the view had acquired new value.

She stood within a crenelle, closed her fingers over sun-warmed stone, and let the breeze caress her face. It smelled of hay and herbs, and perhaps a little manure mixed in. She gazed out over trees clinging to the slopes below, over pale rocks jutting through the bushes, the winding path leading to the gatehouse, and the flat land further off—peasant strips and common land, woods and rivers.

"You shouldn't be up here, my lady."

She hadn't heard him approach, but now she thought about it, she could smell something other than hay and herbs. Leather, and something else subtler. Something indefinably Raf.

"You shouldn't be either," she countered, still facing the view. "We need you in the courtyard, my lord vicomte. I've a castle's worth of servants down there gripping weapons like they would their brooms. I believe you know how to handle a sword?"

"Better than a broom, at least. But truly, my lady, you should not be up here. Ah, forgive me—"

Two hands encircled her waist and lifted her bodily. Eglantine flung a started look at her captor, but she was released almost immediately.

"There." The hands settled on her shoulders and held her in place, her back against a protective stone merlon. Eglantine gazed up into dark eyes blazing with concern and only a hint of apology. "Stay there, my lady," he growled. "When you stand within the crenelles, you give me a seizure."

He had manhandled her. He deigned to tell her what to do in her own castle. She should object, but that look of his swallowed up all objection. It was almost as if he truly cared what happened to her. Ah, it was a seductive thought, and an entirely false one. The vicomte only deceived himself, and she would not be fooled again.

But he was so close, hands heavy on her shoulders, his eyes darker than ever under his shadowing helm, his lips so beautifully shaped. He did not need to care, but he did need to kiss her.

Perhaps he read her thought, for the vicomte's hands dropped from her shoulders. He stepped back and sanity returned.

Dear God, it had been a stupid impulse. She may not be outlined for the invader's benefit any longer, thanks to her manhandler, but she and Raf were in view of practically the entire chateau.

A pity.

"I did not see any Englishmen below," she said.

It was true. She had gazed out over the countryside and seen not a single moving figure. Strange, really. On such a fine day, and well past the midday dining hour, she should have seen peasants moving about their strips or busy about the village. She was inclined to have another look, just to confirm, but Raf was still watching her. It was tempting to make him manhandle her again, but she took pity on the delicate state of his health.

"Oh, they are there, my lady. They simply do not make themselves obvious. I could point out half a dozen archers upon the hillside—or at least the rocks and trees they are stationed behind."

Suddenly she didn't need the cool breeze. The sensation of icy spiders crawling down her nape was entirely sufficient.

"Have they shot at you?" she whispered.

He shook his head. His dark hair was tied back and concealed beneath a foot soldier's iron helm. It provided a rim of shade. Was it even possible to kiss him wearing that? She'd likely crack her head against it.

He noted her gaze and tapped the metal. "A precaution only, my lady—and a touch of sun protection. No, they have not shot at me or anyone else. Yet."

She lifted a hand and ran a finger along the iron rim. It felt uncomfortable and heavy. "I suppose I ought to wear one when I come up here too."

"No." His voice was harsh. "Because you won't be coming up here at all, my lady. Not again. I swore to protect you, and this is the most dangerous and exposed location in all La Roque."

"Sir Garit won't shoot me. He wants to marry me."

It was an entirely reasonable objection, but she said it a little pointedly. After all, this vicomte wanted to trap her in marriage as well.

"He might change his mind," Raf muttered.

Eglantine stood quite still. What did that mean? Was he speaking for himself? He had professed love—ridiculous, unfounded love, of course—but now he was getting to know her, was he was changing his mind? Well, that was good, wasn't it?

Eglantine squared her shoulders. "Vicomte Rafèu, I came up here to fetch you. We have need of you in the courtyard. I have servants to train. Will you come?"

⇶⇇

HE TOOK SOME convincing—he seemed persuaded it was his duty to guard the walls against imminent invasion—but once Eglantine pointed out that two of La Roque's three men-at-arms were already guarding the battlements and he, the vitally important vicomte, would be but a short distance below, Raf succumbed.

They were just in time. Osbert seemed about to dent the stable wall by means of his head in frustration.

"Vicomte. Thank God. Grab a sword, a wooden one, and we'll do a demonstration for these lead-handed rake wielders." Osbert paused a moment, casting Raf a wild-eyed look. "I take it you know how to swing a sword?"

"Does a cow know how to eat grass?" her fake minstrel replied. "What do you have in mind?"

Osbert swiped the back of his hand across his brow. He looked a bit heated beneath his iron cap and padded aketon. The sun was dipping, but the afternoon was still warm. "Have at me, vicomte. Show us your stuff. We'll just give these clods a notion of what a sword's for. Then we'll take it slower and get back to basics."

Eglantine hid a smile. Evidently, training a crowd of servants in blade work with only an overexcitable boy for assistance had stretched Osbert's patience. He needed to work off a little frustration by bashing at an opponent.

That brought a frown. Bashing, at Raf? Her unwanted suitor was a man of music. He was not built like a tree stump like Osbert. He was lean and long and graceful. And she had seen Osbert at sword practice before. It was as if someone had given a bull a sword. A short bull, admittedly. And true, they would only be wielding bits of wood, but still…

But Vicomte Rafèu was already selecting his wooden weapon of choice. He kept his iron cap on, but Eglantine nearly squeaked when he shrugged off his brigandine. He had been wearing the plate-lined jacket on the battlements, but now that he was in real danger, the idiot was throwing it to one side.

"Stand back, you lot. Give a man some room." Osbert shooed his trainees back into a wide circle. "Right, now take note. I got an opponent sneaking up on me. I've got no idea what he fights like, but I figure he'd like to kill me. So lookee, all, and see what you might be up against." Osbert eyed his murderous opponent. "Sure you don't want that brigandine, vicomte?"

Excellent point, Eglantine nearly added. But said nobleman just shrugged. "It's quite warm down here, and it'll restrict my movement. I trust you'll only bruise me, good Osbert."

"Shields, vicomte?"

Raf inclined his head. "Yes. A useful tool to demonstrate."

A useful tool to protect you from undue bruising, not to mention broken bones, she could have said. But thank goodness the man had some sense, even if it was about to be knocked out of him. Eglantine twisted her fingers together, hardly aware of what she did. But she knew better than to intervene between men in matters military—they tended to fancy their very manhoods were at stake.

Osbert struck a martial stance, legs square and slightly bent. Rafèu's stance, if one could call it that, was altogether more casual. He barely seemed to face Osbert at all—his shoulders were cast at a right angle to his opponent. Heaven above, did he have the faintest idea what he was doing? He had looked competent when playing at swords with Con, but his opponent then was only a six-year-old boy.

When the men finally moved, it happened so fast that Eglantine struggled to register the details. Osbert struck, a vicious, sweeping blow destined to crack at least three of Raf's ribs. It never achieved its goal. Raf slipped aside, and his round wooden shield caught the blow and sent it winging aside—leaving her captain wide open to attack.

Raf lunged forward, jabbing his sword directly at Osbert's stomach. Her captain lurched aside just in time, and the impetus of Raf's lunge carried him forward. Osbert raised his wooden shield to bring it crashing down on his opponent's head as he passed, and Eglantine gasped. Helmet or no, that force would surely knock him unconscious.

But Raf was not there. He had simply danced aside. He was at Osbert's back instead, and he was prodding the captain's aketon with his wooden sword, just below the shoulder blades.

"Do you have some proper plate armor stowed away, good captain? An aketon is all very well, but I warrant I just perforated your ribs."

A prod for good measure.

"Aye," grunted Osbert. "Well played, minstrel. I yield." He dropped his sword and shield with a clatter and flung up his hands. "See, you lot? Never underestimate your opponent, even if he's underdressed. He could be a tricky bugger who's too quick on his feet—begging your pardon, vicomte."

Raf ceased poking the captain's back. He stepped forward, scooped up the dropped blade, and handed it to Osbert. "Shall we take it more slowly now, captain? We have established that some of us are tricky buggers, while others swing blows fit to fell an ox. Perhaps now if one of us demonstrates and our trainees imitate? I can move among our troops to adjust the finer points."

"Aye, we'll do that. All right, you lot. Take your weapons and line up. Watch me, and do exactly as I do. The vicomte here will fix anyone who gets it wrong. And for God's sake, try not to kill anyone in the process."

Eglantine surveyed her nascent soldiers. Margery was there, as was Con. Of the two, Con looked by far the more proficient in holding a blade. The middle-aged cook was there too, holding her wooden weapon as if she were about to slice a side of beef.

Eglantine's two manure shovelers hurried up and grabbed a practice blade each.

It hit Eglantine then: her people were all here to learn to defend themselves and La Roque. They were servants, not soldiers. They were forced to pick up weapons because of her—because she refused the alternative to siege.

Should she marry the bastard Englishman for their sakes? What was she condemning them all to? And what about Raf? Shadows haunted his eyes when the word "siege" was mentioned, yet he was staying here for her. Or so he said. Was she just being selfish, subjecting those who depended on her—or thought they loved her—to prolonged suffering?

But the Englishman might just go away. They could wait him out quite safely. She hoped.

In the meantime, she had to do everything she could to unite those within La Roque. She would give heart to her defenders. Together, they would stand firm. And right now, the least she could do was join them.

Eglantine walked over to the near-empty trestle and took up a length of wood cast in the roughest possible approximation of a sword. It felt splintery and awkward in her hands.

Oh well—a soldier had to start somewhere.

Chapter Fifteen

RAF MOVED AMONG the troops to adjust the finer points of their swordplay. In truth, he had to look damned hard to find any finer points at all.

Osbert stood before them, going through the standard drill in slow motion—infinitely slow motion—and it seemed that every servant in La Roque tried to follow suit. And the diminutive Lord Con, of course. Unsurprisingly, the small boy was more competent than the rest of them put together. He had had the benefit of prior training under Osbert's guidance—and just a dash of Raf's own.

Raf grinned at the boy and got a blazing smile back.

Then Rafèu stepped down the line to the next faltering, fumbling swordsman, and his smile fell off his face like a cat from a tree.

What in hell are you doing? he might have growled—if he hadn't had just enough sense not to berate the Lady of La Roque before her entire household. Actually, he might have growled it anyway, but there was no getting words past the sudden blockage in his throat.

She had no idea how to hold a sword, even a wooden one.

He stepped in close and stilled her wavering blade with one hand. "One moment, my lady. Permit me to adjust your grip."

A surreptitious glance at those surrounding showed him no

one had stopped to stare, or more importantly, to listen. He stepped around behind her, the better to position her hands correctly. And to hiss in her ear:

"My lady, this is not seemly. It is not right that you bear weapons."

She stiffened under his touch. "Why? Do I lower myself in your estimation, my lord? Is it not *seemly* that I defend myself against the invader?"

Raf busied himself with unclenching her hands and then repositioning them in somewhat less of a death grip upon the hilt. His fingers tangled with hers, all awareness centering upon his hands.

"There. Do not grip so tightly, my lady. It makes your arm too rigid. Any jar to the blade will transmit itself directly up your arm. You need to retain flexibility in order to retain your sword."

But he did not move away. He was not finished yet, not by half.

"You, my lady, are the queen of this castle," he murmured. "You rule, you command, we do your bidding. It is our task to protect you. You do not need to pick up a blade."

In pure contradiction to his words, he closed his fingers over her own, draped his arm over hers, and guided her sword stroke in accordance with the drill. Only so he could remain close and drive his point home.

"It is not your task to protect me, vicomte. Nor is it yours to tell me what to do."

He was not her husband, was what she meant. He was a stranger in La Roque. Yet Raf's hand continued to guide hers, echoing Osbert's instructions. He could feel her frame against his every time they moved together. One step forward, one step back. Thrust, parry, slash, defend. Like a slow and intimate dance.

Raf knew he was spending far too long on one combatant. He should be moving down the line, correcting everyone's stance and grip and thrust, not melding himself to Eglantine's back. Keep this up, and Osbert would toss him over the walls himself.

"Let me protect you instead, my lady," he murmured in her ear as they stepped in unison. "A true knight proves his love by obeying his lady's every command. If necessary, he lays his life at her feet. Let me do this. I ask nothing in return."

"Don't you?" she retorted. Eglantine slipped her hand from his grip and stepped out from his arms. She ignored Osbert's drill and turned to face Rafèu, chin up. "You ask everything in return. You wish me to hand my possessions, my body, and my very soul over to you, and in return for what? A flimsy promise of love? A lifetime of bondage in the guise of marriage? You are no better than the man who besieges us." Her eyes flashed green fire, and she flicked her sword at him. "Now go and instruct someone else how to gut a man."

Folk *had* stopped to listen and look this time. Con was gazing up at them with open interest, and Osbert's sword dangled from his hand.

Eglantine squared her shoulders. "I tire of going through the motions," she announced. "I am inclined to try my newfound skills on real human flesh." The look she shot him in that moment made it clear whom she'd like to carve up—clear to all the watchers too, unfortunately.

"Drills only for now, my lady," Osbert said. "You'll need something a tad more protective than a wimple if you're to face a man." His brown eyes flicked to Raf and narrowed, but the captain addressed the group at large. "You're looking better, you lot, but I'm not pitting you against one another yet. We'll drill a few more days, build up a bit of strength and skill first." Then, in a lower tone, "I just hope to God we don't get attacked in the meantime."

It seemed the deity had heard him—and had a nasty sense of humor—for Osbert had barely uttered the words before the bell began to toll. It wasn't the bell Con had rung earlier to summon the would-be swordsmen. It was one of the bells upon the battlements.

Raf turned to stone. The past washed over him.

"Mother of God," Osbert swore, not quite under his breath. "Right then, don't panic. Them I've assigned to the battlements, get your arses up there. Don't reckon you'll need weapons. It you have to, chuck rocks at the bastards. The rest of you—"

But Osbert was interrupted by a boy, breathless from his descent from the battlements. "Sir, it's just a couple of men approaching. Don't think it's an attack."

Osbert blasphemed to the tune of one of God's many body parts. Raf felt like seconding the motion, with interest. "What in hell did you ring the bell for, then?" Osbert flung at the boy. Then he bellowed, "Oy, hold back, you lot!"

But a good handful of defenders were already pounding up the stairs.

"Perhaps we need some clear parameters on bell ringing, and who should respond and how when it does?" Raf said.

"Aye," snapped Osbert. "Seems like we do. I'll put you on that task, vicomte. Reckon you've got some prior experience of such matters."

Raf could feel Eglantine looking at him. He fought to retain a bland expression.

"What do we do, captain? Vicomte?" There was a slight wobble to his lady's voice.

"Boy, you sure it's just two of them?" Osbert asked.

The boy nodded vigorously. "Unless the rest of them are creeping around the sides, captain. I didn't see no one else, though."

Osbert raised his eyes heavenward. No help came from that quarter. "Right then, I'd better get up on the walls and see what's what. Vicomte, you're in charge down here. Keep her ladyship in one piece, or by God I'll flay you alive."

THEY ENDED UP in one of the rooms built against the curtain wall.

Eglantine refused to be sealed up in the central keep for safety, but she did consent to retiring under cover. Raf pointed out that she—and everyone else—needed shielding from any stray missiles that might be sent over the walls. The vicomte had accordingly sent all the folk in the courtyard scurrying for cover, unless they were required on the walls. Eglantine herself had ordered Margery to drag Con into the keep and keep him there, on pain of severe pain.

But she *had* to know what was going on. Eglantine was not holing up in her solar and pretending nothing untoward was occurring, no matter how Raf nagged. They compromised on a storeroom near the gatehouse, a room Eglantine knew full well was equipped with an arrow slit.

"No, my lady!" Her unwanted protector grabbed her by the arm as she started toward the bow embrasure.

She shook at her arm. His hand did not shift. "Let go of me, you brute," she snapped. "I need to see what's going on."

She glanced up at him as she spoke. No, she should not have called him a brute. In truth, he was not looking brutish at all. In the dim of the room, Raf's face was all sharply defined angles, the more defined for the determination etched upon it. He looked a little otherworldly, but quite…well, beautiful.

For an instant she forgot why she was here—why he was here. She just looked at him. But the spell evaporated the moment he spoke.

"It is too dangerous, my lady. I will not permit you to come to any harm."

She shook at her arm again. "You will *not* not permit me to do anything, you damned intrusive Frenchman."

"Why do I feel like that is the greatest insult of all?" he murmured. "If I were English, would you listen to me?"

"No! It's because you're a man and you want to control me. And *you* insult *me*. Let go of me, you great lump, or I'll scream for help."

"Promise me you'll not approach the window."

"I'll promise you nothing—No, quiet. Listen!" She threw up her free hand. There were voices outside. Raised voices. English voices.

Then there came a reply from above, bellowed down from the battlements. It was almost certainly Osbert.

"They are parlaying, not fighting," she declared. "It's perfectly safe. And I *will* hear what is going on!" She gave a final yank and forged her way toward the bow embrasure. She only managed it because her captor moved with her, still keeping his iron grip about her arm.

She bundled herself into the embrasure, half sitting, half leaning into it, the better to peer out of the narrow vertical slit to the outside world. Raf leaned after her, still maintaining his grip. She twisted and craned until she caught sight of the men outside the walls. Two men only, standing on the path close by the gatehouse. Both were heavily armored. One was holding a lance, from the top of which fluttered a length of white linen.

The other was Sir Garit of the Ruin. She knew it from his stance, his surcoat—and by the voice that emanated from the sealed helm.

"I come to inquire whether the lady has changed her mind," the helm declared, doubtless in response to Osbert's challenge. But without waiting for an answer, the helm went on: "Know that we are determined. We will remain in La Roque and on the slopes about your castle. Rest assured we find ourselves well supplied in your hospitable village."

Eglantine ground her teeth. Accursed thieves.

"You may tell your lady that I will continue to protect your village and its surrounds until she accepts my enduring protection as her husband."

Eglantine wriggled closer to the arrow slit and opened her mouth. A hand slipped over it. She nearly screamed with frustration, but of course that would only emerge as a muffled bleat from beneath a certain vicomte's palm.

"Do not show him you are provoked, my lady," Raf said

softly. "It will do no good. Besides, he may treat your village better if he believes he has a chance of owning it." Then the man half on top of her paused. She could feel him tense. "Unless you've changed your mind. Unless you now find this English knight an acceptable husband."

He lifted his hand from her mouth at that. Well, praise heaven he deigned to hear her answer. "Of course not," she spat. "Now be quiet. I must listen."

But Osbert was already replying. It was harder to hear his words, for they emanated from far above her and there was a large quantity of stone between them. But it seemed the gist of it was *no*.

Sir Garit inclined his iron-clad head. "So be it. I have patience. La Roque and its lady are most worthy prizes. In time—much time, if necessary—your lady will see reason. In the meantime, enjoy your food stores while they last and pray do not venture beyond your curtain walls. Anyone who does so is at the mercy of my men. And I regret to say they are not renowned for their mercy."

Osbert shouted down something along the lines of *get your stinking hides out of our village* and *La Roque will stand strong until Doomsday.* Sir Garit merely bowed in reply. It did not look easy to bow in full plate armor. It was probably about as easy as it was to trudge up her hill wearing an extra skin of iron.

"I wish you good day, captain. I will return on the morrow. And pray wish my lady-wife-to-be sweet slumbers. For be assured, she *will* wed me. It is as inevitable as the sun rising in the east. She only harms herself and her people by her hesitation."

Eglantine did not hear Osbert's reply, if there was one. The blood was pounding in her ears too loudly. Raf was still leaning partly over her, hand quite close enough to her mouth that she knew he would muffle anything she yelled at the departing dastard.

She watched in impotent fury as the two iron figures clanked out of sight down the path. She stared through the arrow slit and saw nothing but dusty path, parched bushes, and a distant, beckoning view.

For a long time she did not speak. She wasn't sure she had the energy to move. The wave of anger had drained away, leaving...emptiness, and a vague gratitude that her false minstrel leaned warm and near. He wasn't touching her anymore, neither clamping her mouth nor her arm, but he was so close that she could hear him breathe.

"Is he right?" she whispered. "Is it inevitable? Do I harm others by refusing him?"

Rafèu stirred. He looked at her. They were both still half within the bow embrasure, and it was not a space designed for two. Dear God, he was overwhelming at such close quarters. What was more, his *expression* was overwhelming. Dark, deep-lashed eyes gazed unwaveringly into her own.

"Of course not," Raf said, and his tone was absolutely certain. "He is bluffing. He is sowing despair and distrust. They are greater enemies to a besieged castle than any bombardment."

She looked at him. Really, there wasn't much choice in this small space. Not that she was complaining. Beyond a lack of energy to move, it was strangely comforting just to lie here like this, knowing he would protect her. Or at least, that was what he said.

So she told him the truth. "Sir Garit wants La Roque. He doesn't want me. I am just a means to an end, a way to legitimize his theft. I do not even want this cursed castle. I hate this place. I only stay here to safeguard my son's inheritance. This is *his* patrimony. It's the only good thing he got from his father." She stared at Rafèu, willing him to give her answers, or at least to understand. "I am tempted to simply hand La Roque over. I could leave. I could give the whole place to Sir Garit. Con and I could return to England. But I *cannot* marry this man, Raf. I will not be trapped again."

Strange that she should be telling him this. He wanted to marry her and trap her too. But he had also said he would protect her and that he was her own true knight. Of course, it was ridiculous fairytale stuff, and she would be an idiot to believe it.

But a tiny portion of her *wanted* to believe in it, and in him. And when he looked at her like this, her doubts fled like bats from bright sunlight.

Raf's lips quirked. "It seems a pleasant enough castle. What's to hate about it?" But he didn't wait for a reply. "I fancy your son is more attached to these walls than you are, my lady. He might not thank you for giving them away."

She sagged. "I know."

He ran a finger gently over her cheek. Her skin came alive as if to the stroke of butterfly wings.

"You do not have to give La Roque up," he murmured. "You do not have to marry this man—or any man you do not want to. Have you harmed anyone by your decisions so far? I think not. And if we are to believe Sir Garit, no one will be harmed if they stay within the walls."

"But that is not how sieges work, is it?" she whispered. "If he gets tired of waiting—if we don't starve quickly enough for him— he may attack."

A shadow crossed his face. "Perhaps. We shall cross that bridge when we come to it, but for the moment he seems content to wait. He seems very sure you will fall into his arms, my lady."

"That's just because he's blond and broad-shouldered and blue-eyed and passingly handsome," she snapped. "And he's got a big sword."

Raf's eyes widened in a most gratifying manner. "Are you sure you don't want to marry him, my lady?"

"No. What do I want with a husband telling me what to do, shoving me about in bed, and then rutting with every second woman he meets?" Eglantine clamped her lips shut. Now she'd said too much. But she unsealed them to clarify: "That's the problem with handsome men. They think every woman wants them—and they want every woman. But they don't really want them. They just play at love. They…"

Ah. His face. His sculpted, almost too-beautiful face. Did he think she was describing him? Well, maybe she was. He was a man playing at love. He had no idea of its reality.

"I understand," he said softly. "Ferrand of La Roque was a less-than-ideal husband. He was a fool."

"Yes, he was a fool who deluded himself he was in love. He swore undying devotion to me before we married. I thought I had found the perfect husband—handsome, charming, and utterly smitten with me. And how long did that last? Until he fell in love with the next woman, and then the next. And I was just an irritating appendage on whom he had to get a son."

"Not all men are like that."

"Perhaps. But it matters not. I would rather give up La Roque and take my son to safety in England than be chained in wedlock again."

She said the words, and by heaven she believed them, but at the same time, her senses betrayed her. They were full of him. He was the dizzying draft of wine in her blood. He was so very close, and she just wanted him to touch her, lay his lips on hers, *and convince her she was wrong.*

It was simply desire, of course. The sort of passing lust her dead husband had indulged in so many times. She'd just never felt it before, or only to the mildest degree. And the solution? She nearly laughed as it struck her, the irony was so complete. The solution was to do as Ferrand did—give in to the lust, indulge it to the hilt, and get it out of your system. Lust was not love. It did not last. The more thoroughly it was indulged, the sooner it was purged.

Rafèu obviously didn't realize this. For some reason he had taken a fancy to her, possibly because she was unattainable and he was so used to attaining any woman he wanted. Just look at him, for God's sake—all that angular, masculine beauty and the soul of a minstrel. Women would melt in puddles at his feet. Margery was proof of that.

He opened his mouth to speak. Such expressive, fascinating lips. She could not resist them. There was no need to resist them.

She simply leaned forward and kissed them.

❧❦❧

Chapter Sixteen

S HE HAD BEEN telling him about Ferrand, about the thoughtless bastard she'd married. Raf already knew the story, of course—tavern gossip was good that way, although one could not necessarily trust the ramblings of half-drunk men concerning women they barely knew. Then there was Margery's somewhat more trustworthy information. But it seemed Ferrand had not kept his lascivious liaisons a secret, even from his wife. How fitting that the man had died as a result. Indeed, if he had not, Raf would have been inclined to do the job himself.

He saw with absolute clarity why Eglantine did not trust men or their protestations of love. She had a point—handsome or highborn men often indulged simply because they could, although not always so blatantly as Ferrand. Women, on the other hand, had no such freedom. They were required to be the seedbeds of legitimate heirs, faithful and obedient. Ferrand had sworn devotion to his young wife, and she'd believed it. What was worse, she'd loved him too.

Eglantine did not have to tell Raf this—he'd seen it. He'd seen her on her wedding day, a blazing vision of love and happiness. That was what he'd fallen in love with—her beauty, yes, but more fundamentally, the transcendent power of her love.

And Ferrand had destroyed that.

Raf did not know how to react. To say *not all men are like that* may be true, but it wasn't the truth she'd experienced. Words alone meant nothing. How did one prove to a lady who did not believe in love that he was and would forever remain hers?

All of which passed through his mind as he half sat, half reclined in the bow embrasure, a mere hand's breadth from his lady. It was not doing his thought processes any favors.

There was absolutely no reason for him to remain here—Sir Garit was gone, and Eglantine herself was probably waiting for Raf to remove his bulk that she too may exit with dignity. He was about to reply to her last statement with a further, doubtless inadequate reassurance when she leaned forward and touched her lips to his.

It was a hesitant kiss. His lips had been slightly open when she touched them—her mouth, too, was sweetly ajar. It was a questing kiss. It grazed over his lips, coaxing gently. It asked something of him. *What, goddammit?* Was he supposed to prove he was not like her dead husband? Was it simple gratitude? Or was it a renewal of her strange proposal to the Minstrel Raf?

And in the meantime, his body was smoldering, igniting. Her breath was mingling with his, her scent driving out thought, and her soft warmth was so very, very close.

The end result? Raf froze. No, *freeze* was entirely the wrong word for it. He was combusting on the spot. But he moved not a muscle—not even a lip muscle.

"Kiss me, dammit," she murmured into his mouth.

Well, that was a direct command. He had sworn to obey his lady, hadn't he? That was as far as logical thought got him before the barely leashed animal within him broke free.

He obeyed. What followed was not a devouring—not quite. Perhaps that was because she was as hungry herself. It took some concerted maneuvers within the stony window ledge, but he managed to twine his arms around her. She wrapped her arms around his neck and drew him to her. Their mouths were no longer slightly ajar. They were entirely open to each other, tongue tangling with tongue, lips melded with a blinding, all-consuming intimacy.

He didn't want to stop. He wanted *more*. He wanted everything. Raf slipped a hand down her side, learning the dip of her waist, the swell of her hip, before slipping it around to cup her buttock, molding her to him. Fitting against him in ways that felt too utterly right.

She gasped and wriggled just a little closer.

"You see," she said breathlessly, "this is not love. But it does not need to be. You do not love me, Rafèu, any more than I love you. We do not need to chain ourselves in wedlock. Touch me, Raf. I am a woman like any other. Take your pleasure, and then, when you have had enough, take your leave."

He froze, again. This time there was definitely more of a cooling sensation. A slow turning to ice of the blood in his veins.

She equated him with Ferrand. He too was a French nobleman and—Raf wasn't blind—women had been known to find him attractive. And just like Ferrand, Vicomte Rafèu swore devotion to the Lady Eglantine before asking her to wed him. She thought he was pressed from the same despicable mold.

It was a thought to wilt his very manhood, which was probably a good thing right now.

He released her. He ceased to grasp her delicious posterior and slipped his lower arm out from around her shoulders. In fact, it was high time he ceased to lounge here in the window in inappropriate proximity to the Lady of La Roque.

"Excuse me, my lady," he muttered as he removed his person from the embrasure with awkward dignity.

"Excuse you from what? Am I too blunt, my lord vicomte?"

She too slithered out of the window ledge. Her severe gown was crushed and dust-smeared. Her wimple was somewhat askew. His fingers ached to put her to rights—or more likely to remove the offending garments altogether.

"You are certainly direct, my lady. Allow me to be equally direct."

"Directness, from a minstrel? I thought you all spoke in poetry and allegory. And as for vicomtes…"

She did not finish the sentence, but she did not have to. He knew it would not be complimentary. He found himself staring at her lips, pink and a little swollen from kissing him. It would be so easy to close the distance between them and claim those lips again.

But that would only confirm her low opinion of him.

Low? It was ground level, practically subterranean.

"You think my love is illusory. You think it will fade as quickly as Ferrand's. Do you think I came here, disguised as a minstrel, as there was no other way into La Roque, to woo you out of passing fancy?" He felt his brows contract. Was he scowling at his love? "You think I will subject myself to a siege—possible starvation and death—just because I want to tumble the lady of the castle?"

PUT LIKE THAT, and with the accompanying black look, it didn't sound very likely. Eglantine's heart seemed to expand and grow lighter. She knew the very word *siege* conjured up a dark cloud over this false minstrel. A playacting nobleman might embrace a troubadour disguise, but to remain in a chateau under siege went well beyond acting a part.

Well, what of that? Rafèu deceived himself. He believed himself wholeheartedly devoted to her. It was so very tempting just to succumb, to fall into the dream of his love. The wave of feeling was almost irresistible. Someone to care and cherish her, to share the burdens of ruling a chateau, of raising a son, of withstanding a siege. Someone to drive the loneliness away.

But Ferrand had believed himself in love with her too. He'd been entirely convincing, too, and like a fool, she had given him her heart. He had discarded it like an old toy the moment he found a new one. Except she'd been an old toy he couldn't simply throw out—he had to keep her, and he'd resented it. He'd let her know how superfluous he thought her.

She couldn't bear that to happen with Rafèu.

"I think you believe yourself truly in love," she said carefully, but when she looked into his eyes, she saw just how ill-chosen that answer was.

His dark eyes blazed; his face was a collection of sharp lines, none sharper than his mouth. For a moment she was almost frightened. Had she done it? Had she turned his false love to fury? Was it so easy to turn Vicomte Rafèu's affections? Well, better to know now than later. She straightened her spine and waited for the storm burst.

"My lady, I will prove it to you. I will put myself to the test in whatever way you see fit. Command me. Test me. I have loved you since—" He broke off and shook his head. "I have worshipped you for years. Your image displaces all other women and always will."

"Ah, that is my very point, vicomte. My image. You barely know me. You have seen me before, I know not where, and for some reason, that image pleased you. But an image is not reality. You have fallen in love with an idea, not with me."

It was the hard truth. Rafèu, the vicomte with the soul of a minstrel, had taken the romances he sang to heart. In those romances, a hero fell in love with a lovely lady at a mere glance, sometimes only at the mention of her name. That wasn't how matters proceeded in the real world—this harsh world in which women were the chattels of men, chained by supposed bonds of love, until they were widowed and suddenly made free.

She had to say it, but she didn't want to say it.

She wanted to believe, and for that she was a fool.

Someone shouted her name. The sound carried through the wooden door from the courtyard. Osbert. Her captain was looking for her. There, at least, was a man she could depend upon.

She brushed down her skirts and patted at her wimple. It

would not do for Osbert to suspect what Raf had been doing to his mistress. Murder within La Roque's walls would be bad for morale.

"Thank you for your protection, vicomte. Such as it was. If you would obey this lady's whims, present yourself in the hall this evening. We could do with some music to lighten our mood." She cast him a small smile. "Pray sing in whatever language you please. I find I am not so enamored of all things English in our current situation."

"I would sing in the tongue of the Saracens, if my lady commands it."

"Truly, you could do that? Have you fought in the Holy Land?"

"I regret I have not decapitated any infidels, my lady. Would it warm your heart if I had?"

She actually laughed at that. It felt good, especially when she saw an answering quirk on Rafèu's lips. That harsh line needed softening.

"No, blood is not the way to my heart, vicomte. I'm not sure there is one."

The look in his eyes, so fierce moments before, softened. Ah, she could gaze into them forever. She would drown in them and lose all sense of herself—or self-preservation.

"I will find a way, Lady Eglantine. I promise you."

Her knight-minstrel looked about to say more, but he was not given the chance, for at that moment the door to the storeroom rattled and burst open.

"Praise the Lord and all His saints." Osbert stood in the doorway, effectively blocking out the light. "I'd looked everywhere, m'lady." The man-at-arms cast Raf a suspicious look. "I feared—"

"Fear not, captain," Raf intervened. "You asked me to keep the lady from harm or suffer the removal of my skin, I believe? Observe, she is in one piece."

Eglantine wasn't entirely sure about that, but Raf carried on smoothly, "We listened to the whole exchange from the safety of this storeroom, then we discussed…strategy. At length. Captain, I strongly suggest we work out a system of alarms and ascertain who responds and in what manner to each. We do not need to alert the whole castle when Sir Garit simply comes to shout threats at us."

Then Raf directed an inquiring look at her and just a hint of a smile. "Shall we retire to the solar with the good captain, my lady, and debate a little more…strategy?"

Chapter Seventeen

T HEY ACTUALLY DID discuss strategy. Raf very sensibly suggested that a continuous, jangling bell tone should only be employed in cases of imminent attack. That was the signal for all occupants of La Roque to deploy to their arranged positions. A lesser alert was signaled by two strikes of the bell, repeated at intervals.

"Two strikes just means that bastard's approaching under his white flag, or some other such thing," Osbert declared. "I hear that, and I hie me up on the battlements to see what's what. Or supposing I'm asleep or sick or dead, then you go, vicomte."

"Why me?"

"Why not me?"

Eglantine and Rafèu spoke simultaneously. They'd been looking at Osbert, but now they eyed each other.

"You, my lady, cannot venture onto the battlements because it is too dangerous," Raf said. She was about to bite back when he added, "We need our lady commander alive and coordinating matters on ground level."

She narrowed her eyes at him. He had been affronted by her picking up a wooden sword earlier. He was likely just condescending to her now. He couldn't be a noble knight protector if she was capable of protecting herself.

"True enough, m'lady," Osbert added. "Someone's got to

order folk about down in the courtyard."

"Agreed. But I should not be second-in-command on the walls," Raf said flatly. "I am a stranger. I do not know La Roque or its people."

"Aye." Osbert gave the vicomte a level look. "But let's not beat around the bush, my noble lord—you know more of sieges than the rest of us poor wights put together. A bit of prior experience counts for a deal more than local knowledge."

Eglantine watched Raf turn to stone. But he did not deny the charge. He said nothing at all.

"I agree," Eglantine said softly. "Whatever your prior experience, Vicomte Rafèu, you are a knight and a nobleman. You are trained to command. You do not appear to have any sympathy with this English invader. Thus far, we may trust you."

And as she said it, she realized with an odd little thrill that it was true. She trusted this man, at least so far as keeping her from bodily harm. She barely knew him, but she knew that much for certain.

But Raf did not look happy about it. "You have two other men-at-arms, captain. Surely they are capable of command?"

"Neither know naught about siege," Osbert said with a shrug. "I asked 'em."

There was a tight-lipped pause, after which Raf gave a curt nod. "So be it." But the look on his face instructed Osbert in no uncertain terms that he was never to sleep, never to so much as cough, and, for God's sake, not be so inconsiderate as to die.

They talked some more of deployment of people, training, and how they should organize shifts on the battlements. Eglantine got out a wax tablet and stylus and scratched out a roster. Not that most of those rostered could read it, but Osbert could decipher names and times at least. She knew because she had taught him.

That done, Eglantine grew restless. The baskets of midden waste awaited. The sweet siren call of horse manure and rotted hay crooned in her ears. More fundamentally, she needed her haven. Her small paradise—a walled garden to shut out the world. Plants, even thirsty, summer-stressed plants, were so much less demanding than a chateau under siege. Or a certain vicomte.

The sun was dipping toward the western horizon. She could see the lowering light from the solar window. Eglantine wriggled her toes and forced herself to focus on the finalization of deployment details. Raf was making suggestions, remarkably well-founded suggestions that more than hinted at a wealth of experience of siege, and Osbert was grunting agreement and occasional comments.

She watched the two of them—the stumpy, graying English captain and the darkly graceful French vicomte. Her two champions, the two men she trusted to protect La Roque and everyone within it.

But inevitably, she found her eyes lingering on the Frenchman. After all, he was by far the more pleasing to look at.

Was he just like Ferrand? Her husband had been handsome too, but it struck Eglantine now that Ferrand's looks had been far blander than Raf's, somehow unmarked by underlying character. The vicomte was the less conventionally handsome of the two, his face almost too sharply defined, a little too long and angular, but it betrayed an underlying firmness that Ferrand's never had. Yet there was poetry in his face too, in the melting softness of his eyes, the slight husk of his voice as he sang. There had been no poetry in Ferrand, only conventional sweet talk when it suited him.

"Can I have a lend of the tablet, m'lady?"

Eglantine startled. Osbert was looking at her—and she had doubtless been staring at a certain picturesque Frenchman.

"Osbert and I are going to the walls to explain all we've decided, my lady." Raf's voice brushed over her senses, setting them to tingling awareness. "Your roster will help."

"Of course." She seized the wood-framed wax tablet and thrust it toward Osbert. "Are we finished for now?"

She glanced at the window, trying not to seem too eager to leave. She shouldn't be so keen to escape to her garden—she should hammer out the details to the last, then go and put plans into action, just as her two champions were about to. But the pressure, the weight of what seemed the entire chateau, was bearing down on her. This was her fault, her responsibility. At least in her garden she could take some small action toward alleviating it.

Osbert nodded, and Raf looked at her with those melting eyes that saw far too much.

Eglantine rose from her writing desk and fled.

DUSK HAD SETTLED over the landscape by the time Raf descended the battlements. The sun had sunk in a blaze of red gold in a cloudless sky, and the color leached from the tapestry of woods and fields below. He and Osbert had done the rounds, speaking to everyone involved in the defense of La Roque, which was essentially everyone in the chateau. They would run some drills on the next day to ensure their instructions were understood. He did not wish the panic that had ensued at the approach of Sir Garit earlier to be repeated. Likely the bastard would approach on a daily basis to harass Eglantine, and Raf suspected he'd be reduced to quivering aspic given too many repeats of today.

It proved it—he was no good in a siege. After Combret, Raf had retreated from the whole stupid disaster of war and lived the lordly life at Bruniquel. He didn't want to face the soul-destroying act of endurance that was siege anymore.

Raf stumbled down the final darkening steps and eyed the wall beside him with evil intent. The fingers of his right hand were bunched. He was inclined to thump them against the ungiving stone, if only to distract his thoughts with a bit of blinding pain.

But no, his lady had commanded him to play tonight. He may not pluck the strings of his lute as the minstrel girl Azalais did, but it would be damned hard to grip a plectrum if his hand was swollen and bruised.

Slowly, he uncurled his fingers and walked on. Down here in the courtyard, the darkness was almost complete. They should arrange lights, Raf thought absently. A burning brand here and there. Broken arms and legs on the way to the wall was not the best way to fend off a night attack.

Given the circumstances of darkness, abstracted thought, and an urge to hit something, Raf never noticed the figure before he collided with it. It was only surprising that he managed *not* to lash out the moment he walked into something that shouldn't be there.

Just as well, considering it turned out to be the Lady Eglantine.

He stepped back hurriedly, releasing her shoulders as if they burned him. Actually, they probably would. Set him afire, at least.

"What are you doing here in the dark, my lady? And what in God's name is that smell?"

She laughed.

The gossips at the tavern lied. The Lady Eglantine could laugh, and this wasn't the first time he'd heard her do so. But that soft, throaty chuckle seemed particularly out of place in the current atmosphere.

"If you must know, I was closing the garden door, vicomte. Be grateful you didn't happen along earlier, or it wouldn't have been me you crashed into. You'd have upended in a basket of manure instead." Another low laugh.

"You're sounding remarkably cheerful for one who indubitably does *not* smell like roses, Lady Eglantine." Then he frowned. "Did you fall into one of those baskets?"

In the low light, he saw her swipe an arm across her brow. It left a smudge over her pale skin and wimple, visible even in the dim. Before he could think better of the action, he'd reached out and wiped at it, setting her wimple to rights in the process. Now his hand too smelled like horse crap.

His lady moved in her very own cloud of manure scent. Not that that would stop him kissing her. In fact…

"I need a wash." She smiled at him. Her teeth showed white in the low light. "I haven't even finished yet. We talked for so long I only got two baskets dug in. Come…"

Somewhat to his surprise, she tucked a hand in his. She began to lead him toward the central keep. Her hand felt a little gritty in his. His larger hand encompassed hers completely, his fingers folding around hers.

It was probably due to her hand in his—almost childlike in its innocence and friendly trust—that it took a moment for her words to percolate through.

He was inclined to come to an abrupt halt in his progress across the courtyard, but her hand tugged him on. "You were handling that stuff?" he demanded. *"Digging it in,* you said. What is it, for God's sake—horse dung?"

She glanced at him. Her face didn't register outrage but a quirk of quite inappropriate amusement.

"Yes, mostly. There's a fair bit of straw in there as well, but that's all good for the soil."

Raf did come to a halt this time. He dug his heels in and took a firm grip on her hand. "Lady Eglantine, let me be clear. I seem to have misunderstood you. Naturally you had menservants performing the actual digging and dung handling. How it is you come to be so fragrant, I do not know."

"It's quite simple, vicomte. I currently smell of that which makes roses grow *because* I have been handling it myself. I cherish my garden. I do not trust men with their stomping great feet not to trample my plants. I do what work is necessary in my garden, and sometimes that involves manure."

"My lady…" He loosened his grip on the dainty hand in his, which was gritty with what he now knew to have been in intimate contact with a horse's rear. That wasn't precisely why he let it go. Not wholly.

She was looking up at him with her head angled to one side. "Well? Are you going to tell me that the lady of your dreams does not dabble in dung?"

Give or take a word, that was exactly what he was going to say. "Perhaps," he muttered.

"This, my lord, is just one instance in which your dreams depart from reality. I am not the pristine idol of your imagination." She advanced her hand toward his face, palm outward. For an instant he thought she might slap him, but no—it was worse. "Wake up and smell the roses, Vicomte Rafèu. They do not smell so sweet as you imagined."

Her palm hovered just beneath his nose, and it most definitely did not smell of roses. His nose burned and desperately wanted to wrinkle, but he knew he could not let it. He leaned forward, tried not to breathe in, and laid his lips to the proffered palm.

Her eyebrows lifted. "You have strange tastes, my lord."

She withdrew her hand.

Raf took a relieved breath and murmured, "Perhaps. But I find my tastes run wholly to you." Then he frowned and added, "I understand you cherish your garden, but surely you do not need to engage in the manual work? Not all men are equally elephantine. Can you not find someone trustworthy to reek of manure in your place?"

She laughed at that. "Ah, you are full of courtesy tonight, vicomte. And I've only dug in two baskets. I have eight more. Just think how I'll smell at the conclusion! Margery will certainly have to pour me a bath."

A bath. The Lady Eglantine freed of her constraining garments and clothed only in soft skin and flowing hair, slipping into the silky water. It was a vision to banish any quantity of manure.

But the lady in question wasn't finished yet. She stepped a little closer to him, head cocked at an inquiring angle and an expression his bemused brain could only register as mischievous on her lovely features.

"Tell me, O Vicomte of Bruniquel, are you an elephant?"

Rafèu blinked.

"You declare yourself my true knight," she carried on. "You ask me to put you to the test. You had in mind a quest, perhaps—something noble and chivalrous? Well, I have a task for you, and one that I would trust only to you. I would have you prove your worth, my true knight."

His heart should have leaped at her challenge. It was precisely what he'd asked for. He had to prove he was no Ferrand. He was no feckless fantasizer who would toy with Eglantine's heart only to discard it. But he had a dreadful feeling that he saw where this was going.

She was gazing up at him in the gloom, a decidedly wicked quirk to her lips.

"My lady, only say the word," he managed, and awaited his doom.

"Indeed I will. I will say a number of them. Hear your quest, my true knight. You, Vicomte Rafèu, will dig eight baskets of well-rotted manure into my garden on the morrow, and you will trample not a single plant in the process. Do you accept?"

$$\approx\!\!\!\!*\!\!\!\!\approx$$

Chapter Eighteen

E HAD, AND Eglantine felt a little guilty about it. But only a bit. And then they went their separate ways, Eglantine to wash the scent of horse dung off her before the evening meal and Raf, presumably, to collect his lute.

Then followed a strangely peaceful evening, in which it was almost possible to forget they were hemmed in by enemies. Eglantine had watched her minstrel play. Indeed, she found it impossible to look away. He cradled his lute so intimately, his hair drooping over one shoulder and feathering the polished wood of the instrument. His fingers were sure upon the strings— long, elegant fingers, so skilled in coaxing out rippling, magical music. He seemed so utterly absorbed, as if there were no one else in the room but him.

Until he glanced up mid-*canzo* and looked directly at her. Then the words he voiced in husky velvet entered her very heart and gave it a sharp twist.

The words were too beautiful. He was too beautiful, and he was nothing but a fleeting, seductive dream. She could not lose herself in the fantasy of his false promises, for all he believed them himself.

Here, then, was the solution. Nothing like a bit of dung-scented reality to bring a man to his senses.

Eglantine had come to the garden early, just as the day was

dawning and there was still a hint of damp freshness in the air. There was to be a siege drill later that morning—both Osbert and Rafèu had declared it necessary in order that every inhabitant of La Roque knew their role in time of attack. Besides, it was always best to tend her plants before the heat of the day.

She was wearing an old russet gown, made even less appealing by the addition of a voluminous apron. Her wimple was temporarily replaced by a wide straw hat, and her hair bound back severely beneath. It was gardening garb, calculated to dispel any man's romantic illusions.

That and eight baskets of dung ought to do the trick nicely. Why then, as she lugged pails of well water to her various thirsty plants, did she feel a nagging emptiness within?

The bell at the garden door was struck once…twice. Two brassy tones to echo in that emptiness inside her. Eglantine smoothed her apron and checked that her hair was still carefully confined. Then she approached the door.

Raf. Her gaze slipped down from his face, and she registered with a little jolt that he looked as much the peasant as she. A rough-woven linen tunic covered his torso, topped with the plainest of surcoats. His long legs were clad in ill-fitting dun hose, but with thin leather thongs wrapped about them to reveal the shape of the muscle beneath.

"Clothing courtesy of my village acquaintance, who now boasts a fine suit of motley," Raf said. "I did not think it worth dirtying what clothes I have left in pursuit of your noble quest, my lady."

Eglantine felt her cheeks heat. "A wise decision, my lord. You see I have dressed with similar practicality."

And then she wished she hadn't said anything. His gaze immediately traversed her person, to linger on the exposed skin of her neck. She often swapped her wimple for a hat in the privacy of her garden—it was certainly the cooler and shadier option in summer—but now its absence left her feeling almost naked. Not that she minded the intensity of his gaze upon her, the distinct feeling that he would like to lay his lips to her naked neck, but she suddenly wished she were wearing something a little more becoming.

Fool, do you want to rid him of this ridiculous fancy or not?

"Well, my lord, do come in. I hear the manure calling your name. We have work to do. We cannot stand around admiring each other's peasant costumes all day."

He gave her a slow, warm smile in return. A flame licked her innards.

"As my lady wills it," he said, and stepped in and barred the door.

Eglantine's lips tightened. He was doing his best to cast this undertaking in a chivalrous light. He was only playing the peasant, just as he had acted the minstrel. Well, she would see how long his playacting lasted in the face of eight baskets of dung.

She led him through the walled garden to the beds set symmetrically about the central pool. They were mostly empty of greenery now. Eglantine did not attempt to grow her beloved English plants in the exposed central beds in summer. She had tried that in the early years—it only ended in heartbreak.

But this year it was going to be different. It had to be.

"These." She pointed out the four crescent-shaped beds. "I want the contents of the baskets distributed between these. You see I have already started on that one." She indicated the nearest. About half of it was newly turned over.

He cocked his head at her. "May a mere peasant inquire why? Or is it part of the test to engage in a pointless task?"

"Pointless? It is anything but pointless, vicomte. Perhaps you have noticed La Roque is under siege?"

His eyes flickered but he said nothing.

"We have no access to green vegetables now," she went on. "There is not room in the outer courtyard for a kitchen garden, and to venture beyond the walls is a death sentence. We have food enough for many months, it is true, but we have no greens." She waved a hand at the bare beds. "But we *will* do. Behold our new salad garden."

He observed the dry, desolate beds. "I am no peasant tiller of peas, my lady, but I believe it takes a goodly while for vegetables to mature."

"Some vegetables, yes," she snapped. "But I do not aim to keep La Roque in onions. I shall sow fast-growing greens. Salad leaves, orache, sorrel, and radish. I only pray we no longer need them when they mature."

She left the implication hanging. Who knew what kind of situation they would be in a month or so hence?

Raf stared at the bare beds. Perhaps he was considering their inadequacy. The beds would only provide a few leaves of lettuce for each inhabitant per day. Or perhaps he was seeing something else entirely, something even bleaker.

She had the urge to slip an arm around his shoulders, but not in any suggestive way. He simply looked as if he needed it.

Then the vicomte shrugged. "And horse manure is essential to this aim?" One end of his mouth quirked up. It looked a little forced. "I shall regard lettuce in an entirely new light from now on. I shall also ensure it is well washed."

"Yes, manure is essential. Green leaves are hungry for dung."

"Truly? Well, there is no accounting for appetites." His smile looked genuine this time. "Point me toward your shovel, fair lady. I am convinced of the worthiness of my task, although you may have to excuse me from eating any of the produce of our labors."

"Fop," she countered, but softened it with a smile. Then she added, "You'll find a few plants in the beds. Thyme and sage and the like." She narrowed her eyes at him. "Don't, for the love of God, dig them up or cover them in dung."

"Or put my elephant feet on them?"

"That too. Plants like company. My salad greens will be happier in the shelter of stronger plants."

"Plants being somewhat like humans?"

She gave him a look. They had talked enough. The sun was

climbing in the sky and would soon bathe the central garden in its merciless light. Then he would regret wasting the cool of the morning on words.

She pointed at the shovel, the baskets, and the beds. "Dig," she commanded.

RAF DUG.

Actually, he had barely dumped one basket of foul-smelling material on a bed and started to attack it with a shovel before his lady intervened.

"Stand up."

He obeyed, a treacherous hope flickering in his soul. Had he passed the test already? The lady had taken pity on her knight and decided not to drown him in dung in order to prove his worth after all.

She moved around behind him. Then her hands were in his hair, and a jolt coursed through him.

"Stand still. There."

Moments later, Raf found his hair had been bound back at the nape and a monstrous straw hat wedged on his head.

"Was my peasant outfit incomplete?" he inquired.

"Without a doubt. There, you are much better equipped now."

Then she walked away and picked up her pail again. Raf stared after her a moment. She took her pail to the central pool, bent, and filled it to the brim. Then she carted it to a verdant bed against the chateau wall and emptied it about a rosebush. He frowned as she repeated the process, but this time dousing a shrub replete with drooping purple flowers. Roses were about the limit of Raf's plant knowledge. He was happy to sing of flowers in spring, but he had no idea what the majority of them were called.

Did she do this every morning? She said she banned all others from her garden demesne. Christ, did she do all the labor in her garden with her own hands? It was passing strange behavior for a noble lady.

Raf turned his frown upon the garden bed before him. He swiped his brow with one rough, linen-clad arm, nearly dislodging the hat. He had hardly begun and he was warming up. Well, better get it over with.

OF COURSE SHE cast him many glances as she proceeded about the garden. She had to keep an eye on a potential owner of elephantine feet. Eglantine finished the watering and then busied herself with some pruning within strategic view of her laboring vicomte. But it wasn't her vulnerable herbs her eyes strayed to most frequently. No, they barely got a glance.

Her gaze lingered on her gardener instead, the way he bent wholeheartedly to his work, the manner in which he attacked the soil with his shovel, turning it, sifting it, even picking up stubborn clods with his hands to break the clumps apart. The man was going to reek of dung, and he didn't seem to care.

At some point he had divested himself of his rough surcoat. Now it looked as if he ought to strip off his tunic too. He had rolled up the sleeves, but the remainder of the cloth clung to his frame damply. Eglantine found herself watching the way the linen adhered to the muscle beneath. It was an effort to recall her pruning. She had never considered sweat the least bit attractive before, but the dampness seemed to polish Raf's skin, making his exposed throat and forearms seem positively sculpted.

Eglantine's fingers flexed. She would dearly like to see the effect on the rest of his torso. A pity about the tunic.

She gave up on her pruning and moved to the pool. She sank her hand into its cool depths and fished out the vessel submerged there. He must be nearly finished—all the baskets were emptied, and now Raf seemed set on perfecting the tilth of the soil. He was knelt on the ground, leaning over the beds, and combing his fingers through the dirt.

Eglantine stepped up to him and put a hand on his shoulder. That wayward hand yearned to run downward over the length of his back. But she sensed him tense a little, so she made do with the warmth and solidity of his shoulder.

"You have done well, my knight," she said. "Come. Rest from your labors and enjoy your reward."

He angled his head to look at her. His face glowed from his exertions and his eyes seemed more darkly luminous than ever. "Might my reward include a dunk in cold water, my lady? I crave it over a mound of gold right now. By God, I don't know how your average peasant does it. I'll combust if I don't come into contact with cool water without delay."

"Come to the pool. I can at least provide you something to drink."

Raf unbent. He brushed off his hands and rose, dispersing a scent to baffle the best perfumer in Paris. There were definite notes of manure—that could not be denied—but blended in too was the scent of fresh soil, just a hint of thyme, and more than a hint of heated man.

"Why are your eyes closed, my lady?" A light chuckle. "Are you overcome with my aura of horse? I would advise you not to faint, for then I would have to pick you up, and smear the stuff on you in the process."

"Would you, my knight?" Eglantine opened her eyes to find him looking down at her with just a hint of concern. "Sweet heaven, I feel a swoon coming on. Scoop me up in your dung-smelling arms and clasp me to your manly, sweaty chest!"

She clapped a hand to her brow, unfortunately dislodging her straw hat in the process. The ugly thing tumbled to the ground.

Raf simply looked at her, a half-smile upon his lips. There was something about his expression that made her knees feel a little wobbly. Maybe she would swoon after all.

Then he reached out and stroked some stray tendrils of hair back from her brow. "You haven't changed. You know some of the gossips say you are scarred, my lady, for you wrap yourself up so thoroughly."

"Scarred?" Eglantine gave a mirthless laugh. "Perhaps I am at that." But when she saw his brows rise, she added, "But not in the way they think. What do you mean, I haven't changed?" She dipped to retrieve her hat.

He waylaid her arm just as it was lifting the item to her head. "No, don't put it back on. Not yet. Consider it my reward for perspiring in your garden, my lady."

"You sell your labors cheap, sir knight," she murmured, but did as he requested. "But you haven't explained your earlier statement."

He still had hold of her arm. He did not seem inclined to let it go. Instead, he led her to the pool to stand beneath the tamarisk tree.

"Sit in the shade, my lady. I fear you will burn without your hat. Sit, and I will explain."

She sat, dipping her hand in the cool water. "And you, my lord—what about your imminent combustion? I have watered wine for you, kept cool in the pond."

"Ah, the pool." Raf sank down on its stone rim beside her. Unfortunately, there was not shade enough for him too, but he did not seem to notice. He was eyeing the water hungrily—or like a man who had not drunk for a week.

Then he glanced up at her with a glint in his eye.

"Pray forgive me, my lady. My garb and this morning's activities have infected me. I fear I must continue to act the peasant."

And he swung his long legs over the side of the pool and simply let himself tumble in.

Chapter Nineteen

L ITTLE DROPLETS SCATTERED over Eglantine's hands, a sprinkle of delicious coolness. Raf slowly sank back in the pool with a look of infinite pleasure on his face until he lay at full length. He let his head droop back until the water closed over it, entirely submerging his face. Dark hair fanned out like a midnight cloud about his features. He must have untied it.

He stayed like that for what seemed countless heartbeats, so long that she began to worry he'd passed out. Should she sink her arms into the water and haul him up?

Just as she was shoving back her sleeves, he sat up. Water streamed off him, cloth clung to him, and he pushed back his hair with two hands. He was smiling, a blazing, unguarded smile, and Eglantine could not breathe. His hair was slicked back, torso outlined beneath wet linen, and he was smiling at her.

His smile dimmed.

"My lady, do I offend you?" One hand rippled the water. "I saw that you used this pond for your watering. I hoped you wouldn't mind it watering a man." A broadening of the smile. "And believe me, between the heat and the horse turd, I was sorely in need of watering."

She shook her head in negation. And bemusement. "I think you need some wine. The heat has addled your head."

He was not the only one in need of wine. She poured and

proffered. His damp, cool fingers slipped around her own upon the goblet.

"You feel heated, my lady. Perhaps you too need a bath."

For a mad instant she was tempted, but she saw he was joking. Pity. What would it be like to slip down into the water with him? She wasn't sure it would be a cooling experience.

"Drink, then take off your shirt," she returned. At his startled look, she said drily, "I will hang it to dry. You will be no more naked without it," and ran a finger down his chest.

Her fingertip prickled on the coarse linen. Yes, it needed to come off.

He glanced down. "Ah, forgive me. I had not realized." He tweaked the wet fabric away from his torso, but the moment he released it, it clapped back against him like a second skin, albeit a wrinkly one. He sighed. "I am hopelessly indecent, my lady. I can but follow your advice."

He raised the goblet to her, drank, and then he peeled.

And in the breathless moments he was tugging the damp fabric up and over his head, Eglantine could gaze with impunity. Indeed, the gyrations required to remove the clinging cloth made his musculature move in all sorts of interesting ways. And he definitely had musculature. Clothed, Raf had simply seemed lean and long—graceful for a man, but not heavily built. Now Eglantine saw she had been wrong. He was beautifully proportioned—a sculpture of lithe muscle and light olive skin.

The tunic came off. Raf swished it about in the water, then wrung it out with a proficiency that suggested this nobleman had laundered for himself before. Yet another mystery.

"My lady, if I may ask you to array my laundry at your pleasure? I am disinclined to get out of your pond as yet. Besides"—he glanced down—"I fear for your sensibilities when I do."

She followed the direction of his glance. Beneath the water, he still wore hose and braies. They too would cling to him when he arose.

Raf shook his head ruefully. "I regret I did not think this

through." He took up his wine goblet from where it sat by the pool and tipped the remainder of its contents into his mouth. "You were right—the heat had baked my brain. I begin to come to my senses now, and find I have acted most…inadvisably."

Eglantine smiled and took the shirt. She draped it over an outstretched branch of the tamarisk. "You earned it," she said softly. She leaned closer and made a show of sniffing. "And it improves your fragrance no end."

When she glanced up, her heart stilled. He was very close.

She reached out and touched his shoulder. Skin so smooth and firm, still a little dewy to the touch. "You begin to dry." The words were irrelevant. She had to say something.

"Good," he said, and drew her to him.

IT WAS A bad, bad idea, but he was due a little reward, wasn't he? He was seated most comfortably in her pond and must stay there for the sake of decency, and she was perched on its stone rim. Thus placed, they could do no more than kiss. And a kiss was the traditional reward for a task performed in a lady's name. So said the romances.

And then there was her hair. That was part of the reward too. She'd left her hat off as he'd asked, but now Raf's hands did more than cup the back of his lady's head as he laid his lips to hers. His fingers fiddled with her bindings—only the bindings of her hair, mind you. He was not a complete churl.

Her lips were warm against his, and she opened to him like a flower. It became damnably hard to focus on the task of untying her hair. She tasted of the watered wine she'd just drunk, and of a yearning headier than any wine. It was a need to be held and loved, to be cherished and valued. By God, he could do that.

He tangled his fingers in her loosening hair and reveled in the feel of her against his bare skin. Then slipped his tongue inside her mouth in an invitation to dance.

She gasped and moved against him. Beneath the surface of the water, his braies too moved. In complete defiance of cold water. Thank Christ that part of him was safely separated from his lady.

Her hair tumbled around her shoulders, and his too. It curtained them both in soft waves, and Raf threaded the fingers of one hand through its luxuriance. He cupped the back of her head with the other hand, the better to plunder her mouth. Although, come to think of it, the plundering was decidedly mutual.

Then her hands began to roam his chest, her palms flat against his torso. They brushed over his nipples and paused. Then her fingertips strayed over first one nipple then the other, scattering little jolts through him, and prompting most inappropriate thoughts.

Such as doing the same thing to her.

Perhaps it was the slight distraction from matters of the mouth that prompted it. Whatever the cause, Eglantine shifted. She dipped her head down, soft hair brushing his bare flesh, to descend to the angle just where shoulder met throat. She kissed him there. He closed his eyes and simply felt, breathing shallowly as she proceeded to taste him in little licks and nibbles, as if he were some delicacy arrayed at her table, setting his skin afire as she trailed across his chest. Her loose hair caressed his skin, and she gripped his shoulders as if afraid he would wrench away.

By God, no. Raf would not move a muscle (unless involuntarily beneath the water). He would offer himself as a seven-course meal to his lady, should she desire it. He was still safe within the water; she was protected by a couple of layers of cloth. He had caused his lady no dishonor, breached no boundaries of chivalry, and he wouldn't.

For all he desperately wanted to.

She glanced up at him, and her expression should have dissolved him on the spot. It was a combination of innocent inquiry and smoldering need. "I have never tasted a man before, and I find that I like it," she said, and colored a little. "It's strange, I know, but you looked so delicious I had to try. Now I want you to do it to me. Shall I make it your next knightly task, my lord vicomte?"

A shudder ran through him. Perhaps the cold of the water was getting to him.

Raf fought for rational thought. Her hands were still on him—she was gazing at him with sweet supplication. How could a true knight deny his lady's request?

A truly chivalrous and honorable knight would. He would stay firm. It was a knight's part to worship his lady from a respectful distance.

Ah, firmness. His braies tightened yet further. Raf closed his eyes and groaned.

"Is it such a hard task, my lord? I would have thought it more pleasant than dung digging."

He blinked his eyes open. She looked a little crestfallen, her beautiful green eyes were wide and vulnerable, and Raf knew what he had to do.

"I am a minstrel," he said. "Or at least I am in my soul. Let me act the minstrel now, my lady, and tell you a story."

❁

"Once upon a time, a knight attended a wedding," Raf said, settling back in the pool to lean his arms on the stone coping. His gaze dwelt upon the tamarisk tree. He was no longer touching her or even looking at her.

"The wedding was not his own. He had never met the lady in question, and, as for the bridegroom, he barely knew him. The knight had come because he was invited, and because his lands lay in a border region menaced by English aggressors, and it was wise to make alliance with other nobles in the region."

Raf did not look at her, but that did not mean Eglantine could not look at him. His hair was beginning to dry. It flowed down his back like a midnight waterfall. His skin was deliciously smooth…and edible.

She wanted more, and he just wanted to tell her a story.

He went on: "The bridegroom had taken the notion of alliance a step further. The knight was surprised to find many Englishmen at the wedding. Englishwomen, too. The knight noticed one English woman in particular. The bride."

Eglantine stilled. She ceased to explore the landscape of Raf's chest and arms by means of her gaze, and settled on his face instead. His eyes were distant, directed at the tamarisk tree.

"The knight was told the bridegroom was making a marriage alliance with a wealthy Englishman. In return for his noble name and ancient patrimony, the bridegroom would receive wealth, an English ally, and the protection that alliance would give him. He would also receive a bride of transcendent beauty. I wonder which of these gifts he valued the most?"

Eglantine pressed her lips together. She would not answer his rhetorical question. She would hear his story out. It must have a purpose, surely? She had just presented her true knight with a second task to perform, and he answered with this—a dredging up of the sordid past.

"But the knight did not dwell upon the bridegroom's motives. No, the knight was transfixed. For when the English bride was led before her husband-to-be, she radiated joy, beauty, and the very essence of true love." Raf's voice had softened. "The knight saw this, and he was struck, not by the god of love's arrows, but by inspiration. He had found his muse, and she was about to be wedded to another man."

He shifted his gaze from the tamarisk then. Raf looked at her. She could not read his expression. He did not smile, but the intensity made her look away.

"Did that matter?" he asked. "No, not in the least. The knight knew love was not necessarily to be found in marriage. Nor was it necessary to consummate his love in any carnal sense. It was enough to carve her image in his heart. This is the way of the romances, of *canzos*, and *fin'amor*."

Pretty illusions, the lot of them, she was tempted to retort. They fostered fine notions of falsehood, of love that could never last.

But she didn't. She wanted to see how the story would end.

"The knight never spoke to his lady. He simply worshipped her from afar. And she made his heart sing. Throughout those marriage celebrations, she had eyes only for her husband. She was love personified—for him."

Ha! More like foolishness personified.

"It was as well the knight could not wed her," Raf went on. "For he would not have been much of a husband to her in the years that followed. But equally, it was well for the knight that he *had* seen her, for without that image to inspire him, it is certain the knight would have perished."

Story or no, she had to interrupt at this point. "You embroider, my lord. Love does not kill, nor does it save. You stretch the truth too far."

"Do I? I am but a minstrel telling a tale. Am I not entitled to a little embroidery? Hear me to the end."

And the semi-naked man in her pool spoke on.

"As I say, it was as well the knight could not wed her, for it was not long after the wedding that he became embroiled in battle. In a protracted siege, to be precise."

Her throat tightened. Eglantine would not interrupt now. She had wanted to ask this of him for days but had not dared. His reaction whenever the subject had been touched upon had forbidden it. She could not prod whatever wound lay beneath.

But now…

"It was only a small stronghold, but a strategic one. The Companies—those nationless armies of ravening men—were spreading across France like a leprosy. The knight's liege lord wanted a stop to it in his lands. The knight was put in command of a small chateau at a mountain pass. It should have been an easy task to hold. It was well-nigh impregnable." His gaze lifted to meet hers. "Much like this stronghold, my lady. Built on rocky heights, and well supplied with water and food."

She did not answer—could not answer. There was a rock in her very innards.

"The chateau was besieged. The English commander wished to eliminate the stronghold. *Eliminate* it, I say. He could not pass on and leave a force of Frenchmen to attack his back. So he bombarded the chateau. He employed cannon to batter the walls, and arrows to sow death within. The knight found himself in command of a fortification being reduced to rubble and despair. And this went on for months, for the chateau was no easy target."

Raf paused to drag in a breath.

"Honor decreed the knight could not surrender. He had sworn to hold the stronghold for his liege lord. Yet his men were dying. The chateau must fall. In all this death and destruction, the knight had but one thing to hold on to: her image. The vision of beauty, purity, and love. In a world without music, she was his song. He was surrounded by death, but she gave him a reason to live."

He lifted his gaze to hers. Raf had been staring at nothing for the last few sentences. Now she looked into his eyes and saw nothing but darkness.

"Do you see, my lady? I do not embroider. Such things cannot be embroidered."

"I see," she whispered.

After a long moment, he went on. "The knight saw his lady once more after this. After the knight and his men burst forth in a desperate night attack to drive off the enemy, after he'd captured a wealthy lord in the process, long after the siege was over...but not forgotten."

"When?" she asked, seeing his expression turn bleak, sinking into the past. She leaned forward and took his face between her hands. "Look at me, Raf. Those days are over. When did you see her again? Tell me."

His lips shifted into an approximation of a smile. "Kiss me," he murmured.

She could not refuse, even if she'd wanted to. He'd bared his soul to her, and he was as vulnerable as a newborn foal. She bent and touched her lips to his, softly and gently. It was no passionate kiss, unless one counted tenderness as passion. It was a slow embrace of the lips, her hands still cupping his face, and she had never experienced a kiss quite like it. Consuming passion she knew, and polite pecks, but this was something else entirely.

She drew back, a little dizzy.

He brushed her hair back from her brow. "Ah, that's better." And she wasn't sure whether it was her hair or her mouth he was referencing.

"Your story, my lord. Is it complete?"

"Almost. The knight saw his lady one more time, as I said. This time he beheld her at a funeral. Her husband's funeral, that is."

"I detect a certain symmetry to your tale, sir minstrel."

"Life offers strange symmetries," he replied. "The knight had returned to his chateau after the siege and resumed his life, such as it was. And when he heard his lady's husband had unaccountably died, he rode to the funeral. The knight's heart ached for his lady. She had just lost the man she loved. Although he could do nothing to ease her pain, the knight needed to be close to her. He had to see her one more time."

"And? How did this lady look? Did she dance upon her husband's grave?"

He lifted a brow, and the corner of his mouth followed suit. "She did not. Do you think she wanted to?"

"I fancy she is not accustomed to dance at the best of times. Even if that was one of them."

"Truly? Perhaps she should be encouraged to dance."

I would dance with you at this moment, Vicomte Rafèu. Only arise from your impromptu bathtub and clasp me in your arms.

But of course she didn't say that. He was talking of funerals, or trying to.

He regarded her. "No, she did not dance. She did not smile. There was not the least hint of color about her. She was garbed in black, face as tightly wimpled as a nun, and her cheeks were as white as the linen that hemmed them in. She seemed frozen in pain. In sorrow."

Rafèu shrugged, as if to shift the image he had conjured.

"The knight could not approach the grieving lady. What kind of a churl would he be to speak words of love when she'd just seen her love buried? No, the knight rode away with a battle raging in his heart. His lady was free to wed again—in time, he could woo her and win her, God willing. But what of the vision he'd fallen in love with? That had been of joy and pure love for her husband, but now the husband was dead, her heart might well be buried with him. She looked so much like a nun that he half expected her to enter a convent forthwith."

He reached out and traced a finger around the oval of her face, where the wimple would normally rest.

"He feared that, even if he managed to wed her, he might just wed a shell. The love that lit her up may never be kindled again."

He regarded her with velvet eyes. What could she say? That it wasn't grief for her husband he saw on her face that day, that she'd existed as a nun for years before that? But that yes, he was right—he had seen a shell that day. Perhaps she was one still.

"It was a false fire," Eglantine whispered. "It was falsely kindled, and it died a slow death of neglect and disrespect. I know better now."

Chapter Twenty

T HERE IT WAS—THE problem. Her feckless husband had kindled her love and then disregarded it, and her. Eglantine would not render herself so vulnerable to a man again. But what, then, had Raf seen that day? If Eglantine's heart was in the grave, it certainly wasn't in Ferrand's. More likely she'd walled her heart up in this garden.

He glanced around him, at the elegantly laid-out beds, sun-baked in the center, verdant and flourishing against the walls and cliff, all tended with evident love and care. Stone mosaic paths twisted between the beds. It was a small paradise, and he lay at ease in its very heart—reclining like a half-naked gargoyle in her beautiful pool.

Yet she'd invited him in here, admitted him into her sanctuary and entrusted him with shoveling shit. It was a step in the right direction, surely? Especially if the way to the lady's heart was through her garden. She hadn't even denounced his abrupt appropriation of her pool—unless she was making the most of him as a temporary garden statue. Hence the removal of the shirt.

"To the point of my story, Lady Eglantine. Let me shrug off subterfuge. I am that knight. I fell in love with a vision of love and beauty. With you. It was this vision alone that kept me sane, even alive, during the siege of Combret. I cannot sully that vision. I can only hope to kindle the fire I saw in you that day again and hope to bask in its flames." Raf cast a rueful glance down at himself. "Forgive me for speaking of such matters in this indecent state."

Then he looked up at her again, and steeled himself to say it. "To answer your question—much as I would enjoy doing as you ask, my lady, I cannot make free with your person."

"You want me to love you, but you do not want to *make* love to me? Is that it?" Eglantine had drawn herself up quite straight on the pool rim. "You make strange demands, vicomte. My late husband would not understand you at all."

"My lady," he said softly, "perhaps you have not noticed it, but it would be my infinite pleasure to make love to you. But consider your dear, departed Ferrand. Your pardon for mentioning the matter, but he sated his carnal desires with abandon, with many, many women. So I hear it said. I declare Ferrand knew not what love is. How could he, if he neglected and abandoned you?"

She shivered. "After I heard of his lemans, I was content that he *did* neglect me. Then he began to mention the need for a second son, not that he ever paid Con much heed, and I feared then he would *stop* neglecting me." Her fingers twisted together in her lap. She stared at them. "So when he was murdered, I was wicked enough to be grateful he was dead." Eglantine looked up at him then, eyes wide. "You see, it is not me you think you love. You think I grieved for Ferrand when a part of me was quite happy he was gone."

Raf was silent. Did it matter? Did her words shatter his illusion? No, he did not recoil. He understood what she was saying. It made sense.

He frowned. The dream itself seemed to be shifting beneath his feet—his image of her. Yet somehow it did not matter. Come to think of it, it *did* matter. It deepened his feeling for her. He had enshrined a vision in his soul. It had fed that soul for years, but now the vision was resolving into a more complex reality, a reality of warm skin and soft hair as well as of inner fire. She was mother, chateau commander, gardener, and a creature of flesh and blood who craved his skin against hers.

Maybe as much as he craved hers.

The lady of his dreams, of his heated reality, continued to sit still and straight under the tamarisk tree. She spoke on quite calmly:

"You are wrong to think Ferrand had no notion of love. He did. I would not have loved him had he not believed himself besotted with me. And he was, for a time. But, you see, Ferrand's love was tethered to his desires. This is what I came to realize. He did not think of himself as a philanderer—he truly thought himself in love which each woman who caught his fancy. But then, after a period of fleshly indulgence with that woman, he found his love flitting away like a butterfly to the next pretty flower. And so it went on."

She gave him a level look, only belied by the twining together of her fingers.

"I put it to you that you are no different, Vicomte Rafèu. Perhaps I am no different myself. Our bodies make fools of our heads. We think ourselves in love when it is only a trickery of lust. I love my son. *That* is lasting love. But lechery veils itself in a glamour of love. It is not real. It is merely the stuff of minstrel song."

His lady took a slow breath and then decreed the terms of his quest:

"I propose I put you to the test, my true knight. I will put myself to the test as well. Let us indulge this lust. Let us wear the glamour of love out and see what emerges at its end. I contend you will be heartily glad to leave me and La Roque at its conclusion."

RAFÈU ROSE FROM the pool. One moment he had been leaning back against the pool's rim, legs outstretched in the greenish depths, and the next he was standing before her, water streaming from his braies and hose. Eglantine couldn't help but notice said items of clothing, for they were in her direct line of sight now that he was standing. She also noticed the degree to which they molded themselves to his form.

It almost distracted her from the imminent storm.

Then Eglantine rose too, one hand steadying herself upon the tamarisk. It was not a big tree, it had a flexible and drooping habit, and it was not holding her up with anything like the firmness she needed. She had just insulted this knight. She had attacked his beliefs. She had compared him to Ferrand. Now he had no compunction about exposing his whole glorious form before her eyes—because he no longer cared what she thought.

It was for the best.

Eglantine squared her shoulders and looked up at the vicomte in her pool. Rafèu's eyes were dark embers singeing her soul. Eglantine wanted to back away, but she could not. The tree was in her way. Besides, this was her garden.

"And the duration of this test, my lady? How long will take for us to tire of each other, do you think?"

His voice was like velvet dragged over gravel. Gooseflesh prickled her arms. Was he actually considering her proposition or was he only mocking her?

"I…I do not know." She closed her eyes, trying to think, unable to think while he looked at her like that. "I heard of Ferrand's first leman about a month after we married. I didn't believe it at first. But…well, I would say a month is a fair trial."

She ventured a look at him then. Eglantine expected mockery or outrage. She saw—what? Something barely contained. Like the sun, it hurt to look upon it.

"So we are to spend a month…doing what, my lady?"

The gravel was more evident now. Eglantine dug her fingernails into the poor tamarisk trunk as she struggled for words.

She only *wanted*—she had never formulated precisely what it was she wanted. Him, of course. His hands all over her, the graze of his skin over hers, the fire of his lips. It was an all-consuming need that must surely be transitory, for no person could endure such combustion for long. She had not felt this way about Ferrand, perhaps because she had been so naive before their marriage, and then afterward…well, proceedings in the bed-chamber had not inspired her to seek more.

So what in heaven did she want now?

She raised her hands, palms to the sky. "Everything," she whispered. "Anything and everything you would like to do to me. It is not a true test unless all avenues are exhausted."

There. That sounded like a thorough, well-thought-out reply. She was quite happy with it. Until he started laughing.

A little line appeared on either side of his mouth when he laughed, and two little lines at the outer edges of his eyes. The laugh itself would have been infectious…if it hadn't been directed at her.

"Oh my lady." He took one sloshing pace through the water and slid his bare arms around her shoulders, drew her to him, and dipped his head to hers. "Anything and everything. Are you sure?" The lines deepened at the corners of his eyes. "And only a month?"

She managed a nod.

"And if, at the end of this month of bliss, we are neither of us tired of the other—will you marry me?"

She froze. That was not part of the plan.

"I said nothing of marriage." He was very close. She could feel the solidity of his chest, the clean scent of him dizzied her, and her skirts were growing damp against his thighs.

"There must be some reward in this quest for me, my lady," he murmured. "Just think of the difficulty of the test you put me to."

It was very hard to stay frozen against him. She did *not* want marriage, but then, she didn't think he did either. Or he wouldn't once the month was out. She just had to prove it to him.

"Am I not reward enough?" She raised her head to his, star-tled at her own brazenness. Then she slipped her hands around his neck and touched her lips to his.

He responded instantly—a searing, open-mouthed kiss that left her breathless and weak. An eon later, he backed away sufficiently to say, "The stakes are too high, my lady. You forget—you ask me to set aside honor and the dictates of a chaste and noble love to undertake this quest. I must know the goal is worth it." He smiled, a slow and bone-dissolving smile. "If, of course, we find this feeling is not a fleeting fantasy."

The enormity of it. To chain herself to another man for life, and a Frenchman, too. But what were the odds? It was inevitable he would tire of her. She would exhaust his ardor and expose the fiction of love.

She cupped her hands on either side of his jaw. The slight roughness of his stubble sent tremors through her palms.

"I—" she began, and got no further.

The bell interrupted her. Two strikes of the bell, one swiftly following another. A pause, and then the two strikes repeated.

This time they both froze, listening. The brassy tones continued, insistent.

"He is here," she said.

"That, or we are being called to our siege drill," Raf countered. He shook his head, a twist to his mouth. "Christ, I ought to know better. I am not caught with my braies down, but I may as well be. My lady, you drive military matters fair out of my mind." He bent and kissed her, hard and fast. "Say yes," he murmured against her lips, and it wasn't a request.

"Yes," she breathed back, and felt the jolt travel through him. She hurried on: "Yes, I will *consider* wedding you. If we are not wearied of each other before the month is up, I will give the matter serious thought. That is as much as I will promise."

He grinned at her, a grin to outshine the sun. "Well then, it is up to me to convince you, isn't it? I accept the challenge, my lady." He took her hand. "Come now, let us make ourselves semi-decent for the aggressor at the gate."

✦

Chapter Twenty-One

His lady's second suitor was not at the gate. It was in fact the call to drill. Raf was expected to play an integral role in said drill—for heaven's sake, he had suggested it in the first place—and now he was turning up with his lower regions sopping wet. There had been no time to run to the hayloft for a change of clothes. That was the point of a drill. It mimicked the inconvenient immediacy of attack.

His lady, by contrast, looked anything but inconvenienced. She had had a wimple at hand in the walled garden, and she'd bundled up her hair and bound it beneath linen within a few nerve-shredding jangles of that infernal bell. She'd reached the courtyard before him, and now she stood beside Osbert, breathing a little quickly perhaps, but otherwise looking quite composed.

"Right, listen sharp," Osbert bellowed. "There's not a soul outside La Roque's walls, praise God, nor even an Englishman without a soul, for that matter. So you can stop browning your braies. We just got you here to practice what we do if them besieging bastards do see fit to attack."

It was a good start, Raf reflected. A pity it deteriorated steeply from there. The chateau's two men-at-arms remained watching on the walls—someone had to—so the folk in the courtyard were assorted servants with little idea of military discipline or action.

They knew what they were *supposed* to do, for Raf and Osbert had told them, but when it came to the actual doing, the courtyard turned into chaos.

With a sick feeling in his gut, Raf stepped in and began to assert order, servant by servant. At least he had commanded trained soldiers at Combret. It had been a military garrison, designed only to keep invaders from his overlord's land. His men had been a pleasure to command…until they started dying. But this reputedly impregnable chateau was garrisoned by maidservants, cooks, and laborers. Oh, and a grand total of three soldiers. Four, if one counted Rafèu.

By the time he'd helped ensure everyone knew their post— and knew what to do with themselves when they were there—his lower regions were entirely dry. But his gut had not ceased to roil. Here he was in a chateau under siege, and somehow he was in a position of command again. Of course Osbert was officially in command—he bellowed the orders—but the captain continually looked to Raf. Sometimes it was just a glance, but more often it was outright consultation.

Eglantine too looked to him. If the walls were attacked, she was to take charge of the courtyard. That was what they had agreed, and she was making a valiant effort to understand exactly what everyone under her command ought to be doing, but she needed guidance—his guidance.

In fact, everyone was looking to Rafèu. Curse them. By some devil-driven insight, everyone seemed to realize that he was the one with most experience. These poor, deluded fools seemed to think he knew what to do in a siege, that he could save them. Dear God, if they only knew.

They were looking to him for salvation, yet in the moments before the bell had been struck, he had been lost in another world. He had been blissfully thoughtless of siege, of command, of anything but his lady. *He* was the true fool.

A bell on the walls began to clang. The sound shivered through Raf's very bones. After some moments, the tones resolved into the dual pattern of a minor alert, and Raf unpetrified sufficiently to survey the general reaction around him. His servant-troops had paused in their various actions. They stared around at each other, then up at the walls.

Raf's heart sank yet further. All this practice, and still they had no idea what to do.

"Drill's over," Osbert bellowed from the battlements. "We got company coming up the hill, and he's waving a white flag. Likely enough he just wants to wag his tongue at us. Go about your business for now, but stay alert. If you hear the bells ring without cease, you know what to do."

Raf had his doubts. Pray God the bastard currently plodding up the path *had* only come to wag his tongue. Raf fancied the occupants of La Roque would benefit from a few hundred drills yet before they faced a real attack.

Those occupants were dispersing slowly. Some clusters of servants remained in the courtyard, whispering among themselves and casting looks toward the battlements. The rest were scattering into various buildings. As for the Lady Eglantine, Raf saw her lift her chin and step swiftly toward the storeroom by the gatehouse. That convenient little room furnished with an arrow slit.

He was about to follow when two things stopped him.

The first was the remembrance of the last time he'd been in there, of the deliciously secluded proximity to his lady that made his groin stir even now.

Christ, man, the alarm is clanging and you are thinking only of your cock. And the man who would force your lady into wedlock is approaching the damned gate.

The second was the sight of a small boy slipping out of the central tower door, glancing about and looking decidedly furtive. No one else seemed to notice as Con trotted off in the direction of the stables by a circuitous route, one that avoided passing near any servants remaining outside. Raf might not have paid any attention either, if it wasn't for the way Con moved.

The boy was up to something.

"You and you—keep the Lady Eglantine safe," Raf flung at a couple of doughty servants as he passed. He jabbed an arm toward the storeroom, then strode into the stables.

Eglantine would sever his balls with her pruning shears if he let anything happen to her son.

Chapter Twenty-Two

IT WAS THE midday meal—the most substantial meal of the day, and one no one in La Roque ought to miss, unless they fancied a gnawing stomach the rest of the day or were on duty on the battlements. And Eglantine sat down beside an empty chair.

Con should have been in it.

She looked about for Margery. The maid, too, was nowhere to be seen. Oh well, doubtless she and Con were simply late.

Then, of course, she looked for Raf. Dear God, she was going to turn into an owl with all this twisting about of the neck. No, the minstrel-vicomte was also absent. Eglantine frowned. Had the drill driven thoughts of food out of everyone's mind?

But no, the table was well tenanted for all that. A couple of men were missing, but they were probably up on the walls and would eat later. Osbert stumped down the hall and plunked himself onto a bench near the head of the table with a sigh.

"Sorry I'm late, m'lady. Too much to do." A gesture toward the battlements. "Some of them up there wouldn't know how to scratch their... Ah, beg pardon, m'lady." Osbert scratched his head, as if that were the body part he was referring to all along.

"Have you seen Con?"

Osbert shook his head. "Came straight from the walls, m'lady. The lordling knows he didn't ought to be up there."

Which didn't mean he *wasn't* up there. Con had a habit of

turning up where he shouldn't be, although more out of curiosity than willful disobedience. But surely Margery was keeping an eye on him?

Eglantine frowned at her unfilled trencher for a moment.

"And Raf? Ah…the Vicomte Rafèu? Did you leave him on the battlements?"

It was her captain's turn to furrow his brow. "No, he's not due up there till later. He's to help us with weapons training first."

A fist seemed to close around her heart and give a squeeze. But it probably meant nothing. People were late for meals all the time. Delay the serving much longer and the food would be cold, and what good would that do anyone? She gestured to the servant who doubled as pantler and butler to begin serving. Then old Father Andrieu who'd taken refuge up here from the village offered a blessing.

Con bounced into the hall halfway through the second course, Margery close on his heels. Bits of dried grass decorated his tunic.

He came to a halt beside her and executed a bow that nearly had him scraping the floor rushes. Then, in perfect English, he said, "Lady mother, I apologize for my tardiness. I hope I have not caused you anxiety."

It seemed to Eglantine that her brows disappeared up into her wimple, possibly never to return. "Sit, wash your hands, and eat," she managed. "You too, Margery."

A servant delivered the finger bowl to her son, and a degree of splashing ensued. Then there was the loading of the trencher. It was well loaded. It was some time before Eglantine was able to put the question to her son.

"Where were you? What delayed you?"

The boy paused in his stabbing at chunks of pottage. He didn't look up. "I stayed inside for the first alarm, just like you said. I watched from the solar window. I *am* the lord of La Roque. I need to know what's going on."

Ah, she could see where this was going.

"And the second alarm—the real one, when Sir Garit came to the gate? Were you inside then?"

Con jabbed at an offending onion. The thing was skewered, but he didn't look inclined to eat it.

"Umm, kind of." He looked up at her. "I was inside the stables. That's inside, isn't it?"

"Con, I told you to stay inside the central keep whenever the bells ring. You *are* the Lord of La Roque. If you are not safe, the whole siege is for nothing. You must take command of the keep. This is your responsibility."

"But I *was* safe. Raf was with me. You've seen him with a sword, Mother. He's even better than Osbert."

"Raf?" Eglantine threw a sharp glance at Margery, who was evidently straining her ears in their direction. "In the stables, with Margery?"

"No, Mother. He followed me in. I heard the bells and Osbert shouting, and I wanted to see Sir Garit for myself. He is my *enemy*. I had to see him."

"No, Con, it's too dangerous. What if he saw you? You know what they say about Englishmen and bows, don't you?"

"Yes!" Con bounced in his seat. "They're the best in all the world, save for Welshmen, that is. Osbert's been teaching me. I can shoot a longbow too."

Eglantine pressed her lips together. They wanted to twitch into a grin, and that would send entirely the wrong message. All the longbows she'd ever seen were approximately twice Con's height.

"But don't worry, Mother. He never saw me." Con pulled a face. "Raf stopped me before I could climb onto the roof."

"What?"

"That's where Raf hid when you told him to get out of the chateau. He says it's got quite a good view."

Eglantine gripped her eating knife with rather more force than required to carve well-stewed meat. "Is that right? And where was Margery in all this, pray?"

Would she find pieces of straw clinging to Margery's clothes too? Eglantine closed her eyes and shook her head. Of course not. Raf was all hers, at least for now. That was how men and their desires worked—total absorption in one amorous object until the magic waned. Only then might he glance toward Margery.

"The little lord slipped away from me, mistress." The maidservant had risen from her seat and was standing beside Eglantine now, wringing her hands. "One moment we were in the solar, then I looked round and he was gone. I searched for him everywhere, I did. I was so worried, what with the alarm and all. I never heard the dinner bell, I was so frantic."

"You see?" Eglantine looked severely at Con. "You ought to bow and say pretty words to Margery too."

Oh, and she had a good idea where those pretty words came from now.

Eglantine turned to the maid and softened her expression. There was no evident hay on the girl's gown. "That's all right, Margery. Con won't do it again—will he?" A raised brow in the small lord's direction.

Vigorous nodding from a tousled blond head. The speared onion was being chewed, which spared Con the trouble of replying.

And that was that, apparently. Con would not do it again, and Margery had been acting the exemplary maid, save for turning her back on Con for one instant.

Except it did not explain why Raf was still not here.

Nor did he appear in the hall at any point during the rest of the meal.

Eglantine picked at her food, forcing herself to eat every last sop she'd spooned on her trencher. Food was plentiful now, but who knew how long that would last? Not that anything on the trestles would go to waste. Temporary pigpens had been erected in a corner of the courtyard. La Roque was not normally a farmyard, but someone had thought to bring a handful of pigs, a goat or two, and a goodly number of chickens within the walls just before the gates were barred.

Maybe Raf had preferred the battlements to explaining to Eglantine why her son wished to clamber onto the stable roof. But no, that didn't seem in character. Not that she really knew what his character was—or did she?

Her vicomte had revealed so much of himself in the garden, quite aside from his torso. The past he had brushed over, the siege he had endured, hinted at pain, at a vulnerability beneath his evident skills and charm. Yet it made her flinch that he thought she'd helped him survive that past. He deluded himself. He had simply used her as a talisman. But now he would get to know her—every last inch of her, she hoped—and come to his senses.

At least she would enjoy herself in the process.

The meal ended and the afternoon's activities began. Eglantine descended the chateau stairs to consult with the kitchen staff. She needed to assess their supplies on a daily basis and work out where economies could be made if necessary. Most chateaux employed a steward to manage the household. Not La Roque. The Lady Eglantine was both chatelaine and steward. She'd learned enough from Ferrand's old steward that when he retired, she'd been able to do what he did. The place was small enough that the role had been manageable before. Now, she wasn't so sure.

The responsibility for keeping so many souls alive under siege weighed on her, and they were only a few days into the blockade. And it was nothing to what Raf had experienced.

Not yet.

The thought was quite enough to get her out of the kitchen and into the courtyard, ready for some more weapons training. Besides, her vicomte would be there, guiding her strokes. Heaven knew Osbert needed some help in polishing them up.

Again, a good proportion of the castle's inhabitants swarmed into the courtyard to brandish wooden weapons under Osbert's instruction. Except it wasn't her captain who stood before them, moving slowly through the motions so they could mimic him this time. It was Rafèu, Vicomte Bruniquel, stripped down to a loose tunic and hose in the unforgiving afternoon sun.

Osbert was striding up and down the line in Raf's stead, correcting and encouraging his motley troops by gruff monosyllables.

Eglantine grabbed a wooden weapon and joined the line. Her sword-swinging minstrel would not be laying his hands on her this time, correcting her grip and murmuring in her ear. But on the positive side, he wouldn't be berating her for picking up a weapon in the first place. Did this mean he was reconciled to the notion of his perfect lady holding a sword? One little chip away from that false image?

Probably not.

The wooden sword felt heavier than yesterday. Muscles twinged in strange places. Her thrusts and parries felt more awkward than ever in comparison to her instructor's easy grace.

Ah, but he *was* graceful. Yesterday, Osbert had been solid and shiveringly forceful. Her vicomte, however, wielded a sword like he did his lute—with nonchalant dexterity that made it look easy. And Eglantine was finding it most certainly was not.

But it was worth the ache in her arms just to watch him. She had to watch him, didn't she? He was their instructor, the model of artistry for a legion of incompetents. She had to watch his smallest shift of posture, the beautifully controlled movements, the play of his muscles, and the way he never, ever looked at her.

He looked at Con frequently enough. The little lines would flicker at the edges of his mouth and he would execute a stroke as if solely for the boy's benefit. Sometimes he caught others' gazes too, correcting their stance by a look or flashing them a smile to melt Eglantine's bones. Did it melt theirs? By God, he was making love to everyone but her by means of his eyes and mouth alone.

And at the end of it all, when Eglantine was sure she could not hold her wooden blade up for one more stroke, he simply disappeared. The flurry of people replacing their practice weapons blocked her view for mere moments, and when the view cleared, the courtyard was bare of Raf.

Was he deliberately avoiding her? Surely not.

Yet as the afternoon wore on and dimmed into evening, Eglantine saw not a hair of her supposed suitor. At least he appeared in the hall, armed with his lute. But when he coaxed a ripple of notes from the instrument and began to sing, it was not a love song that emerged. Instead, his voice had a martial tone.

Con, at least, was pleased. Raf sang of battles and valiant warriors. He sang solely in English. And when her minstrel launched into an ancient epic that involved some serious slaying of monsters, Con could contain himself no longer. He practically bounded to Raf's side. He liberated a stick from the pile of fuel by the hearth and began to slay dragons with it. Eglantine feared for the health of her tapestries.

And at the end of the monstrous epic, once he'd combatted the barrage of questions launched at him by one small boy, Raf finally looked at her.

He bowed deeply and gracefully, offered a slight smile, and then strode out of the hall.

Chapter Twenty-Three

IT WAS CHILLY on the battlements. At first, Raf had welcomed the breeze. Now, close to midnight, he'd almost appreciate an attack in the dark simply because he needed to move. It wasn't just the cold. The action would stop him endlessly thinking…and dreading.

He didn't actually want the ruinous bastard to attack, but at least Raf would be ready if he did. Unlike earlier, when the alarm had caught him half undressed and dallying in a pond.

The memory of which only set his thoughts off again on their endless, circling permutations.

As if he'd conjured it by pure power of wishing, a cloak-swathed silhouette emerged at the head of the battlement stairs. It moved slowly to the nearest crenelle, as if to stare out at the gray-black landscape.

It did not.

Raf stayed quite still and watched to see what it would do. What moon there was had already dipped beneath the horizon, and the stars did little to illuminate the walls. But he knew who it was.

The shape looked around, up and down the walls. Raf was familiar with the parapet's contours now, even in the dark. This was the second night watch he'd taken up here, and tonight he planned to stay up here until the sun was a red jewel in the east.

He'd be exhausted the following day, but that was the point. He would have an inarguable reason to sleep most of it away in the hayloft.

But now this silhouette had come to disrupt his plans. Maybe she'd just come to see the walls for herself. He'd asked her not to, but perhaps she thought the chill hours of night were safe.

No, a canny enemy knew when a chateau might be taken unawares. No hour was safe, by night or day.

But maybe if he kept quite still, she would not notice him in the shadows. He had taken the easternmost position, the one farther from the stairs she had mounted. A second guard watched to the west. Doubtless he had seen the silhouette too.

The shape began to move. Away from Raf. One hand upon the outer wall, it made its careful way westward, toward the other guard. Then he could hear low voices. What on earth did she have to discuss with a guard at midnight?

Something inside him twisted. He'd like to think it was his gut, but it might well be a lower location. Had she changed her mind? Had she decided to capitulate to Sir Garit's proposal-by-siege? Perhaps the slight distance he'd managed to keep from her today had encouraged her in that direction. She had come up here at the dead of night to tell her guards that the situation had changed. They could go to bed.

He should feel relief at the thought. No more state of siege. No more leaden responsibility thrust upon him.

Then the silhouette turned and was moving eastward. Toward Raf. And sanity returned.

Even if Eglantine had decided to capitulate to her ruinous suitor, Sir Garit would not know it yet. Raf had heard everything the knight had been told earlier. He and Con had been straining their ears in the hayloft. Indeed, Raf had his hand clapped over the boy's mouth—in part so Con would not interrupt, but also to restrain the lad from making a break for the roof. Con declared he *needed* to lay eyes on Sir Garit, but Raf needed to hear every last snippet of the exchange. Besides, he also needed Con not to make a target of himself on the stable roof *or* tumble off it in his haste.

The English knight's visit had played out much as before: a few insults (mostly from Osbert), a few threats (primarily from Garit), and absolutely no capitulation on either side.

Thus the besieging bridegroom could still attack, and the best way to assault an impregnable castle was by stealth, to slip a ladder up in the dark when fewest people were alert. Eglantine was not up here to tell her guards to go to bed.

Or if she were, Raf would refuse.

However tempting it would be to join her.

But if she'd decided to wed the handsome English bastard, she would reject her superfluous French vicomte.

Oh, the circuitous tangle of his brain. And the shadow was padding slowly toward him.

Rafèu stood. She obviously knew where he was. If she hadn't originally, the first guard would have set her straight. He was not going to be an absolute churl before his lady.

When the shadow was close enough for him to see faint details beneath the hood, he greeted her with a small bow. "You should not be up here, Lady Eglantine."

She halted. "You said that before. Will you manhandle me again to prove your point?"

He ignored the last sentence. "It is as true as it was first time. It's too dangerous for you up here. If you are killed, what will happen to your son?"

Or to me? he did not add. He would have choked upon the words.

"It is dangerous for both of us to present ourselves as targets against the night sky, wouldn't you say? We should sit, Vicomte Rafèu. And not here, where we have made ourselves so visible. Let us move closer to the tower. I must talk to you."

Her arm was a dark line, pointing further to the east. A small tower punctuated the walls at that point. He couldn't argue with her logic. They *had* presented themselves as targets. It *would* be safer there.

Except she shouldn't be up here at all, and not just for the sake of her safety.

But he also knew there were stairs in that tower. All Raf had to do was coax her inside and convince her to descend them.

"Yes," he said. "You go first. Let me do my watchman's duty a moment."

He needed to gather his thoughts, but he also had to assure himself there was no imminent attack, not when his lady was so exposed.

Rafèu leaned into a crenelle, molding himself to its contours to lessen the chance of being seen, and gazed out over the hillside. It was a patchwork of black and darker black. Sometimes pale rocks jutted through, almost luminous by contrast, and the path that wound to the gatehouse seemed to reflect the Milky Way above. If men were present on that hillside, he would only see them if they moved, preferably against the rocks or track. Worse, the breeze ruffled the bushes, tricking his eyes into believing them men. Sneaking up for a night attack.

There was a soft rustle of cloth beside him. His heart lurched. Eglantine too was peering through the crenelle, not quite touching him, but far too close.

"If you stare at it long enough, your eyes start playing tricks," she whispered after a while. "There could be anything out there."

"Yes, although you'd soon notice the difference if there really were men advancing up the slope. Trust me." He slithered back, doing his best not to brush against her. "Come. You said you needed to speak to me. So let us speak, and then you may return safely to bed."

She regarded him in the dark. He could only hope she saw nothing of his features. They would likely belie his words.

"Yes, Vicomte Bruniquel, we do need to speak." And she walked toward the tower.

THE STONES WERE warm and rough beneath her palm. They steadied her. The darkness and height were the least of her fears. He was so distant and coolly correct. It was as if whatever he had expressed in the sunlit garden simply evaporated up here. Dried up like rain in summer, leaving no trace it was ever there.

But that was good. She didn't need a suitor, let alone two, and she definitely didn't want a husband. A lover might have been nice, but…well, she wasn't even sure why she wanted one of those. It wasn't as if proceedings with Ferrand had ever inspired her to seek out more.

She reached the darker mass of the tower and leaned a little shakily against its wall. Rafèu was right behind her.

"Sit," he said.

She sat. He did likewise, not touching her. She felt the distance like a gaping gulf.

Well, best to get straight to the point. "You have been avoiding me," she said.

A slight hesitation, then the careful words: "Surely that should please your ladyship?"

It was not denial.

"Raf, tell me! Have I only one suitor to worry about now? Has the mere mention of consummation turned your ardor cold? By God, you put Ferrand to shame for speed. Only this morning—" She broke off, shaking her head. "No, I do not berate you for being a man. I am content that I only need to rid myself of Sir Garit now. Only inform me to my face. Tell me where I stand."

In answer, he reached out and ran a finger over her cheek. That simple touch, the mere grazing of a finger pad over skin, raised every hair on her arms and nape. But what did it *mean*? She couldn't read his face in the gloom. Was it an apology, a farewell?

"Speak, vicomte."

The finger removed itself. "My lady, I regret to inform you that you still have two suitors to worry about."

He *regretted* it? But did she? Certainly she ought to.

"I see." She did not, and in more ways than one. If only she could read his face in addition to his words. "So why avoid me?"

She would not mention the garden or the agreement she thought they'd come to. She would not sound so desperate, so downright wanton.

"My lady, I cannot be two things at once. I should be on watch this instant, not talking to you."

"Put your mind at ease. I have asked a second guard to come up onto the walls. See?" She gestured down the crooked length of the walls. Here against the tower, they were nearly out of sight of stairs she'd mounted, but she could just make out a hooded head moving into place.

"Ah. Well considered." But he didn't sound convinced of his statement.

"You weren't due to stand watch this night anyway. You took his place. I checked."

He inhaled slowly and let it out. She heard the soft passage of breath beside her, and waited.

"I thought it best to remove myself from temptation. Believe me, my lady, you would tempt a saint."

The way he said those words, so soft and deep, sent a little vibration through her. A mad sparkle of hope.

But he was not finished. "As I said, I cannot be two things at once. I cannot be both lover and castle commander. The one would inevitably undermine the other. I would fail you. I cannot let that happen." A pause. "Today, in the garden, I completely forgot myself. In your little walled paradise, I failed to recall we were in a castle under siege. If Sir Garit had attacked then, he would have found me a man without a sword, clad only in wet undergarments, and thinking only of his—"

He broke off, shaking his head.

"You err, vicomte. You are not in command here. That is my role, and Osbert's. This is not Combret. We are not your responsibility." She said the words gently but firmly. "Nor will I let it become a second Combret. Should Sir Garit truly begin attacking us, I will give him what he wants. People shall not die for my marital whims."

"No!"

She saw him reach out, then withdraw.

"Touch me, Raf." She spoke so softly that her voice barely carried above the breeze. "We are not under attack, and if Sir Garit chooses to do so tonight, you are on hand. I am not such a distraction as all that."

"Are you not?" All the same, he did reach for her. His fingers found her cheek, then trailed slowly down, tracing her neck, her shoulder, and finally closing over her hand. "The English fiend will not have you. It will not come to that."

His fingers wrapped around hers, warm and strong. He still belonged to her, whatever was to come. Who knew what tomorrow would bring? There was only tonight.

Eglantine rose on her knees, careful not to show her head above the parapet, and closed the distance between them. Refusing to consider quite how brazen the action was, she slipped a leg over his thighs and straddled his lap.

A sharp intake of breath, a tightening of the fingers on hers, but he did not push her off.

She wriggled a little, in part to arrange her skirts, but more to revel in the feel of the long, strong legs beneath her.

"Stop that." Half a gasp, half a whisper.

Then her hand was released, his arms wrapped around her, and she was pulled to him. His arms were about her shoulders, hands cradling the back of her head. His mouth found hers, a hand tugged back her hood, and he showed her precisely how little he wanted her to stop.

Ah, there was a power in sitting as she did, her knees pressing into his buttocks almost as if he were a horse, her head angled down over his. She was taking command. She was slanting her lips down against his and opening to invite him in. And his hands were tangling in her hair, left loose beneath her hood. His tongue sought hers, and they simply devoured each other.

"My lady, this is unseemly—" he broke off long enough to

murmur. "The guards…"

Yet at the same time, one hand was tracing over her ear, her neck, along her collarbone. She arched her back, simply *feeling*. The slight movement shifted her hips against him, and she felt more.

A distinct solidity at the juncture of his thighs.

Warmth flooded through her. Mad, melting warmth. Who cared about guards? The feeling was just too delicious to resist.

Then the world was moving. Somehow—she wasn't quite sure how he did it—Raf had risen to his feet. He'd scooped her up into his arms and was even now nudging the door to the tower open with his shoulder.

Eglantine tensed. Her overbearing vicomte had decided proceedings were too unseemly. Without consulting her, he was putting a stop to them. He was manhandling her on the battlements. *Again.*

Once inside the tower, he set her down against the wall.

And left her there.

It was utterly dark. Her nerves prickled to the sound of wood rasping against wood. He was bolting the door. That done, all she could sense was the cold stone behind her, a scuffling, scraping noise at floor level—dear God, not rats?—and emptiness, within and without.

"Raf?" she whispered.

✦

Chapter Twenty-Four

"ONE MOMENT, MY lady. Let me light the tinder."

More scraping noises followed, mercifully resolving themselves into iron striking on flint. Sparks followed, and an infant flame cupped between long-fingered hands. After a few moments, the flames caught sufficiently in the small hearth for Raf to retreat. She could see him now, a dark shape against the amber glow, at first crouching, but now rising and stepping toward her.

Eglantine held herself quite still. What now?

He stood before her, not touching. She could see nothing of his face, for the firelight was behind him. Hers was likely illuminated in all its uncertainty.

"Do you still wish to put me to the test, my lady?"

Did he mean what she thought he meant? But she'd been brazen one too many times tonight. She couldn't bear to voice the words, just in case she was wrong.

So she simply inclined her head. And waited.

He stepped a little nearer, still not touching her.

"Just to be clear, my lady—you hold that what I feel for you is a mere dream. You think a little indulgence in the more tangible aspects of love will dissipate the dream. I declare it will not. You challenge me to put this to the test. Do I understand the matter correctly?"

It could have been a cold accounting of a difference of opinion. It was not. She could not see his face, but his voice was as warm as the flames growing behind him.

"You do," she replied, voice a trifle unsteady. "Save for one thing. No *little* indulgence will do. I will have no half measures, Vicomte Rafèu. We must test this feeling to the hilt. Why, Ferrand probably thought he still loved me after the first bout or two."

"No." A finger came to rest across her lips. "Do not speak his name again. He is not part of this test. Just you and me. *N'est-ce pas?*"

She nodded and waited for the flames to grow. She needed to *see* him.

A light chuckle. "And as for half measures, you will get no such thing from me, Lady Eglantine. My days henceforth will be divided into two parts—protecting all in La Roque from harm, and bringing you to bliss by every means I can devise."

The words shivered through her. They entered her blood and set her toes tingling. She should correct him—his goal was to bring *himself* to bliss, over and over until he was replete. Satiated and gorged till he wanted no more. There was little enough bliss in the matter for a woman.

She frowned. His mouth and his hands had already given her more pleasure than she'd ever felt at Ferrand's touch. And something deep within her craved more with an insistence that defied all prior experience. But what did men care about bliss in a woman?

"You frown, Lady Eglantine. Are you sure this is what you want? It is not too late to—"

"No. I am sure." She closed the gap between them, put her hands on his shoulders, and looked up into his shadowy face. "Do your worst—do your best, Vicomte Rafèu. Let us begin."

RAF GAZED DOWN at his lady. Her face was tilted to his, delicate, vulnerable, and quite magical in the firelight. What was he waiting for? This was his chance to convince her. She thought he would lose interest after a few intimate encounters, but now he began to wonder what truly drove her strange quest. There was more trepidation in that lovely face now than desire.

He reached out and ran the tips of his fingers over one cheek and along her jaw. Her eyes fluttered closed.

"What do you want of me, my lady?" he murmured.

He would not ask how Ferrand had touched her—that name should not be spoken—but he did wonder how much care that excuse for a husband had ever taken of this exquisite creature.

Her eyes opened. They seemed to flicker in the firelight. "Just touch me. Do what men do—whatever you want to do."

"But what do *you* want, my lady? Why do this at all? You do not have to subject yourself to an ordeal, if that is what it is. Just tell me to go away. Say you won't marry me."

Raf couldn't believe he was actually saying these things. But he, too, wanted no half measures. He wanted all of her, body and heart. Most especially, he did not want her giving herself for the wrong reasons.

"I don't know what I want!" Her fingers dug into his shoulders. "I want to prove that this lust of the flesh is but a passing madness. Just like…" But she did not say the name. Then her voice dropped to a raw whisper. "I feel it too, vicomte. This madness inside. And I do not want to be made its fool. Drive it from me. Remind me how it is to be used for a man's pleasure."

Rafèu swayed a little where he stood. Her eyes were huge, full of warring emotions. She wanted him, but she was frightened too. Of herself, and of the act too, he guessed.

Do your worst—do your best.

He could only hope it was good enough. For her.

SHE'D HOPED HE would begin with a kiss. Whatever came afterward, at least then she'd have that knee-weakening experience. He did not. Instead, he took her by the hand and led her toward the fire. There was a low pallet nearby, a rough sack stuffed with hay. He unpinned his cloak and laid it over the pallet, crouching to smooth it. Still crouching, he turned to look up at her.

Now she could see his face more clearly. It seemed a collection of sharp, firelit lines and shadows. He looked almost fey. But wholly breathtaking. He did not smile.

"Not a bower fit for a lady," he said. "You may yet change your mind."

"No. Better here than my chamber in the solar." With Con and Margery sleeping nearby, and the ghost of Ferrand haunting her bed.

Abruptly, she too unpinned her cloak and began to fumble with the buttons at her sleeves. There were so cursed many of them, and they were particularly tricky to negotiate in the dim. She favored close-fitting sleeves secured by multiple buttons and avoided impractical, flowing sleeves that would obstruct her work, but normally Margery assisted with the buttoning.

A hand closed over hers, stilling her efforts. She looked up.

"Are you any good at buttons?"

How many hundreds of women have you unbuttoned in the past, or do you bypass that problem and simply throw up their skirts?

Oh. Maybe she need not get undressed after all. She recalled a few such incidents with Ferrand when he…

No.

Her vicomte's eyes were gentle and deep as midnight—and getting nearer as he bent to kiss her. Ah, why hadn't he done this in the first place? He stroked back her hair and cradled her head so he could brush his lips over hers. Just lightly, leaving her craving more. Then he drew back and examined her buttons.

"You do wrap yourself up well, don't you?" he murmured, slipping a few buttons free with a disturbingly practiced touch.

"We don't have to… You can just…you know." She tweaked at her skirts.

The dark eyes widened. Then he abandoned the buttons, and his lips descended on hers for a second time. And this time it was no mere grazing of skin against skin. He demanded entry, and she opened to him, welcoming the possession, daring to slip her tongue alongside his, to join its dance. He kissed her until they were both breathless, and then he drew back sufficiently to growl, "I want to see *all* of you, my lady. I want to lay my lips to your every curve. I want to feast my eyes on your loveliness, *without* these nunlike garments. Yes, the buttons must be assailed."

And while she took in those words, he proceeded to free the remaining buttons of her left sleeve. He proposed to lay his lips to her every curve? A shiver rippled through her. She felt quite wildly exposed, and he'd only bared one forearm.

"Wait!"

He'd just taken hold of her right wrist and was teasing the first button loose. He paused, looked up at her, and raised her hand to his lips. Then he opened his mouth and nipped her skin ever so slightly.

"Yes, my lady?"

The action flustered her. Whatever she was going to say flew out of her mind. Instead, she gazed at him and said, "You have too many clothes on."

She reached out and scraped her fingers down his iron-scaled jacket. What was it, a brigandine? Some kind of protective outer garment. Sensible enough clothing for guard duty, but now…

He smiled, slowly. "An excellent point," Raf said, and began to unbutton the jacket.

"No, let me."

"As my lady wills it."

He held his arms wide, and she was glad enough to focus on something other than his face. She could not bear to look on it, this feeling that would so soon dissipate. Easier to unbutton him, run her hands over his shoulders and arms in pushing the heavy canvas off him, and then—why not?—continue with the tunic beneath. The only problem was a heavy sword belt wrapped his hips about, complete with sheathed weapon. It had pinned the base of his tunic down. She'd tugged the tunic free, but that still left the obstructive belt. It must go.

Eglantine began to work the leather at the buckle loose, but it was hard to see, bending over it, so she knelt to put the buckle at eye level. And then, with the sudden clarity of vision, she couldn't help but notice something else.

She paused in her buckle tugging.

Dare she? Oh, she wanted to. The craving to touch was too strong, so she dipped her hands below his belt, skimming the cloth, until her fingers contacted what she'd noticed.

The body beneath her fingers jolted. She traced the evidence of his need, wondering at its size and the way it stirred, restless beneath the cloth.

A groan, and then Raf was lifting her up by her elbows, back to a standing position, the better to pull her to him for a third dizzying ravishment of the mouth. But she could still feel that stirring energy just below his belt, pressing against her. It wanted to be freed. Her fingers itched to do the freeing.

"May I unbutton the rest of you?" he said, drawing back infinitesimally.

His eyes were entirely black in the firelight. She shivered at their expression, the strangest blend of hunger and worship.

"Take off your own clothing first," she commanded. "I want my knight wholly disarmed before I lower my defenses."

"As you wish it," he said softly.

The belt was unbuckled and thrown aside, the shirt removed in one swift movement. Eglantine barely had time to feast her eyes on his naked torso before he was bending to shuck off his short boots—no decorative crakows for the battlements—and loosen the ties on his hose. Long legs emerged, dusted with dark hair, and now his hands were at the belt of his braies...

Eglantine stepped forward. She put her hands over his. She

helped them loosen the rolled fabric that held the braies up, then urge the linen down. Of course, the process was not aided by what lay beneath.

"It is not normally so awkward to remove my drawers," he said, with a chuckle. "Pray excuse me a moment while I adjust myself, my lady."

"No, you are not excused. You require my assistance."

He cast her a decidedly wolfish smile. "Who am I to say nay to a lady?"

Then he took her hand and guided it beneath his braies belt.

Silken, heated skin encasing an immense hardness. A curl of crisp hair. The aliveness of him. A welter of sensations, transmitting themselves through her palm and fingers, and shooting like flames to her core. And then he was helping her ease the fabric over, letting it drop down his legs, and standing before her quite naked. Her knight exposed.

✦

Chapter Twenty-Five

S HE LOOKED AT him for long moments. Raf made himself stand quite still before her, letting her gaze her fill. She needed him wholly exposed before she dared unloose another button. But it was a risk. What if she didn't like what she saw? What if the sight brought back memories she'd rather forget?

"Well, my lady," he said at last. "Does the test continue?"

Oh, he felt put to the test, all right.

She lifted her gaze to his face. A smile flickered upon her mouth. "You are nicely made, Vicomte Rafèu. I like my knight peeled." Then the smile slipped. "I only fear you will not find anything so pleasing beneath my clothes. But then," she murmured as if to herself, "perhaps that is the point." She lifted her chin and extended her arm. "Unbutton me if you will, sir knight."

The remembrance of that conversation with the blacksmith returned. *Reckon she's maimed or scarred or the like.* Was she after all? It was another test. Would it shake his love?

Raf stepped in close and began to unbutton, beginning with the rest of her sleeve. And as he touched her and felt the slight tremor that shook her, a wave of tenderness washed over him. By God, he would not show the slightest shock at whatever these clothes concealed. He would sooner have his tongue cut out.

As he unbuttoned, she laid her free hand on his chest, over his ribcage. At first tentatively, then increasing in confidence, she began to explore. Eglantine traced the muscles of his abdomen. She dipped lower, and Raf tensed, pausing mid-button.

"If you touch me there, I won't be responsible for the safety of your clothing," he growled. "There will be mending to do."

A breathless laugh. "And I refuse to explain to Margery why she has so many buttons to repair. Fear not, sir knight. I will not assault you while you are so focused."

He had moved to the line of fastenings running down from the center of her bodice. That meant she had both hands free now, and she was currently running them over his naked buttocks. Her soft, questing touch was setting his skin afire. His fingers were trembling upon the buttons now.

But they were just about done. He knelt to fiddle with the last two. They were set below the level of her waist, just before the skirts flared out over her hips. Of course, that meant an end to her exploration of his buttocks. Her palms slid over his bare skin as he descended. Then her hands were on his hair, stroking it back, letting it slip between her fingers.

Thank God he'd given his hair something of a wash that morning.

"You have long hair for a man," she murmured above him.

He looked up to see her finger-combing a length of his hair slowly, her head tipped to one side.

"I will cut it short if my lady wills it."

"Don't you dare." She tightened her fingers on his hair. "It gives me something to hold on to."

"You can hold on to it as long as you like, my lady." *Until it turns gray*, he did not add. She was not ready for that. "Your buttons are all undone. You see, you have me at a disadvantage." He spread his arms wide. "I may catch my death of cold while you, my lady, remain snug beneath your wool and linen." He reached for the base of her gown, the same unadorned russet she'd worn in the garden. "May I?"

"Only my outer dress," she whispered. "Leave the chemise...for now."

Raf smiled at that. He liked the sound of *for now*. He took the hem of her woolen gown in his hands and lifted. It was like peeling an onion, but the most delicious onion he'd ever tasted. She raised her arms like a child as he rose, peeling the dress with him. He eased it over her head and then turned aside to find a clean place to lay the dress and to give her a moment to…to what? Grow accustomed to appearing semi-naked before him? He wanted her a lot more naked than that. Or put a halt to proceedings altogether? His groin was already as hard as La Roque, and he'd likely do himself irreparable damage if he did not do something with it.

A touch on his shoulder. Immediately followed by an indescribable sensation at his back. Skin. Warm, smooth, indisputably naked skin against his.

"Put my dress down. It doesn't matter where you lay it. It's nothing fancy."

That much was true. His lady wore clothes more suited to a serving maid than a…

He turned slowly around, half afraid what he might see, but determined not to show any adverse reaction. Her skin slid against his. So unbearably arousing. She was aligned to his front now, and seemed not to want to give him a full view of her.

He had turned his back for one instant, and she'd taken her chemise off. Now she hid against him, her body shielded by his.

He would kiss her. That was the solution. She seemed to like that. Oh, he wanted to kiss her all over, but he would start at the conventional location for now.

Rafèu cupped her exquisite face in his hands and gazed down into wide green eyes. Her pupils were dark with desire—and fear. So vulnerable. He dipped his head slowly and kissed her quite chastely on the lips. He lingered a moment there, waiting to see what she would do.

She pressed her body a little closer to his and opened her lips.

Raf needed no further invitation.

THIS WAS IT. He'd required her clothes off. A fumble beneath the skirts was apparently not enough for this discerning minstrel. But in a moment of wild bravado, she'd pulled off her chemise. Now he'd get on with it. The slaking of his lust, his imitation love. He was worried about guarding La Roque. Now he'd distracted himself from his duty so long over her buttons, surely he'd just set to and plunge that hardness rearing between his thighs into her?

Eglantine shuddered against him. The thought was not as displeasing as it ought to be.

But now he was kissing her, and all thought was submerged by feeling. She wound her arms about him and gave her mouth up to his invasion. The sensation of his skin against hers was incredible. She wanted to rub herself against it like a cat. She experimented a little. Ah. Her nipples grazed his chest. Little sparks shot through her. She gasped, and did it again.

"Enough, my lady." His lips left her mouth, and he growled in her ear. Then Eglantine startled. His tongue tip was tracing the whorls of her ear. He settled on her earlobe and nibbled.

Eglantine squeaked, half from surprise, half from the melting pleasure of it. And then she squeaked again as he scooped her into his arms and stepped toward the pallet.

Now. He would do it now. Making the beast with two backs, old-fashioned fucking. A deadly sin, but not so deadly to Eglantine as the chains of marriage. How many times would Rafèu do it before he tired of her?

He stooped and laid her on the pallet. Eglantine froze. In the next instant, he would lean back and look at her. He would survey the terrain he was about to conquer and he would find it inadequate.

She was not built on buxom proportions. Her breasts were not pillowy mounds or her hips the lush bed men liked to sink into. Ferrand had often muttered that she might put on a little flesh. He'd even complained that her gardening gave her unwomanly strength. Her husband hadn't complained for long, though. He'd found alternatives.

Eglantine shut her eyes. She didn't want to see the disappointment flash across Raf's firelit features.

Which was why she was wholly unprepared for what came next.

Something brushed over her left nipple, something damp and slightly rough.

Eglantine nearly shrieked. She remembered to muffle the sound just in time. One did not shriek on the battlements of a beleaguered castle, even if a man had just lapped one's nipple with his tongue. Her back arched of its own accord and her eyes flew open.

His hair was just slipping down over his shoulders. Soon it would brush her bare skin as he dipped to pay his respects to her right breast.

She could not stifle her gasp. She saw it this time—the simple stroke of his tongue over her nipple that sent a starburst of sensations through her. She squirmed, scarcely able to bear the feeling, yet begging for more.

He glanced up at her and smiled—a smile to create instant combustion.

"I told you I wished to lay my lips to every last part of you. Do you object, my lady?"

She wasn't convinced about the rest of her body, but she wouldn't complain if he repeated his attentions to her breasts. His hair was brushing her chest now, featherlight touches that set her skin alight.

"I find your wishes strange, my lord, but"—she gasped at a third stroke of his too-clever tongue—"not wholly objectionable. Pray continue, if it pleases you."

The pallet sank beneath him as he settled beside her, his flank just touching hers.

He laughed softly. "Oh, it pleases me, my lady. Far too much. It may be that I must curtail my lips' exploration somewhat tonight, but be assured it will continue later. At length."

His fingertips trailed over her cheekbones and brushed her lips.

"You are so very beautiful," he murmured. "Never be afraid to show yourself to me."

She wasn't sure if she should believe his words—they were probably just the product of fleeting desire—but they freed something within her, something she hadn't even known was chained.

So Eglantine opened her mouth and answered him in kind. She licked at his trailing finger experimentally, and then, more daring, she nipped it.

His eyes darkened, if such a thing were possible, and he dipped to cover her lips with his own. He draped his body over hers in the process, so wonderfully warm, hard and heavy, his arms on either side of her. He wasn't wholly atop of her, but suddenly she wanted him to be.

This was lust—*this* was the maddening force that men chased from woman to woman. And now she understood it, this wild craving for union. Would she too desire man after man? She hadn't done so before. She couldn't imagine wanting anyone but Raf, but he would inevitably tire of her and leave. What heinously sinful nature had the man unlocked in her?

But in this moment, Eglantine didn't care. She wound her arms around her minstrel and answered his kiss with open-mouthed abandon, slipped her leg up and over his own, and gripped his buttock.

His mouth wandered down her neck, along her collarbone, then traced the circumference of one breast. Which was all quite delightful, but it meant his body was no longer heavy upon hers. He had pulled back a little to trail his tongue and fingers over her torso and—dear heaven—close his mouth entirely about her nipple.

She arched her back and tugged him closer.

"No more," she whispered. "Just do it, Raf."

The dark head lifted. His palm traversed her torso, just slightly rough, leaving tingles in its wake as it descended.

"No more, my lady? Is it such a trial?" His eyes crinkled at the corners, but they burned at their core. His hand wandered over her hip.

"I…" She frowned. The progress of his hand was distracting her. How to express what she wanted without losing all dignity? She tugged his buttock closer. "What are you doing, Raf? I just—Ah!"

His hand had slipped between the juncture of her thighs. He parted her with a single finger, and ran it slowly along her core. Oh God, she *would* shriek. There was no stopping it. The wild intensity of the feeling was too much.

He anticipated her. Just as she opened her mouth, his lips covered hers. He ran his finger lazily up and down, and she writhed against his kiss. She just wanted…wanted…

Raf lifted his head and held her gaze. "Now, my lady?"

She nodded breathlessly. Need he ask?

"As my lady wishes," he said softly, and shifted his weight between her legs.

She felt the hardness of him against her inner thigh. She twined her legs about his. Closer, she needed him closer. He propped himself on his elbows and looked at her. No, *look* was too inadequate a term. Her minstrel's expression was frightening in its intensity, blazing not only with desire but tenderness. Love. A love that burned too hot. It would burn itself out.

He entered her, a breathtaking solidity pushing deep and deeper inside her. With such controlled slowness.

She closed her eyes, just feeling. Him, filling her to completion.

"Look at me, Eglantine."

His minstrel's voice, so deep and heartfelt. He made love to every woman he sang to, but his voice had never sounded so sincere before.

She made herself open her eyes, look at this beautiful man as he drew himself back only to slip his manhood into her, then again. And it was so hard to look at him. The expressions that flitted over his face seemed so real, so true. Driving desire, adoration, tenderness—all directed at her. As if this would last forever and not for mere moments.

It could not last. Of course it couldn't. The rhythm of his movements was becoming more insistent, forceful. And Eglantine ceased to think. There was only the plunging thickness of his filling her, the spiraling, near-unbearable tension within her, and finally his expression at the last and deepest thrust. A blaze of pure sweetness.

She fragmented at the sight. She convulsed in his arms, writhing against the anchoring weight of him. He was just too beautiful and perfect.

And it could not last.

Chapter Twenty-Six

RAF CRAWLED BACK to the hayloft exceedingly late that night. His original aim had been to see the sun slip above the eastern horizon, and he wasn't far off. But he didn't care about the chill beauties of dawn today, however song-worthy they might be. His minstrel's soul was filled to the brim with a wonder to outshine the mere sun.

His lady, naked in his arms by firelight.

Unfortunately, it would not do to compose a *canzo* celebrating anything he'd seen and done tonight. Unless he crooned it for Eglantine's ears alone.

His soul was so full he almost succeeded in ignoring those niggling pricks to his conscience. *You have dishonored your lady. You have neglected your duty in time of siege.*

Almost, but not quite. They were to reappear with inconvenient frequency over the following days.

Time passed—days of bliss in which Raf forgot for long stretches that the enchanted chateau he wandered through was actually under siege. He returned to assist Eglantine in her garden each morning, although how much horticultural assistance he provided might be debated. But his lady had set him a task, and by God, he was going to show himself worthy. Rafèu must put his love to the test in the most physical manner possible. He must prove this was no fleeting feeling born of lust.

And if the lady commanded, who was a mere knight to question?

So Raf witnessed the garden beds he had prepared sprout tender shoots. He helped his lady water them, pluck off encroaching caterpillars, and erect a light linen sheet to protect them from the midday sun. Raf had never paid any attention to growing plants before. Flowers, yes, but the nurturing of infant seedlings to adults? No, that was peasant work, or the glorious mystery of nature.

His lady possessed strange complexities to her being, and some of them involved horse dung. Manure had never smelled so sweet. Yet slowly he began to understand her fascination—the daily tending of plants, coaxing them into slow beauty, small seeds of hope.

Ferrand had derided her gardening, Raf gathered. That was part of the reason she loved this walled paradise of greenery so—it was entirely hers. In a chateau that had been all Ferrand's, Eglantine's garden was her own. Her husband's presence had never tainted it.

Yet she allowed Rafèu inside. She let him sing her songs as she bent over her plants, and then she let him slip his arm around the curve of her waist, nibble her ear, and unbutton her bodice. Even better, she let him bring her to wild bliss beneath a bower of roses. Another day—a particularly hot day—they both ended up naked in the spring-fed pond. The slide of her smooth, wet skin against his was unbearably arousing. He only managed to hold himself together long enough to seat her on the pool rim, kneel between her legs, and push himself slowly, deeply inside her. Watching the magical expression in her eyes.

Whatever his feelings, her pleasure must come first. This was his quest. She had specified that he satiate himself, but Raf had a different agenda. He guessed Ferrand had never paid much attention to Eglantine's experience in bed—or out of it. Raf would show her that love could be expressed by physical means too. He would demonstrate his devotion by every means he could devise.

Besides, the writhing of her body, the expressions that flitted across her face as he put lips or fingers to her, played mad havoc with his nether regions. And the region of his heart.

At the same time, Rafèu must not do anything to taint her garden paradise. This was her English haven against France, and she had let a Frenchman in. He just had to convince her by means of his body that his heart would never change.

And if he failed? Her garden would never be the same for her. He would tarnish her haven.

Perhaps Eglantine would tire of him. She said her husband had drifted from woman to woman, mistaking lust for love, indulging until disinterest made him move on. She declared she didn't want to remarry. Perhaps she too was just using her minstrel for passing amusement.

As Raf had himself with so many other women, he realized. That was a humbling thought. His intimacies with previous woman had been consensual and kindly, true, but his heart had never been involved. He had left every one of them without a second thought. Could he say as much for all those women? It would serve him right to be so treated in return.

He might yet lose Eglantine if his lovemaking grew tiresome to her, if he could not also capture her heart.

But if Raf failed to protect La Roque itself, he would lose his lady to a ruinous knight.

HE WAS GROWING impatient. Eglantine could hear it in his voice.

"Show yourself, my lady." Definitely an undercurrent of a growl to his tone.

He had demanded she appear on the battlements, but Osbert would not permit her to step between a crenelle.

The captain laid a hand on her sleeve. "Just let him hear your voice. For all we know, he's got an archer stowed nearby."

So Eglantine stayed where she was, cupped her hands about her mouth, and attempted to project her voice through stone. "I am here, Sir Garit. Say what you will."

"I tire of talking to minions," the answer floated back. "I will speak to my bride. I will see her face."

Raf stirred on her other side. He muttered something French and decidedly uncomplimentary.

But Garit was still speaking. "I offer you no violence, Lady Eglantine. Look, I will remove my helm." Then the English accents wafted up again, much less muffled now. "There. You will not shoot me—for such would precipitate a wholesale assault by my men—and I will not shoot you, my bride-to-be." A pause. "And just to set your mind at ease, my companion will likewise unhelm."

A moment later, a ripple passed along the battlements. Something of a collective gasp, murmur, and craning of heads. Eglantine frowned and took an involuntary step forward.

Raf snaked a hand about her arm. "No you don't, my lady."

Osbert on one side of her, Raf on the other—two human manacles holding her back. It was infuriating.

"What is going on? Let me see!"

Her manacles glanced at each other over her head. Osbert shrugged. "I got archers at the ready," he murmured. "One sniff of danger, and they'll turn yon bastards into hedge pigs."

Her manacles softened their grip, and Eglantine stepped forward, flanked by two men. It made the crenelle rather cozy and presented all three of them as a convenient target, Eglantine reflected—then ceased reflecting at the sight that met her eyes below.

Sir Garit was standing there, helm in hand, his short blond hair ruffling in a light breeze. And beside him stood a woman.

Eglantine understood the collective gasp. This was not just any woman. Sleek midnight hair spilled out over mailed shoulders. A pair of large, pitch-dark eyes gazed up at them, set in a face of deep olive tone. She was smiling too, a knowing smile with a hint of wickedness about it. As if she knew the effect she was having on the defenders and reveled in it. She looked like a Saracen, a heathen. A strange and very foreign woman.

Sir Garit caught sight of Eglantine and sketched a bow.

"Thank you for your courtesy, my lady-wife-to-be. It has been weeks since I saw your face. You understand my anxiety to ensure my intended is still at home and in health."

"You think to provoke me, sir," she called. "It is unmannerly of you. It is also useless. I have not changed my mind since I saw you last. You will not starve us into submission. Leave La Roque. Find yourself another castle to occupy and another woman to bed."

If you haven't found her already, she almost added, for the woman by the English knight's side was undeniably beautiful. But such insinuations would be unmannerly in Eglantine. She would not stoop to Sir Garit's level.

"Summer is nearly over," he called back. "I will not subject my men to a winter without a secure roof. Yours will suit me very nicely, as will you. You may be assured I will be a respectful husband, Lady Eglantine. I will permit you to remain here in La Roque, your son's patrimony. Or you may abide in England if you prefer."

Eglantine sucked in a breath. How did he know to say that? Someone in the village must have mentioned her dislike of France, her craving to go home to the land of her birth. Had she been so obvious?

Sir Garit thought to tempt her. Was this why he wanted to speak to her face to face?

She felt Rafèu stiffen beside her. Her minstrel-vicomte knew her dislike of all things French and thought she was tempted. Well, perhaps she didn't dislike *all* things French. But now was not the moment to explain, not while Sir Garit was staring up at the battlements, scrutinizing her face.

"Summer is nearly over," she called back. "Move on while

you can. La Roque is not for you."

The body she knew so well relaxed beside her somewhat.

"Think, Lady Eglantine," the Englishman called back. "Should you spend the winter sealed up in your fortress, you may have food to eat, but will you have the fuel to cook it, or to keep yourself warm? And what will you serve your meals on once you've burned your tables for firewood?"

"I thank you for your concern, sir, but I would worry more about your own men and supplies if I were you," she shot back.

"Ah, my men. Indeed, that is a problem. They grow restless, my lady. Some of them wish to try their hands at the cannon we have acquired. You have heard of cannon, have you not? Are you familiar with the damage it can do?"

Raf's frame had turned rigid beside her. It was more for his sake than her own that she shouted back, "Empty threats, knight. You do not want a damaged fortress. And I have better things to do than bandy words with you." *Like dally with a French vicomte in my garden of love,* she was tempted to add. But no, that was still officially a secret, although she had caught a few speculative looks, particularly from Margery and Osbert. "I bid you goodbye, Sir Garit. Pray do not come again."

She stepped away from the crenelle, set her back to a solidly protective merlon, and let it absorb the trembling that suddenly pervaded her frame.

"Take me away from here," she whispered to her vicomte.

"I COULD GO over the walls by night. It would take me a few days on foot to reach Bruniquel, then a week to raise a force and return. They have threatened you, my lady. The time for waiting and hoping is over. Let me drive them out."

They were in the solar, she, Osbert, and Rafèu. And her lover had just declared his desire to leave her.

Why?

"It was an empty threat," Eglantine repeated, as if repetition would make it true. "He wants a fortress for the winter, not a ruin."

That last word echoed hollowly in the room. This was Sir Garit of the Ruin she was speaking of. That was the name he went by, and he had it for a reason.

"He might use the cannon to target the gate, leaving the rest of the walls whole," Raf pointed out. "A gate is easy to mend afterwards, far easier than stone. All he needs is an open gate to force entry."

"He would lose a good many men doing it," Osbert growled. "I would see to it."

Eglantine stared at him. It was true. Between the two of them, Osbert and Raf had drilled the castle inhabitants into a half-decent defense force over the last few weeks. She knew it because she was one of them. Yes, Sir Garit would lose many men if he attempted to storm La Roque, but her people would suffer too. People would die. Because of her.

"He's just threatening us," Eglantine said, yet again. "He wouldn't risk harming the woman he wants to marry."

She felt Raf's gaze on her, but she did not turn to him. If she did, she might see why her minstrel actually wanted to leave La Roque.

He said he wanted to raise a relieving force, but was that the real reason? It had been nearly a month now. Weeks of delirious lovemaking. She was certain he had kissed every curve of her body now. Indeed, some of those kisses had been quite startling. But perhaps his mission was nearly accomplished as a result— there was nothing left to explore. He knew her, though and through. Now his interest would wane, even though he swore it would not. He probably didn't even realize the true reason he wanted to leave.

She should just let him go. She had always known this would happen. But...

"It is too dangerous, my lord vicomte. Sir Garit has sworn to target anyone who dares depart. It is a risk even by night."

He smiled at her. Quite a restrained smile, probably because Osbert was watching, but it still turned her insides to molten honey.

"I am flattered my Lady Eglantine cares what happens to this humble minstrel's hide."

"Humble?" She snorted. Unladylike, true, but it was either that or crumble and admit that she did care. How hard it was to keep up this pretense in front of Osbert. "You propose to rescue La Roque single-handedly, and you call yourself humble? Can you raise a force sufficient to combat Sir Garit at such short notice?"

"I can but try. What is the alternative—sit around in La Roque and await Sir Garit's pleasure?"

Or attend to mine...and yours. But no, her lover was growing restless. La Roque and its contents could not hold him much longer.

She should let him go, but in this way? Into the teeth of English arrows and Sir Garit's fury? Should the English knight capture Raf in the process, then find out what Raf had been doing with the woman he aimed to marry, a quick death would be the best Raf could hope for.

"Reckon we'd do better to wait this fellow out." Osbert's words, thank goodness. "I don't know much of sieges, vicomte, but your plan'll cost lives, and not just your own. Yon bastard down the hill has a reputation. His men have fought with him for years, and you reckon you can defeat him?" Osbert broadened his stance and eyed Rafèu. "To be blunt, my lord—what's in it for you?"

Eglantine knew: Raf wanted out. Perhaps, once he was safely out, the Vicomte of Bruniquel would find good reasons not to come back after all. There would be no shortage of good reasons. Osbert had just pointed some of them out.

Raf hadn't answered Osbert's challenge, not yet. He was looking at her, and Eglantine did not know how to read his expression. He was holding something back.

"I cannot stop you if you wish to leave, my lord vicomte," she said. "It is dangerous to attempt the walls, but if that is what you desire…"

"My desire has more facets to it than that," he said softly.

A weighted silence, broken at last by Osbert.

"We wait," he decreed. "Yon knight of the ruin likely wanted to provoke us. He'll be extra watchful for now. Whatever your desire, you'd do best to contain it for a tad, vicomte."

Chapter Twenty-Seven

T HE GARDEN SEEMED ethereal in the dawn light, the petals of its roses still scattered with diamonds of dew. The sun was rising noticeably later these days, and the dew lingered longer. His lady did not have to water quite so exhaustively now. Which was good—it left her more time for him.

Raf was sitting in the garden paradise, back against the tamarisk tree, legs draped over the outer rim of the pond. Eglantine wasn't here yet, which was unusual, so Raf focused on his lute and the words he was shaping to a new melody. It was a *canzo* inspired by flowers, tender seedlings, prickling rose brambles, and all the things that thrived and grew in his lady's garden. He was composing it in English, and it was causing him some trouble.

The garden door creaked slightly. The bolt scraped back into place. It was a sound to warm Raf's minstrel heart. He was locked in here with his lady. No one could interrupt their idyll.

"Don't stop playing." Eglantine's hand rested on his shoulder. "Sing for me while I water, Raf."

"Let me do the labor." He captured her hand and raised it to his lips. "I've seen you do it often enough. Surely you can trust me?"

It was an old argument. Raf had repeatedly tried to relieve Eglantine of her watering bucket.

"What? Are my hands so rough with labor that you think you

kiss a peasant? I cannot strum a lute, so each to his own skill, minstrel—mine is watering. Sing to me as I do so, and I may show my gratitude afterwards."

It was a lure to set his heart singing.

Raf did not air his *canzo* of flowers. That was not fit for her ears yet. There was something missing from it, something not quite right. He watched her move about the garden as he sang, bending over her plants, showering them with love. Maybe he should offer himself up for watering too. If she would shower him with such tenderness, he would happily consent to a bucket being dumped over his person. She might allow him access to her body now, but she had yet to unlock the garden of her heart.

"You sing such sad songs, my minstrel," Eglantine murmured as she approached the pond for yet another bucketload. "Is it such a burden being trapped inside La Roque with me?"

Trapped.

His fingers stumbled and the music died. No, he was not going to let the siege intrude here. He set the lute carefully aside. He took her bucket, and set that aside too. Then he removed her hat and ran his fingers through loose waves of golden-brown hair.

"As soft and silky as a kitten," he murmured, and cast her a grin. "I believe I must check if you are as silky elsewhere."

"I think you already have the answer to that, my lord. Not that I object if you wish to confirm your findings." Then she tangled her hands in his own hair and tugged him down to her sweetly uplifted lips.

As always, the gift of her mouth took his breath away. It drove all thought from his head, and it inevitably led to other actions.

He trailed his fingers down her throat, traced her collarbone, along her neckline, then dipped to the swell of her breasts, and…she broke the kiss.

"I must ask you something, my lord vicomte."

She was breathing a little quickly. His gaze lingered on the pulse at the base of her throat, the visible flutter. If he laid his lips to that exact location, would he feel it too?

"I am not your lord. I am your Raf."

"Are you?" she retorted. But before he could answer, she went on, "You fear Sir Garit is about to enter a new phase of assault. The cannon he mentioned, have you experienced this sort of attack?"

Something cold trickled through him. It did not belong in this sunlit garden.

"Yes, my lady. I have known what it is to live in a chateau being slowly demolished by cannon fire. I have been woken at dawn by the very walls about me shuddering, cracking, and tumbling. It does not do wonders for one's sleep."

"I am sorry to make you remember those times," she said softly, reaching up to stroke his hair back. "But this siege has been quite different from Combret, has it not? You need not fear it will happen again."

"We cannot know. Sir Garit grows impatient. He may decide he no longer wishes to wait. He may act."

Enough. He would speak of warfare no more.

Raf gathered Eglantine to him. He scooped her up in his arms and strode to a sheltered corner of the garden. There was a blanket draped there. It had been the first thing he'd done upon entering the garden at dawn. Now, by God, he planned to use it. He would drive all thoughts of cannon from her head and his.

He knelt and arrayed her upon the blanket, but before he could join her, Eglantine sat up. She took hold of his tunic and held his gaze. "I know you do not wish a repeat of Combret, Raf. I can only guess at the scars it has left inside you. I will not inflict more. Know this: if you wish to leave, I understand. I release you from your vow. After all, the month is nearly up. What do a few more days matter?"

Raf turned to stone. His heart was a lump of rock within his chest.

What was she saying?

Sir Garit had offered to take Eglantine home to England. He

declared he would safeguard La Roque for Con, and his lady wife might return to the land she loved. Then the thoughtful fellow had threatened her with cannon. Caught between a lure and a threat, had Eglantine decided to surrender?

The month was nearly up. She had tired of Raf. They had spent a sweet idyll in a summer garden, but now it was turning to autumn. Sir Garit beckoned. Eglantine had no need of a French minstrel-knight who would only hold her in the land she hated. She had sampled his charms. He was of no more use.

"That is not why I offered to leave."

But even as he said the words, he doubted himself. Was there something in what she said? The very notion of that shuddering, unrelenting bombardment shredding the walls of La Roque was the stuff of nightmares. Did he simply want to run?

She looked at him, green eyes interrogating his soul. She ran a gentle finger over his lips.

"If you wish to leave, I will not keep you. I will think no less of you, Rafèu. You should think no less of yourself."

It struck him then. It was a blow to the gut to knock the breath out of him. *She thought he had tired of her.* She probably thought he feared an assault by cannon as well. She believed he would leave and never come back.

His lady would think no less of him? What the hell did she think of him now?

THE FIRST THING he did was kiss her. He was not feeling gentle. Raf pushed her back against the blanket and swooped down on her mouth to silence her. She kissed him back with equal ferocity, her tongue tasting his, her arms twining about him.

He never got on to the second thing he'd planned. If there ever was a plan. For somewhere in the midst of the passionate duel of mouths, tongues, hands, she managed to reverse their positions. She tipped him onto his back, sat on top of him, hair gloriously disarrayed about her shoulders, then planted her palms on his chest and stared down at him.

"You, minstrel, have spent the last three weeks seducing me. You have played the master musician upon the instrument of my body. You have made every fiber of my being shiver with bliss. I wonder, though, whether your repertoire runs to an end. How many more songs do you know?"

"No true minstrel ever runs out of music," he said softly. "He composes more. There are endless variations on the theme of love."

"And the instrument on which you play—do you not long to try your hand at a flute or tabor or vielle instead? Speak the truth, minstrel. I will not shy from it." She ran her hands down her torso. "Does your eye begin to wander from this meagre instrument? Do you tire of me?"

"How can you ask that of me?" he said hoarsely. "Can you not feel the answer straining against you even now?"

She settled her buttocks more firmly about his groin. "That is not an answer, however pleasant it feels."

"Pleasant?" he managed.

A smile touched her lips. "Truly, your plectrum plays a very pleasant tune, minstrel man. But I have been your instrument and pupil long enough. It is my turn to play. I will try my hand upon this instrument while I can." She trailed a finger over his chest. "Before it leaves me. Now take off your clothes."

RAF WAS UNDER bombardment. He had a beautiful woman sitting on his groin, insulting him and seducing him by turns. And she thought he was about to abandon her. It was enough to bamboozle a man.

But she'd given him an order. That much he could do. He

wrapped his hands about her waist and, reluctantly, lifted her from his thighs. Then he stood and, holding her gaze throughout, began to disrobe. She watched him, head slightly to one side, taking in each and every part of him as it was revealed.

Oh yes, he felt very naked at the end of it. Naked and wanting.

"And you, my lady—do you remain fully dressed?"

"The lute does not ask what its musician wears. It is the instrument. It is played upon."

She stepped toward him. She laid her hands upon his shoulders, then trailed them slowly down, over the planes of his chest, abdomen, and ever further down. She skimmed over his hips and completely bypassed his groin—to its everlasting disappointment.

But he was the instrument. He would stand still and let her play.

At which she stopped playing.

Eglantine stepped back and, in no evident hurry, began to unbutton her sleeves. Then her bodice. Raf swayed on the spot and watched her. Tapering fingers, just a little begrimed with gardening, deftly freeing button after button. Her delicate face was angled down, focusing on each little fastening as if there were no need for haste, as if his body were not thrumming from her touch.

All the buttons negotiated, she glanced up at his face, smiled a little, then let her gaze wander down between his hips and rest there. He felt himself solidify to rock. He was not a comfortable rock. Pray God she liked what she saw. Raf was not used to being the instrument—he was the player. He strummed upon his lady's finest fibers and brought forth sweet music. He *needed* to play.

And besides, this was his quest. He ought to be convincing Eglantine of his love by means of fingers, lips, and...well, admittedly that same organ she was scrutinizing at the moment.

"Stay there. Do not turn around," she commanded.

Then the maddening woman stepped behind him. The wool of her skirt just stroked his calf in passing, and that was it. Raf was left standing erect in the sun, wondering if it were possible for his cock to get sunburned.

There was rustling behind him. It took a good deal of self-control to not crane his head around, but Raf managed it. Then her scent stole over him. She was standing directly behind him. His nose was quite certain of the fact.

Of course she smelled of roses, but Raf knew by now that no two roses smelled the same. Indeed, some didn't smell at all. Those were not real roses, in Raf's estimation. But this rose smelled sun-warmed and musky-sweet. With just a hint of lemon. And woman.

The perfume sent a shiver through him. He wasn't going to get sunburned.

Her hands touched his hair. She ran her fingers through it a few times, then lifted it to drape over his shoulder. That achieved, she leaned in to lay her lips to his nape. Raf knew she leaned in, because her hands cupped his shoulders and her nipples brushed his back.

The sensation was electric. It was a lightning strike to his groin. The damned woman was naked, and he couldn't see her. He could barely feel her, but his imagination did the rest.

Then her palms were slipping down from his shoulders, molding the contours of his back, to linger on his buttocks.

"I hope you're enjoying the view," he growled.

He wasn't.

A light laugh. "Oh yes, it's a very nice view. But I don't suppose you've seen it." Her hands roamed his backside with abandon.

Then she moved closer. Praise heaven. He felt her warmth an instant before her skin touched his. He sucked in a breath, then soft contours closed against his backside, back, and legs. Raf bunched his fingers in an effort to remain still.

Her hands were at the front of him now. Raf looked down to see fingers wander over his chest, her nails scraping his skin a little in the passage, then dip slowly lower. He watched, feeling her warmth behind him, her hands wandering down his abdomen, lower, to slip into short, dark hair.

When she found his shaft, there was no controlling the jolt that ricocheted through him. Her fingers lingered upon his aching hardness, stroked tentatively, exploratively, then curled around its breadth.

Her second hand delved lower still. It curved its fingers around his balls, and Raf could watch no more. He closed his eyes and uttered a groin-felt groan. Watching those fingers indulge their curiosity did nothing for his self-control.

The fingers stilled.

"Did I hurt you?"

"No, and absolutely yes," Raf managed between tight teeth.

She immediately released him. Curse it.

"I'd better see what I'm doing, then," she said, placing one palm on either hip and steering him toward the blanket. "An apprentice musician ought to pay close attention to her instrument. Lie down, my lute."

Raf was all obedience. Of course, he wanted nothing more than to twist around and gather her naked gloriousness to him, but a knight knew better than to question his lady. A lute obeyed its minstrel.

He lowered himself to the blanket, resisting the urge to turn around, even closed his eyes as he reclined. No peeking at his gift before it was ready to reveal itself.

"Look at me, Raf. I will not have you replacing me in your mind's eye with another woman."

His eyelids flew open at that.

"Never," he said.

All the same, her words sliced too close to the bone. In times past, Raf had been known to close his eyes and imagine a different woman beneath him than the one present. In the years he despaired of ever approaching Eglantine, he'd succumbed to other women. And sometimes he'd pretended that woman was her—Eglantine, the true lady of his heart. An unworthy urge, insulting both the woman he touched and the woman he dreamed of. But it was all he ever thought to have of her.

Then he blinked, near dazzled. She knelt beside him, her hair alight with filtered sunlight. She was quite naked, as he had known she would be, but the reality was beyond glorious.

He lay back and drank her in. She was a wood nymph, a magical creature of creamy skin, fairy frame, and eyes the dappled green of forest leaves. Her hair slipped loose and alive about her shoulders. One tendril curved about a nipple in a perfect crescent.

"Is it me you see, Raf?" she said softly. "An ordinary woman who lacks any great bounty in her curves, and whose stomach is puckered from childbirth?" She ran her hands along the sides of her breasts, then down to her hips, framing her stomach.

Yes, there were silvery lines on her stomach. Bearing Con had stretched her beautiful skin. The marks were not ugly, and her stomach was a little more rounded than it might once have been. It was only one more indication of the truth: she was not the pale perfection of his dreams. His love had dirt beneath her fingernails. She dabbled daily with manure. Her arms were not the soft white appendages ladies prided themselves on, but almost as strong as a peasant girl's. The songs were not always right.

He began to see where his own infant *canzo* needed adjusting.

"I see you, Eglantine. I will lay my lips to every little line upon your stomach. I will trace them with my tongue—"

"No. You are my instrument to play with today. While I can."

He opened his mouth to protest, but she dipped down and swallowed the words, her lips over his. Her hair descended in a curtain around them, her nipples grazed his chest, and her hands pressed his shoulders down, holding him firm. His lady was growing more confident with her kisses now. She did not wait for his tongue to invite her, but slipped her own between his teeth and took possession.

Raf shifted restlessly beneath her, needing to touch her, stroke her hair, wind his arms about her elusive frame. But he knew he must let her take the lead. He would show that he didn't want to dominate her…and maybe then she would trust him.

Her mouth abandoned his. It traveled down, lapping his neck and descending to circle first one nipple, then the other. Raf grasped two handfuls of blanket, set his teeth, and let her explore.

Too soon—not soon enough—she sat back and surveyed her victim.

"Have you quite finished torturing me yet, my lady?"

Her gaze wandered over him, a half-smile upon her lovely lips. "You respond well to torture, my lord vicomte." She extended a single finger and stroked the length of his shaft.

Raf could not argue with her logic. He was not in the mood for argument.

But Eglantine had more to say. "Do you remember how shocked I was when you…" She hesitated, and rose pink stole over her cheeks.

Raf grinned. "Was it perhaps when I made good on my promise to kiss your every curve, specifically those between your legs?"

A tiny shudder coursed through her. It was perfectly delightful. It made her lips open and her nipples pebble.

"Perhaps," she said. Then she glanced down at him, her blush deepening. She was not looking at his face. "It occurred to me that, shocking though it might be, I… Well, I am curious to return the favor while I can."

Raf frowned. He did not like the sound of this. Her words had a note of finality to them. Was there something she hadn't told him yet?

She lowered her head over his thighs. A curtain of hair shielded her actions from view. And then, sweet heaven, her tongue—it could only be her tongue, warm and damp—trailed up the length of his shaft. Christ, he nearly whacked her in the face with it, so pleased was it with the attention.

A low laugh. Her breath cooled his heated member. Her tongue traced his length again, so very slowly. He couldn't see a bloody thing, and that *was* torture. To add insult to injury, he felt fingers curl about his balls. He lay at her mercy. Would she slowly lick him to death, like a cat grooming its kitten?

No. Worse. Her mouth closed over him. Warmth and wetness encircled his manhood, and Raf had to anchor his hips to the blanket to restrain the almighty urge that took him.

She withdrew, leaned back and regarded him.

"You *do* look tortured, Raf. Perhaps I should take pity and leave my poor minstrel alone." She trailed an idle finger along his cock.

Raf's fingers flexed on the blanket. Heaven help him, he wanted to clamp them about her waist, haul her on top of him, and impale her upon that poor, tortured part of him that screamed for release.

"The priests frown on it, you know," she went on.

"My lady, sacrilegious as it may sound, at this moment I care not a fig for any cleric's opinion. Confess afterwards, but do not leave me in this state, I beg."

Raf began to rise. This instrument was tired of being played. It desired to do some playing itself, and without delay.

Eglantine pushed him back down. "The priests frown on a woman mounting a man. They believe she is the horse to be mounted."

Having announced that bit of canon law, the Lady Eglantine slipped one long, creamy leg over his and knelt astride him.

Raf froze. It was the only option. If he permitted himself to move, his cock would act and he would think later.

"I trust you do not mind my endangering your immortal soul, vicomte."

"The priest will have an entertaining confession of it," was all he could think to reply.

"Well, then…"

Holding his gaze, Eglantine reached down and grasped his shaft with a purpose. Raf could not breathe. Air was immaterial. He watched her sink down, down, until his craving tip met warmth, wetness.

She gasped and guided the head of him along her seam, slipping slowly back and forth. He simply watched her face, the wonder of the feelings flitting over it. His cock was throbbing with need, but he held back and watched her revel in the feel of him.

Then the bell began to jangle.

Chapter Twenty-Eight

I T WASN'T THE bell at the garden gate. It was the alarm bell on the battlements. Two strikes, repeated. Over and over.

Eglantine held quite still, one hand clasping a nicely thick male member, the other resting upon Raf's shoulder. She had been just about to end the torture—hers as well as his—and sink down upon that straining solidity.

Now reality intruded.

His hands interrupted her thoughts. They shaped over her hips, over the dip of her waist and up to cup her breasts. An errant thumb brushed a nipple. Eglantine gasped.

"It is only the minor alarm," the owner of the thumb murmured. "Trust the ruinous knight to interrupt us. The man has no manners. Shall we ignore him, my lady?"

The bell jangled her senses, insistent. Calling to her.

The thumb moved again—a musician's fingers, playing her, sending spikes of need through her.

She looked down into black, black eyes. The thumb brushed again, and Eglantine broke. The bells could go to hell and take Sir Garit with them. She sank down on his thickness, holding his gaze, letting him fill her to aching completion.

His eyes were black stars. They shone for her. She lingered there a moment, feeling all of him, letting the emotions wash over her. Lust-fueled emotions, no doubt, but they felt so very real. He belonged in her. Only her.

He would stay.

Then the bells got to her. They infected her with their urgency. She rose on her knees, feeling the slip of his shaft within her, until she almost left him. Then she permitted herself the bliss of plunging down on him again. The bells sang their two-tone song, and Eglantine obeyed their rhythm. Up and down. The bells meant only this—the slide of Raf's shaft within her, the fire in his eyes. The expression she could almost mistake for love as he watched her rise and fall upon him.

Until it seemed he could endure no more. He closed his hands about her waist, as if to impale her ever further onto his cock. The bells jangled on, and Raf paid no notice. His rhythm exceeded theirs, increasing, thrusting ever more fiercely, until she tightened about him, in back-arching ecstasy. His fingers clenched her waist. His hips bucked beneath her, and he gave a low, ragged cry.

But his eyes never left hers. They never closed, even at the moment of his bliss. And they told her this was not simply lust.

She never noticed when the bells ceased. She sank against him, shuddering in aftershock, her legs about him, breasts against his heaving chest.

He wrapped his arms around her. His breath stirred her hair.

She lay like that, sprawled over him and completely boneless, the sun warming her back for long moments, before he spoke, very softly.

"I will not leave you, lady of my heart. I *could* not leave you. I sing only for you. Are you convinced yet that this is no glamour?"

Eglantine could not answer. She had no breath, no energy. She did not want to interrupt a perfect moment with words. She sank into sleep in his arms.

SHE HAD CONQUERED him.

Raf paced the walls and wondered if every other inhabitant of La Roque saw it writ plain across his features too. After he tore himself away from her, he'd gone straight up here to the battlements, just to check that all was as it should be, and that Sir Garit had merely been delivering his daily round of threats. Apparently he had. The bastard hadn't demanded Lady Eglantine this time, praise heaven. Worse timing could not be imagined. He hadn't even mentioned cannon again, according to Osbert.

All the same, Raf had failed in his duty. He understood Eglantine's reasoning that he wasn't solely responsible for the protection of La Roque. He even believed it, to a point. That belief had allowed him to live this strange double life over the last few weeks—safeguarding a chateau under siege, punctuated by bouts of ecstatic lovemaking. Saints be praised, it wasn't only the lack of cannon fire that marked La Roque as different from the Combret.

But La Roque was still under siege, and he had ignored an alarm. It was not a habit he intended to cultivate. So Raf imposed on himself the punishment of remaining on the battlements over the midday meal.

He stalked along the crenelated walls, hungry in the heat of the day. He stared down at the scrubby hillside below, eyeing in particular the clump of twisted holm oaks he was certain secreted an English bowman.

He punished himself thus because he had allowed himself to be distracted, so very distracted, to the point that he couldn't care less if the chateau was facing imminent invasion. It wasn't just that his cock had demanded instant satisfaction, it was the words she'd spoken. They added urgency to his quest.

The month was nearly over. She thought he had tired of her. He wondered whether she tired of him. After all, she had said he could leave, and she would think no worse of him. Did she *want* him to leave?

And yet...he'd caught an expression on her face this morning in fleeting, unguarded moments. That expression had made his heart expand sharply, almost unbearably. It was a softness, a trust, a wonder. It almost looked like love.

Save that it vanished almost the moment it arrived.

He had to convince her. He must prove his love would never evaporate, that he would stay.

There was movement below in the courtyard. Strange, given that every castle inhabitant should by rights be at their main meal of the day. Raf gave the baking landscape one last raking perusal, then turned his gaze inward to La Roque.

It was Margery. Easy to recognize even from a giddy height by her golden curls. She was hurrying, then stopping and glancing around, then hurrying on. She was calling something, too.

Raf grinned. No need to second-guess Margery's mission. Her small charge had failed to turn up for the midday meal again. Where was the little wretch this time?

Then he felt a stab of worry. Had Con clambered onto the stable roof at the warning bells earlier? He had been determined to get an eyeful of Sir Garit, but Raf had talked sense into the boy. He'd hoped.

Raf's gaze roamed the rooftops of La Roque. They were all bare of human inhabitants, even small ones, so far as he could see.

Please God, don't let him have fallen. Con was surefooted, practically half mountain goat, but even a mountain goat slipped sometimes.

Margery disappeared into the stables. Her voice floated up to him still, muffled now. She was still calling for Con.

Raf began to pace the walls again, but this time he only cast cursory glances through the crenelles to the outer landscape. Now he was more concerned to rake every possible angle of La Roque for a small, overly adventurous boy.

Surely he would turn up for the afternoon weapons drill?

Eglantine's heart had deserted her chest entirely. It now seemed to beat in her throat. Perhaps that was why she was breathing so shallowly.

Con hadn't appeared at the midday meal. Her son had slipped away from Margery earlier, when the warning bells began to clamor.

"I'm so sorry, mistress. He's been so antsy of late. He don't like being shut up. Can't say any of us do. He's got away from me a few of times, 'specially when the alarm rings, but he's always turned up again. When he's worn himself out."

That was Margery's announcement, accompanied by much twisting of hands. It was delivered at the dinner table, well into the first course. Eglantine immediately lost all appetite for pottage and manchet. Her impulse was to shove back her chair, abandon her trencher, and join Margery in the hunt.

The impulse had to be denied. She was the Lady of La Rocue. She did not show panic. She most certainly did not leave her precious food uneaten. The meal must be endured.

Besides, Margery was right—Con always turned up when he was ready, a little dusty or scratched perhaps, but in one piece.

"Thank you, Margery. Sit and finish your meal for now. Search afterwards." Eglantine's hands curled about the ornate wooden arms of her chair. Her fingers squashed wooden tendrils and flowers. "And when you find him, bring him to me. There will be no weapons drill for him this afternoon."

It was a dire punishment. Con loved the training sessions. But now hours had passed since the midday meal, and now he not arrived for his beloved sword swinging.

Eglantine curled her hands about a leather-wrapped hilt. The sword felt perfectly well balanced in her grip—a little heavy, but reassuringly so. All the better for smiting with. Heaven knew, she felt like doing some smiting right now.

They had long since moved beyond wooden weapons in the drills. It wasn't wood they would raise against an invading enemy. Raf and Osbert had agreed that their troops needed to handle the real thing.

Today, half of them would attack the wooden practice posts, imagining a man before them—an Englishman with a snarl upon his face and murder in his eyes. The others would engage in actual fighting, one against one, with wooden swords and bucklers in hand.

Surely all that din of wood and iron would bring Con scurrying from wherever he'd holed up?

She attacked the post. She aimed blow after blow at its offensive wooden surface, and chips began to fly.

When she ran out of breath, she stepped back, shoulders heaving.

"You wear yourself out, my lady," came a voice behind her. "This is the moment your enemy would step in and slip under your guard." A soft prod against her ribs. "Pace yourself. Always hold something in reserve."

She whirled on him. She stared up into dark, compassionate eyes.

Too compassionate. She felt tears spring to her own, and blinked them back.

"I *can't*. Not while my son is missing. He should be here. I thought he'd come. Where is he, Raf? I've looked everywhere."

"I don't know, my lady. I too have searched."

"I should have been here! The alarm…" Her sword quivered in her grip. Con had last been seen just before the alarm rang on the walls. She had heard those bells too, and instead of watching out for Con, she had…

"Dear God, where is he?" she whispered.

She shouldn't be showing her panic out here in the courtyard. People were pausing in their strokes. They were looking at her warily. Fearfully.

She had been outwardly calm so far. But now, with a sword in her hand and Raf looking at her as if he wanted to wrap her in his arms and hold her close, the feelings would not be shoved down.

Raf raised a hand. It wavered toward her, then stopped. Withdrew. People were watching.

Then the bells began to toll.

It was Sir Garit of the Ruin. For the second time that day.

Raf watched the ruinous bastard clank up the hill and hoped he was basting inside his layers of iron and padded cloth. The fellow who accompanied him with the obligatory white flag was evidently not the woman of the previous day. She had moved with an almost serpentine grace. This armored figure stumped up the hill in the wake of his master, using his flagpole as a handy walking stick, about as graceful as a plough ox. He was the gargoyle to her serpent.

Eglantine stood beside Rafèu. There had been no question of keeping her off the battlements, even though this was the first time Sir Garit had approached twice in one day. That should have been ominous enough to keep her far from the walls. But Con was missing. Raf could see by her face that the dreadful thought had occurred—had the English knight somehow got his hands on Con? Eglantine needed answers.

Raf leaned toward his lady. "Don't say anything about Con. No need to mention that you've temporarily mislaid him."

Osbert jabbed a nod. The captain stood to the other side of Eglantine, glowering down at the two figures laboring up the path. "Aye. Dunno what the bastard wants, but it won't be naught to do with the little lord. Can't be."

His lady said nothing. She stared down at Sir Garit and tightened her fingers on the hilt of her sword. She had run straight from weapons practice, blade in hand. He would have to get her a sheath if she kept this up. Damned dangerous to sprint up narrow stairs with a naked blade in hand. Not that anybody could have stopped her.

Sir Garit stood before the walls. The Ruin's pet gargoyle set his white flag on the stony soil and held on to it, breathing hard. The face through the open visor was distinctly pink. Sir Garit, on the other hand, appeared cool, calm, and in possession of all the air he needed.

He looked up at the battlements. His gaze flicked dismissively over Raf and settled on Eglantine. He bowed slightly.

"God's greetings, Lady Eglantine. I am glad I need not summon you from the depths of your chateau. I come to address you, and only you."

Raf set his teeth. Harder. Did the fellow mean to aggravate, or did the words simply reflect a habitual lack of tact? He would not endear himself to Eglantine as a future husband by ordering her about.

"Speak, Sir Garit," she called back. "Say your piece and go. The sooner you are out of my sight, the better I will be pleased."

"Perhaps you would prefer to rest your sight on this, Lady of La Roque." Garit tugged at an item tucked into his belt. His gauntlets caused him some trouble, not being adapted to handling fabric. For that was what it was.

The item tugged from the belt materialized into a tunic. Garit held it up in clumsy gauntlets for all to see. It was a small tunic of distinctive green hue, and it had evidently received some rough treatment. There was a jagged hole down one side.

A faint gasp beside him.

Raf's gaze flicked to Eglantine. His lady swayed where she stood. If possible, her cheeks were whiter than her wimple. Raf extended a quick arm to support her, but she shook him off.

"Do you recognize this item of clothing, my lady?" Sir Garit called up politely. "I have its owner in my custody. I thought you would like to know."

Was she going to faint? She wavered like a tamarisk in the breeze. She did not want his hand on her arm, but by God, he would catch her if she fell.

Her wide green eyes were fixed on the tunic. On the jagged rent in it.

"What do you want?" she whispered.

Garit angled his head. Eglantine was forced to repeat the question, louder. Her voice did not sound her own. It cracked around the edges.

"I want what I have wanted from the very beginning of our acquaintance, Lady Eglantine—your hand in marriage and the guardianship of your son and castle. Nothing has changed. As I mentioned before, I swear I will not deprive your son of his patrimony."

Raf saw his lady's knuckles turn to bone about the sword hilt. That should have been a warning sign.

"You swear falsely, knight," she cried. "My son cannot inherit if you have killed him."

Raf stared at the little tunic, at the hole in its side. He stared till his eyes ached. He had seen Con wear that shirt. He remembered now. The boy fancied the green hue turned him into Robin Hood. But what had made that hole? Was that blood darkening its edges?

Below them, Sir Garit straightened. His voice took on a hard edge. "That is unmannerly of you, lady. I do not swear falsely. Your son lives. He is well. Surrender La Roque, wed me, and he will inherit. This I swear."

He paused, fixing her with an ice-blue gaze.

"If, on the other hand, you remain obdurate in your castle, perhaps your son's future is not so assured."

Eglantine leant forward so abruptly that Raf feared she would tumble over the battlements. He sprang for her arm. Osbert grabbed the other.

"No!" she shouted. "I do not believe you! I see nothing but a tunic. Your threats are empty. This is a ruse. You do not have my son."

Sir Garit shrugged. "Perhaps I have the wrong boy, then. He said he was Constantine, Lord of La Roque, but then, boys like to boast. Be at ease—I shall tear out the little pretender's tongue so he can never blacken your name with such a charge again. Doubtless you have your son safe within La Roque this moment."

Eglantine made a little keening noise. It sliced through Raf's very soul. She sank against him. Raf directed a hard stare at Osbert and jerked his head toward the English knight.

"Say something," he growled. "I cannot. Demand we see the boy. We will do nothing until then."

"Yes, I must see him," Eglantine whispered. "I must know…" Then she straightened against him. "No, you will not speak for me. Let go of me, both of you."

Raf and Osbert exchanged glances, but obeyed. Eglantine leaned into the crenelle and spoke clearly and slowly.

"You will not harm the boy. You will bring him before the walls tomorrow morning, alive and whole. Whoever he is. You will have your answer then."

She paused, and Raf saw her grip the stone for support and heave a deep breath.

"Swear, Sir Garit. Swear on whatever you hold most holy that you will not harm this boy."

The helm below tilted up and blue eyes gazed steadily at Eglantine.

"There is nothing I hold more sacred than my word, Lady of La Roque. Should I swear on a relic, it would be but half an oath." Garit clapped one gauntlet to his chest. There was an audible thump. "I swear that the boy who wore this shirt will remain in as good health as when he came to me. I will bring him before the walls of La Roque tomorrow."

The knight bowed. The tunic fluttered in his hand. "Until tomorrow, my lady-wife-to-be."

And Sir Garit turned and receded down the precipitous path, his gargoyle in his wake.

Chapter Twenty-Nine

E GLANTINE STARED OUT of the beautiful glass window in the solar. She saw only Con, and he was not there.

"I have to marry him," she told the glass.

The silence behind her was heavy. She could feel eyes on her back, thoughts leaden in the air.

She whirled around. "*Why* does he want to marry me, for God's sake? He just wants La Roque, not me. I never wanted to marry again. And I definitely don't want to be wed at swordpoint. Nor with a sword to my own son's throat."

Her voice cracked over those last words.

She didn't even know if Con was still alive. That rent in his tunic—what did it mean? If Sir Garit had Con, why hadn't he paraded the boy before her this afternoon? Why just the shirt?

Eglantine sank against the window ledge. Her legs wouldn't hold her up.

Raf took two hasty steps toward her. She flung up an imperious hand, palm outward.

"No. Do not touch me."

She gave him a long, hard look. Osbert was here too, so she could not say the words, but she let her expression speak them loud and clear: *If I hadn't been in the garden with you, this might never have happened. You will not distract me again.*

Then she looked at Osbert. At her reliable captain, who had

been with her in La Roque since the very beginning.

"I could give up the chateau. In exchange for Con, I could agree to abandon La Roque and its lands. I will return to England with my son. I will beg shelter from my family. I would have left years ago, only…" Her voice failed her, and she shook her head. "Only I needed to safeguard my son's patrimony. But now…now it is all for nothing."

She clenched her hands. Her nails dug into her palms. She welcomed the pain.

If Con were alive, that was all that mattered. She would do whatever it took. But if he were alive, would he ever forgive her for throwing away his inheritance?

"No," she answered herself. "No, I have to marry him." She held her captain's gaze. She willed him to speak the truth. "Osbert, tell me—is this knight's word to be trusted? Will he permit my son to inherit if I marry him? Can I do this thing?"

She saw Raf make a convulsive movement. Eglantine ignored him. She must ignore him completely from now on. In fact, she should order him from the room this instant. He had no place in La Roque. She should have thrown him out the moment she realized he remained.

No, she should never have let him through the gate in the first place.

Eglantine opened her mouth to order him out, but Osbert was answering. "My lady, he seems an honorable man. He has not done anything contrary to his word thus far." Her captain shot a glance at Rafèu. "I think the vicomte would confirm that this siege has been a remarkably peaceable one as sieges go. Sir Garit has offered us no violence."

"Maybe so, but he has threatened violence enough," Raf growled. "And it's not to your advantage to encourage this match, captain. Do you think you'll be kept on when Garit garrisons the place with his own men?"

Osbert snapped some kind of rebuttal, but Eglantine wasn't paying attention. Osbert. She hadn't even considered her captain's future. And what of the other inhabitants of La Roque? Ah, she was tied to some torturous rack and was being slowly dragged in different directions. She was coming apart.

Raf, at least, would be fine. He would just wander back to Bruniquel and find himself some other woman to love. He would have left soon anyway.

She would not think how it would feel when he left. Besides, it was better this way. At least now she could pretend he might have stayed.

The man she was on the point of ordering from the room approached. She would not look at him, she *could not* look at him, even when he was standing directly before her.

He spoke.

"Marry me instead, my lady. Let Con grow up safe in Bruniquel. Do not trust your life to this Ruin. You do not know him. You *do* know me."

Oh, how she knew him. The deliciousness of his body, the midnight-dark eyes that told her she was everything, the skill of his fingers upon the lute…and upon her.

"You know I would never hurt the boy," he continued. "Abandon La Roque to Sir Garit for the moment. The time may come when we may take it back. Marry me and come to Bruniquel, Eglantine."

Velvet words to stroke her senses. Warm and tempting as the devil himself.

Eglantine shivered. She wouldn't look at him. His words tugged at her so.

She would still be chaining herself to a man. Her son's future would hang on her new husband's whim, and she would have given up La Roque.

At least Sir Garit would not break her heart. She would enter that marriage with wide-open eyes. She could keep her garden. And if Sir Garit's word was to be trusted, Con would keep La Roque.

By contrast, the only reason she would wed her vicomte-minstrel was for love. Such a flimsy basis for a life decision. Love could not be depended upon. It might dissipate the moment the next pretty girl crossed her husband's path. Then she would be trapped again, helplessly loving a man who did not love her. Worthless and rejected.

It would be worse this time.

"No." She steeled herself to look up into Raf's eyes. "I cannot abandon my son's future. I have endured France all these years. I have stayed in a land I hated solely because, if I left, I would lose La Roque. My son would never forgive me. Con is everything. I will do what I must, and I must marry this English knight."

SHE WOULD NOT talk to him. Raf had requested an audience alone with her, but Lady Eglantine refused. She would not even look at him.

Dusk fell, and Vicomte Rafèu tuned his lute up in the hayloft. The evening meal approached. He would sing to her in the hall. She could not shut her ears to his song. He must woo her as never before, must soothe her terror for her son.

For surely Con was safe? Sir Garit would not bluff over such a vital matter. The man must know Eglantine would never marry the man who murdered her son.

The plectrum slipped from Raf's fingers. Damn it, the sliver of horn was swallowed by the hay. Raf had to rise to his knees and scrabble about in the stuff, digging for a plectrum in a haystack.

It reminded him of Con. The boy had often come up here. He loved the hay. He had burrowed in it like some furry animal, and Raf had had to pick stalks of dried grass off the lad before letting him run to his mother.

Raf's hands tightened on fistfuls of hay. The stuff did not feel so soft when it was being ground into one's palms.

Con. The boy *must* be safe. Raf's throat closed up. He swallowed, hard. Shouting out his helpless fury would not improve the quality of his song. And this was only a fraction of the pain his mother must be feeling.

And all he, Rafèu of Bruniquel, could think to do was croon love songs while a boy was in danger and the woman he loved was being forced into marriage?

He drove his fist into the hay—and nearly impaled it on a stray plectrum. Well, thank God for small mercies, if not the larger ones.

It was as Raf's fingers closed around the little implement that the thought struck him. There was a better use for his lute tonight.

EGLANTINE COULD NOT eat, so she stayed in the solar, pacing by the light of a single candle. There was no point in descending to the hall for the meal that evening. True, as Lady of La Roque she ought to appear before her people, reassuring them with her calm composure. Pretending that everything would be all right.

But that composure was a brittle mask. One stray thought of Con would crack it, and she would fall into fragments. Eglantine could not do that in front of her people.

Besides, she could not risk encountering Raf.

He was temptation personified. He was a dark devil luring her with promises of heaven. And he had asked her to marry him. Again.

Why?

She paced in the dim, a frantic energy urging her to do something, anything. It was likely approaching midnight now, and she could not be still. But what could she do, beyond wear a track in the rugs?

Raf had suggested she marry him as a means of escape. Rather than return to England, possession-less, humbly begging shelter from relatives, she could wed him. He would keep her and Con safe. They would be close to La Roque, should it ever become possible to take it back, and it would be in Raf's interests to retake La Roque, for then he would hold it in guardianship for Con. He would profit from it as her husband in the meantime.

It was a solution. Part of her cried out just to seize it. She did not want Sir Garit. Most particularly, she didn't want to be subjected to his attentions abed. The knight already had a far more interesting woman than her to see to his needs, but he would still feel obliged to consummate the marriage. Just to make things legal. In fact, he'd probably do it a few times, until he tired of her.

Eglantine squeezed her eyes shut. It did not erase the image of the blond knight, his hands reaching for her.

She just wanted Raf.

She could not have Raf. Their month of bliss had ended, and it had worked too well. Raf had suggested marriage today, but he made no mention of love. Nor had he pressed his suit after she refused.

His passion was ebbing.

The vicomte had merely proposed marriage out of obligation. He had sworn he would still love her when the month was out, and knights were known to take their oaths more seriously than life itself. Raf felt himself honor-bound to wed her.

No, Sir Garit's loveless marriage was preferable to a lie. She could not look upon her minstrel-vicomte every day and feel this ache within. Never to be filled. Never again to be reciprocated.

A rap at the door. Eglantine startled. Shards of alarm ripped at her composure. She was in no state for surprises.

"Who is it?"

The bolt was drawn. She did not want to see anyone. Margery could sleep elsewhere tonight. There was no Con for her to tend to, and Eglantine could undress herself for bed. Not that she was likely to sleep, or even lie down.

"Me, m'lady. Osbert. I got someone here to speak to you."

At this hour? What did it mean?

It didn't matter. If it wasn't Con, she didn't want to see them. Had Raf talked Osbert into helping him? Likely enough. Osbert had not looked at all surprised at Raf's proposal that afternoon. That someone was probably Raf.

"Go away," she said dully.

"M'lady, you'll want to hear what he says."

"Will I? Has he news of Con?"

Silence.

"No. But—"

"Who is it?" she snapped.

By God, if it was a certain dark-haired minstrel-vicomte, she would not unbolt the door until Judgment Day. Or at least until Sir Garit brought her son, alive and well, before the walls.

"It's Matheu, my lady. He's just off duty on the walls. Something happened—"

"Oh, for heaven's sake!" Eglantine heaved the bolt back and flung the door open. "Enter! Get it over and done with."

Eglantine recognized the man who entered hesitantly in Osbert's wake. Before the siege, he had been a man of all work about the chateau, a sometime dung digger. Now, under Osbert and Raf's training, he had become a competent soldier. Should Matheu survive this situation, he should probably consider a change in career.

"What is it?"

She had heard no warning bells. It could not be news of an attack. Besides, why would Garit attack when he was practically guaranteed a surrender tomorrow?

Unless Con was not alive to bargain with.

Osbert turned to Matheu. "Right, spit it out. Tell m'lady what you told me. Every bit."

The man looked at her. His eyes were wide and beseeching. Eglantine's stomach lurched.

"Speak, Matheu."

"I was on the walls, m'lady. I stood guard duty from sundown till just a short while back. Had to wait till the next shift relieved me before I could come tell Osbert, y'know."

"What happened?" she gritted. "Why didn't you ring the bells?"

"No need for bells. We only ring if we see them bastards approach."

Eglantine's hands were fists. "If it wasn't an alarm, what was it?"

"That vicomte. The minstrel fellow. He came up on the walls just after dusk. Had his lute with him, of all things."

"Yes?" she said, and the man flinched at her tone.

"Well, he's in command, isn't he? After you and the captain, that is. And he told me to tell you what he'd done."

"What—did—he—do?"

Matheu flashed a look at Osbert, who nodded grimly.

"The vicomte got us to lower him over the walls. He had a rope. He slung his lute on his back, some other stuff too, and had me slink round to the very back of the battlements. Close to the rock face. I lowered him there, where there was least chance of them English seeing him." A pause. "I think he got away with it too. Didn't hear any disturbance afterwards."

The floor beneath her feet did not feel so steady. Osbert took a step toward her. She waved him away.

"You lowered the Vicomte of Bruniquel over the walls. He has gone."

It was a statement, delivered in an admirably flat tone.

"Yes, m'lady."

"Why? Why did he say he was going?"

But she knew already. Whatever it was he said, she knew the truth. The month was over, the game was up, the passion extinguished. Rafèu had asked her to marry him once more, and she had refused. He had no reason to stay in a doomed chateau any longer.

"He said he was going to get Con. Um, the little lord, I mean. But he said Con."

The world blurred about her. She must have misheard.

"What?"

Chapter Thirty

RAFÈU SLIPPED ON his crakows in an alley off the village square. They were the only remaining part of his minstrel costume, thus vital, but he was damned if he was going to walk in the ridiculous things any further than he had to. Especially in the dark.

He missed his motley. Those garments had shouted *minstrel* so loud it verged on a farce. All he'd needed was a bell or two to complete the foolery. But he'd swapped his bright patchwork for peasant brown to sneak back into the chateau unnoticed all those weeks ago. Back when the siege was only a threat. He'd not thought he'd ever need his motley again.

Oh well, not every minstrel gadded about in multicolored gear. William and Azalais hadn't, and no one had mistaken them for anything but minstrels...until Alain herself had revealed she was Lady Azalais.

Raf had a lute. He had his voice. That was all that mattered—he sincerely hoped.

He lingered in the alley for long moments, watching. Listening. But he could not stay here too long. Someone might notice him. The village of La Roque was practically a garrison, and soldiers were suspicious bastards. That was how they stayed alive.

There wasn't much activity in the village. Everyone seemed to be indoors after dark, save for the couple of sentries he'd avoided on the way in. He knew where they were because he'd watched so long from the walls. Thank God. Otherwise he'd have likely stumbled over them in the dark, and then where'd he be?

Likely dead—or the sentries would be, which was almost as bad. For that would raise the alarm.

What activity there was seemed to be centered on the inn. Which was exactly as he'd hoped. Light spilled from the open door. Noise, too. Occasionally a man came stumbling out, mostly for the purpose of washing down the cobbles with surplus fluid. Most of that flowed from the depths of their braies, but one inebriate saw fit to throw up his ale. Raf wrinkled his nose. He could only hope it would rain soon.

But not tonight. Rain would be most inconvenient tonight.

Raf straightened. He'd established the most important point—no music emanated from the inn. The stage was bare and waiting for Minstrel Rafèu. It was time to make his entry.

Raf padded across the *place de La Roque*, toward La Roque's only inn and the current haunt of English soldiers. Yes, it was nerve-racking. Raf gripped his lute's neck as he might his sword hilt. A pity it wasn't one. He'd stowed his weapon in his lute case. Better not to swagger around enemy soldiers obviously armed.

The only weapon he needed right now was his lute. Raf closed his eyes and tried to sink into minstrel mode. He was not a vicomte, he was not even a knight—he was a mere wandering minstrel who'd happened upon a village full of soldiers.

Well, even English cutthroats liked a dirty ditty, didn't they?

He entered the inn.

And nearly collided with a man attempting to exit said inn.

It was a near thing. The fellow lurched like a boat at anchor. Raf only managed to avoid crushing his lute between a stone wall and a soldier by a quick sidestep. The fellow cast him a bleary look, but did not stop to grab him by the throat and demand to know who the hell he was.

It was a good start.

Raf walked farther in, then paused to look around him. A few heads turned his way. Male heads, mostly. English heads.

He moved toward the bench that passed for a bar and the woman who stood behind it. He really needed a drink.

Raf blinked. It was the same woman as all those weeks ago. He was surprised she'd stayed—or been allowed to stay. Still, with a village full of thirsty soldiers, he hoped she was raking in the silver.

He bowed. "God's greetings, honored madam," Raf said. "This humble minstrel craves the joy of filling your worthy establishment with song. In swap for a place to lay my head and a little something to fill my stomach, if it please you."

She looked him up and down, a little frown crinkling her brow. She recognized him, he could see. And it confused her. There was only the hint of a doe-eyed look for him this time, only a slight heave of the bodice, the contents of which were considerably better covered than when he saw her last. She'd probably had to pack it away for safekeeping, what with so many soldiers about.

"Don't reckon it's me you've got to please, minstrel man," she said at last. "More's the pity." That said with a stirring of her former bodice turbulence. Then her gaze shifted from him to glance with meaning behind him.

Ah, truly he missed his sword.

"Who're you, and what're you doing here?" The words were uttered in bad French and cast in a growl.

Raf composed his features and turned with all calmness toward the growler.

It wasn't Sir Garit, thank goodness. It was just possible the English knight would recognize him, having eyed him on the battlements more than once. But then, Raf had been wearing a protective helm and a brigandine. He prayed he appeared quite different now.

He didn't recognize either of the men who stood before him, legs akimbo and raking him with narrowed eyes.

Raf bowed. Then he raised his lute.

"You see before you a wandering player, my lords. I desire a place to sleep, not to mention something to wet my throat. I thought to find it here, in swap for some song."

They looked at each other.

"We've got entertainment enough, I reckon," said one.

The second narrowed his eyes again. "How'd you get in?" he demanded. "The guards sent us no word."

"What guards?" Raf looked from one to the other in all innocence, then shook his head ruefully. "Forgive me, my lords. I lost my way after dusk fell. I took a track that wasn't a track and stumbled around in circles for a goodly while. I saw no guards, but God knows, I've developed a royal thirst."

"Don't reckon we need entertainment," the first fellow repeated. He glanced at his companion and jerked his head to the door. "Safer to…"

There was a stir at the door thus indicated. The narrow-eyed fellow glanced over his shoulder.

"Hmph. Speak of the devil." Then he turned back to Raf and raised a brow. "Well? Reckon you can compete with that, lute twiddler?"

Raf craned to spy this newly arrived competition.

It was the woman who'd accompanied Garit to the walls.

And no, he could not compete.

In a taproom full of half-sloshed soldiers, no male minstrel was going to outshine that lithe and utterly feminine figure. She was not wearing armor now, but a deep red gown that clung to her every curve. She positively sashayed into the room, dark hair loose down her back, evidently aware that every eye was upon her. And that she was quite safe in the sea of their appreciation, for Garit of the Ruin stalked in behind her.

Then—hell and all its devils be damned—the woman was sashaying up to Rafèu. One glance about the taproom, and she had clearly decided that he and his audience were the most interesting thing it contained. Worse, far worse, the ruinous knight was accompanying her.

Raf *really* needed his sword. Perhaps he could wallop the English knight over the head with his lute? At very least, he should smash Garit's bollocks so hard that he never gave Eglantine any trouble. Even if she had to marry him.

What would happen to Raf after that ungentlemanly action, he chose not to consider.

The dark woman reached out and ran her fingers over the curve of his lute. Elegant olive fingers, trailing slowly and seductively over the polished pearwood.

"Ah, my dreams come true, Sir Garit," she said in her strange accent, never letting her gaze drift from Raf's. "I wish for music, and here is music."

The man so addressed also had his gaze locked on Raf. It was not a pleasant feeling. Raf had seen Garit enough times now to know the fellow wore a habitually impassive expression. But he had only ever seen that stony countenance at a distance. It had never been directed at him.

"You dreamed of this fellow?" Garit replied.

The man's tone was also expressionless. But the words…oh, Raf did not like the words at all.

"Yes!" The woman whirled from Raf and twined her hands up around the blond knight's neck.

Raf blinked. A moment later, the woman had actually mounted Sir Garit. Somehow, she'd hooked both her legs about his waist. She had her hands in the knight's hair and was slanting her lips down on his. She was too short, Garit too tall, for her to have achieved her aim otherwise. Now she was kissing the knight, quite brazenly, in front of the whole taproom.

No, Raf definitely couldn't compete with that kind of performance.

There was a general cheer, some clapping, and the woman unglued her lips and slithered down from her prominence.

"Yes," she repeated, her voice husky, her hands still on Garit. "I dream of music, and here it is. Now he will play—and I will dance."

AND THAT WAS how it was. Raf played so the dark woman could dance. Not that he'd ever seen dancing quite like it before. Whirling, intricate finger movements, the use of a strange percussion instrument. At one point, she even leaped to swing from the beams overhead, revealing loose trousers beneath her red skirts. And the energy of it had Raf's fingers flying to keep up. He was exhausted by the time she abandoned the floor for Sir Garit's lap.

"You were lucky, minstrel man." The innkeeper settled herself on a stool close by Raf with a sigh. She'd brought Raf a beaker of wine, and by God, he needed it.

He raised it to her in thanks. "How so, madam?"

"Don't reckon they'd have let you stay if *she* hadn't turned up." Madam's gaze dwelt upon the figure perched upon a knightly thigh.

Raf looked too. Sir Garit seemed as impassive as ever. Perhaps he was accustomed to being used as a seat.

"Does he always do as she asks?" Raf asked mildly. Maybe this was Sir Garit's vulnerability. Maybe Raf could use this dancing woman…somehow.

The innkeeper chuckled. It made her bosom jiggle. "Oh Lord, no. Not mostly. But tonight… Well, I've heard tell he's extra pleased with her tonight." The woman leaned in close to Raf. Her breath tickled his neck as she murmured, "She did him a service no one else could do."

"Really?" Raf raised a brow and directed a look at the woman on Sir Garit's lap. She seemed to be whispering in the man's ear. As he watched, the dancer ran her tongue along its outer whorl. "Dear me, I wonder what?"

The innkeeper gave herself up to a full-bosomed laugh at his tone.

"Oh no, old Garit can have *that* any day of the week. Just look at the leman, will you? Do you think she keeps her legs closed to him? No, that's not what's got Garit sweet." The innkeeper stopped for a portentous breath, inflating her bodice in the process. "That heathen tart put an end to the siege—or she will by tomorrow—and she did it without shedding a drop of blood. Well, only a few drops, anyway. She fetched him the boy."

THANK HEAVEN FOR lady innkeepers with soft spots for minstrels. Unlike the first time he'd met her, Raf did not rebuff her attentions. No, he lapped them up. He even encouraged them, just a bit. Her name was Penelòpa, he learned—Pené to him. Her husband had died in the war against the English, which meant she was sole proprietor of the inn, and free to bestow her affections on whomsoever she saw fit. Within the bounds of matronly propriety, of course.

Raf didn't think those bounds would hold her long.

But in the meantime, he planned to take quite unconscionable advantage of her.

They wandered around the village. Very slowly, and with much wavering and propping up of walls. Raf had his lute tucked under one arm and Pené tucked under the other. She felt nothing like Eglantine. She was the wrong height, the wrong build—she even smelled wrong.

Still, he desired fresh air and the delight of Pené's company all to himself. That was what he told her. He wanted to sing to her beneath the stars. He did sing to her, and he knew it was a damned odd choice for lusty minstrel to croon to the object of his desires.

Hearken, good yeomen,
Comely, courteous, and good,
One of the best that ever bore bow,
His name was Robin Hood.

It was a ballad of that bow-wielding outlaw, sung in English. Which probably meant that Madam Penelòpa had no idea of what he actually sang. Raf bawled the refrain over and over as he wandered the meagre streets of La Roque. Well, he was a drunk minstrel with a buxom woman on his arm, so what could one expect? A refined and elegant lament?

And he halted frequently to lean against a wall, strum his lute, sing some more, then listen for a space. Oh, and a piece of polished pearwood against his torso came in handy for keeping a certain innkeeper at a distance too.

He got a few less-than-subtle suggestions that he ought to take his caterwauling—and his woman—somewhere less public as he progressed about the streets. But for the most part, the Englishmen grinned at him. Raf was singing them a little slice of home. They understood the woman part of the scenario too.

It took a while, but eventually it happened.

Thank heaven and its full coterie of saints.

He was leaning against the wall of one of the more substantial houses. Raf was beginning to wonder how often he could repeat the same old ditty about rollicking Robin before his voice went hoarse or some irate Englishman choked the words off in his throat. Pené was insinuating one of her rounded arms about his waist when a voice repeated the refrain.

One of the best that ever bore bow,
His name was Robin Hood.

Raf went quite still. Pené took this as a sign that she might press her substantial forefront to what she could access of Raf's own forefront. Her arm wound closer about him.

He ignored the woman. Almost absently, he crooned the opening verse over again. Then paused, waiting.

The answer came again, echoing his own last words. Clearer now. Then a deeper voice interrupted, grumbling some rebuke. The first voice was silenced, but that didn't matter. Raf knew.

Con was alive. He was being held just the other side of this wall. And someone was guarding him.

IT WAS SAFE to assume that Madam Pené had extensive experience of drunken men. Perhaps, then, she was a little surprised and definitely disappointed when this particular drunken man staggered into a nearby stable and subsided, semiconscious, onto the horse litter. With all her experience, she probably reckoned that this particular drunk was up at least for a brief roll in the hay.

Raf was not.

Oh, he felt guilty for employing the delectable innkeeper as a convenient cover for a ramble about La Roque, but not *that* guilty.

So Raf refused to be budged. He groaned and muttered a bit, but persisted in sinking himself determinedly into the hay. Pray heaven Madam Pené did not feel obliged to keep him company. It wasn't a comfortable patch of hay, and he had heard at least one rat scarper on his wavering entry.

Should he snore to dissuade her?

Raf was just preparing himself for a tonsil-vibrating breath when Pené shook him one last time, then sighed and stood. Then he listened to her footfalls receding into the blessed night air.

He lay there some moments more, thinking furiously. Planning and attempting to allow for all possible outcomes.

It was dangerous, horribly dangerous. Raf might easily find himself with a sword in his gut for his troubles.

But that wasn't what gave him pause.

He would be putting the boy at risk. If he simply let well alone, Con would remain safe. The ruinous knight would return the boy to his mother in the morning, and Eglantine would marry the bastard. She would keep La Roque for her son. Maybe.

What alternative could Raf offer? She didn't want to marry him.

But she didn't want to wed Sir Garit either.

If Raf could somehow extricate Con from the English bastard's grip and then let Eglantine know her son was safe, she would remain free to choose.

Even if she didn't choose him.

He might lose her anyway. He certainly would if Con was harmed in some kind of bungled escape.

Finally, Raf stood and brushed himself down in the darkness. He picked up his lute, pressed the smooth wood to his lips, and then laid it carefully in a corner of the stable. It had done its job. It was time to wield a different weapon now.

Chapter Thirty-One

RAF WAS GONE. Con was gone. Eglantine was adrift in a chateau that had no meaning.

It contained her garden, at least. That was where she was this very moment, standing in a midnight garden, a chilly blotching of grays and blacks. This space was her English paradise. It was her world away from France, her haven of beauty.

And it was a hollow shell. It was haunted by an absent minstrel-knight. It was a gray shadow of the love they had made in the sunlight, of the seedlings they had nourished together.

He had gone after Con.

But had he really? Or was that just an excuse to leave La Roque?

She wrapped her arms around herself and shivered.

Con and Raf…their mock battle, the stories, the camaraderie that existed between the pair when Raf was just a minstrel. The evident affection. Eglantine remembered the look on Raf's face when he had seen the tunic that afternoon.

It wasn't an excuse. Her idealistic vicomte had genuinely gone mad. He was off to rescue her son single-handedly. Or to avenge his death.

And he would probably get himself killed in the process.

A sob rose before she could choke it back. She clapped a hand over her mouth. No, she would not weep. Once she began, she would fall apart, and that would achieve nothing.

But if Con was dead, and if Raf died too as a result, what would be left?

Nothing. Absolutely nothing.

Eglantine kicked savagely at a garden bed. Plants? Who cared about plants when she was stuck helpless in here, powerless while the two people she loved most were in danger?

There it was. That word.

Now Raf was gone, the realization slapped her in the face. It was an open-palmed whack that left her breathless and reeling.

True, these feelings had been pestering her for a while now. A craving for his nearness, trust in his judgment, reliance on his strength in the face of a siege that she knew secretly terrified him.

He had endured it for her, and she loved him for it.

Ah, what was love?

She loved his hands upon her, his lips, the way he made her feel cherished and adored. These things fed her lonely soul, her neglected body, and that was how Eglantine had known she was deceiving herself. Raf was too good to be true. The illusion could not last. His interest would wane. She would be a fool to let her guard down. She would be a fool to let himself tangle about her heart like an unruly rose.

But she had done so just the same.

And it was tearing her apart. Garit would return Con to her if she agreed to his conditions, *if* her son were alive, but Rafèu was lost to her. He had slipped over the walls to take on a whole company of soldiers. Even if by some miracle he survived this night, she would still have to marry Sir Garit.

But even that would not be so bad if she knew her love was alive.

That did it. Eglantine began to unbutton herself.

She was quite good at it now. After all, she'd made a habit of undressing in the garden of late. The thought almost made her smile.

The smile never made it to her lips.

She shrugged off the practical, plain russet gown. Then she fumbled with the bundle she'd brought with her. She'd fled the solar after Osbert and Matheu brought her the news. The walls were trapping her, burying her alive. She needed air, needed the peace of her garden—that was what she had told Osbert before she fled down the stairs. For if her captain knew what she really intended, he would try to stop her.

For one last night, she was the Lady of La Roque. She would not be stopped.

She had a lantern. She set it on the pond rim so she could see what she was about. She had not worn what she drew out of the bundle in an age.

The low light illuminated a flow of lustrous green. It picked up glints of gold too—intricate embroidery around the sleeve tips and hem. It was the most beautiful gown she'd ever owned, and she hadn't worn since it before Con's birth. Eglantine's breath lodged in her throat as she gazed at the object of beauty…and revulsion.

It was the gown she'd worn to wed Ferrand.

She dragged it over her head, praying it still fit. Of course, her wimple did not survive an expanse of heavy silk being hauled over her head, but that was fine. It too had to go.

Once the complexities of the green silk were navigated and Eglantine was satisfied that not only was it buttoned to propriety, but it also fit her to perfection—almost too-great perfection, given the immodest manner it clung to her form—she combed her hair.

She tugged ferociously, paying no heed to the odd knot. Margery normally combed her hair and then arranged it for her, but the maid, Eglantine hoped, was soundly asleep. Besides, her hair needed no braiding or binding tonight. She would wear it loose, virginal and bridelike, about her shoulders.

She almost snorted at the thought, but it threatened to turn into a sob. She swallowed it back. Nearly done.

One more thing. She walked to the little storage room where she stowed all her gardening equipment. She rummaged in it by lantern light until she found a long, slim pole. It was the sort of pole she used to support her plants. She would put it to a different use tonight.

FIRST, SHE CLIMBED the stairs to the battlements. The damned dress threatened to put an end to her plans at every step. It clearly thought a broken neck was the preferable alternative. The hem dragged, heavy with embroidery and tangling her feet.

The men on sentry duty were surprised to see her. The first fellow's eyes kept skittering over her gown, his brows shifting like uneasy caterpillars.

"You will not raise the alarm when you see me exit. Do you understand? Do not ring the bell. Do not alert Osbert. The gate guard will tell him all he needs to know."

The men nodded, incomprehension obvious on their faces.

Then she looked at each in turn. "Thank you for your loyalty, and for all you have done in these past weeks. It will be over soon. God be with you, always."

Eglantine descended the stairs, skirts in hand. She collected her long, slim pole, checked that its attachment was firmly in place, and approached the gatehouse.

The guard took some persuading. He emerged from the depths of the gatehouse, hair awry, and evidently still thought himself asleep when Eglantine bade him open the gate for her.

"What? No. You don't want that, m'lady. No, Osbert's orders. Gate stays bolted and chained. No one in nor out."

"Osbert took his orders from me. I am the Lady of La Roque, and I command that you let me out of this gate. Now."

Pray God she was not already too late.

"But—"

"Open the gate."

"Osbert'll gut me. He'll pull out my innards and use 'em for a bowstring."

"No he won't. You'll tell him I ordered you to. You'll also tell him that he is in command of La Roque if anything happens to me tonight. But you will wait to tell him at first light. Do I have your word?"

The guard muttered and blasphemed, but he gave Eglantine his word. And he opened the gate.

Just a crack. It was sufficient for Eglantine to slip through, her skirts jagging on rough wood and iron. And then she was out of La Roque for the first time in a month.

She stood there a moment, grasping her pole. The bolts rasped back into place behind her. The gate was sealed.

Sir Garit had threatened death to anyone who set foot outside the walls.

Eglantine gripped the pole in both hands and lifted it. Slowly, with just enough speed to unfurl the square of white linen at its peak, she waved her flag from side to side. It was a pole that had last propped up flowers, the most peaceable things in the world. How apt.

Then Eglantine began to descend the path. She employed her flagpole for support in low light. The path was pale, mostly fragmented limestone, which meant it was visible enough. But it was rocky, courtesy of the limestone, and Eglantine was not dressed for a country stroll. Falling would quite spoil her appearance.

For all her care, she nearly did stumble when a man stepped out of the bushes, sword in hand.

"Halt!"

It was an entirely unnecessary command. Eglantine was already rooted to the rocks.

She looked at the man, or what she could see of him under a helm and an enveloping coat of plates.

"Take me to Sir Garit," she said in as firm and calm a voice as she could muster.

RAF EXITED THE stable with all apparent casualness. The very best way to draw attention to himself would be to sneak and slink. Raf was just a drunken minstrel ambling about in the dark. And what did drunken minstrels (or drunks of any stripe, for that matter) do? Why, they were caught by the sudden need to enter a side alley and decorate it with the contents of their guts.

The side alley Raf chose for this important activity just happened to run alongside the house he'd most recently sung to. Pure coincidence, of course.

He leaned against the wall and made the appropriate noises. Necessarily, there was a lack of material evidence, but Raf did not think anyone would bother to check. He was not going to take verisimilitude *that* far.

And as he leaned against the too-solid wall and retched, Raf racked his brain. How was he to extract Con, safely, and without alerting the entirety of the village to his activities?

He could attack and probably dispose of one guard. He might even do it silently. But what if there were more than one?

Raf needed more information. There was no point in just rushing in, sword in hand, hoping to hell he could strike before he was struck. He would watch and wait for a while. He would wander around the back of the house and listen for voices. He would see if there was a back door or a loose shutter. Just maybe an opportunity would present itself, and then Raf would be on hand to seize it, sword in hand.

Men would die tonight, and it was possible one of them would be him.

It would be nice if Sir Garit were another, but that was too much to hope for. The ruinous knight would not be guarding his small captive. A commander had better things to do. Garit would more likely be using some poor villager's mattress to conduct an intimate dance with his lovely dancer.

Raf gave one more heartfelt retch for good measure, and then paused to listen. The village was nearly silent now. Sensible men had sought their borrowed beds. He hoped the delightful Pené was safely in hers. Raf could only pray that Con's guard or guards were similarly inclined.

But there was a noise. Footsteps on the cobbles, drawing ever closer. Raf leaned against the wall, motionless. Damn, maybe he should have attempted to throw something up after all. Had someone grown suspicious of a mere drunk?

Two sets of footsteps, one lighter, one heavier. A strange swish of fabric too, alongside the usual muted jingle of an armed man.

He didn't see the figures until they passed directly by the entrance to his alley. *Passed by*, praise the Lord.

Not that that brief flutter of relief lasted more than an instant.

For in the next moment, Raf was as winded as if a lance had caught him in the kidneys.

A moonlit dream had passed by the entrance to the alley. A vision from years past. Eglantine as he'd first seen her on the day of her marriage. A shimmer of green and gold, with gloriously loose hair. An impossible angel.

Except she wasn't that impossibly perfect image to Raf anymore. He had peeled back the wimple. He knew the woman within now, and she had shattered his notions of perfection. She was more exquisitely real, earthy, prickly, commanding, and deeply loving.

Or, at least, Raf *thought* he knew her.

For the Lady Eglantine was gliding through the village of La Roque in her wedding dress, accompanied by one of Sir Garit's soldiers. She bore a white flag.

She had not waited for proof that Con was alive. She had not waited for Rafèu to rescue her son.

She could not wait to wed Sir Garit.

Chapter Thirty-Two

THE MAN LED Eglantine to one of the nicer houses in the village. A merchant owned it, she recalled. Or, at least, he had.

She strongly doubted he was at home this evening.

A soldier was lounging just outside the door.

"What're you doing out here?" her captor asked him. "Sir Garit throw you out? Didn't fancy an audience, eh?"

The lounger grunted, busily eyeing Eglantine. "Things were getting strange in there." He jerked a thumb at the door. "Stranger than usual."

Her captor guffawed, and Eglantine stiffened. She did not like their tone *or* the implications behind it.

"Take me to Sir Garit," she commanded the door lounger. "I am the Lady Eglantine of La Roque, and this is my village. Open the door."

The fellow straightened. His brows rose more than the rest of him. "You sure you want that, my lady? I—"

"Now," she snapped.

It worked. The guard cast her a bow, rolled an expressive eye at her captor, and then turned to open the door.

Eglantine let her makeshift flag fall to the ground and entered the lion's den.

SIR GARIT WAS in a state of disarray. Which was to say, he wore an undertunic and that was it. No hose. No shoes. Eglantine didn't like to wonder whether he wore any braies. Mercifully, his tunic reached to mid-thigh, and any more compromising view was concealed.

His short hair was also unruly, but the worst of the disarray lay in his expression. Sir Garit of the Ruin was not impassive anymore. There was something wild about his eyes. A barely banked fury.

Perhaps it was something to do with the woman on the bed behind him.

The lovely, dark-haired woman Eglantine had seen from the battlements no longer wore armor. She was dressed in dark red gown, and she reclined on the bed with her wrists and ankles tied. She smiled at Eglantine when she entered the chamber. Like a cat.

Sir Garit did not smile.

"What in hell is this?" he growled, gaze flicking from Eglantine to the man who'd accompanied her down the hill.

She wasn't sure which of them he addressed.

"That is no way to speak to your wife-to-be." It was the woman on the bed who answered. Her voice was melodious and decidedly foreign. She also sounded amused. "Look at her, Ruin. She has put on all her finery just for you, while you—" Her gaze caressed the hem of his tunic. "Well, let us say we do not want a stray breeze to toy with your shirt."

"Be silent, Zhila," Garit growled, then he cast Eglantine the slightest of bows.

Yes, probably best not to bend excessively in that tunic.

There was some kind of noise outside. Scuffling. Garit glanced at her guard and jerked his chin. "Go, Donal. See what's amiss."

The guard departed, and his master turned back to Eglantine. His expression did not look promising.

"To what do I owe this pleasure, Lady Eglantine?"

His tone was even less promising. It was flat and hard, and anything less loverlike was hard to imagine.

So she took a quick breath and just said it. "I come to offer you my surrender, Sir Garit. I will marry you. You may use the chateau as your own. But on two conditions, applicable immediately."

"And what would they be?"

It was barely a question, the intonation was so flat.

Eglantine shivered. This man was rock. Even standing before her in a state of undress, having evidently been engaged in activities no prospective husband ought to be caught doing, he was implacable.

And here she was, proposing to spend the rest of her life with him.

All the same, Eglantine went on: "You will return my son to me, safe and whole. You will swear to keep him safe henceforth. And you will *not* permit the Minstrel Raf to come to any harm."

"No!"

The exclamation came from behind her, from the entrance to the chamber. She knew that voice.

She did not turn, although her heart certainly did. She fixed her gaze upon the knight before her and willed him to reply.

"Do you agree, Sir Garit?"

Behind him on the bed, Zhila tipped back her head and laughed. "Ah, it is better than a play. I would clap, but sadly, I find my hands are tied."

"Do not harm him! Do you promise?" Eglantine cried.

Garit's brows lifted infinitesimally. She saw his gaze slip between her and whoever had just entered the room.

"I, harm him? I rather think it's the other way around, my lady."

Garit gestured, and Eglantine bit her lip and turned. Slowly.

Of course it was Raf standing just inside the doorway. He held a naked sword in his hand. The steel was marred by streaks of red. His chest was rising quickly, and his expression seemed to burn with a dark flame.

"Con is alive, my lady," he said. "I do not know if he is unharmed, but he is alive and conscious."

"Thank you," she whispered.

"This, I gather, is the Minstrel Raf," Sir Garit said. He looked at her, then at her minstrel-knight. "My lady, do you not find it a bit rich to beg favors for your lover as a condition of marriage?"

Another peal of laughter from the bed behind.

Something twisted in Eglantine. She flung a glance at Raf, still standing, sword at the ready. "Seize him," she said. "Seize the bastard!" And she slipped a dagger from her skirts, just in case Garit thought he could attack her.

The ruinous knight was unarmed, almost undressed, and Eglantine knew how skilled Raf was with a sword. She hadn't thought it through, but suddenly it seemed there was a different choice. Perhaps she didn't have to marry this cold Englishman after all.

Raf raised his sword and stalked toward the knight-in-undress.

"Surrender, Sir Garit," he growled. "Give me your bond or I will run you through."

Garit looked at him. "Run me through, minstrel, and you'll still have to deal with the rest of my men."

"And what of your woman?" Eglantine demanded. "Do you care if she is run through?"

She strode to the bed and leveled her dagger at the bound woman's throat.

Zhila chucked. Yes, she actually chuckled. "You miss your mark there, my lady. He'd consider it fair payment. I tried to slit his throat just an hour past."

Garit, though, had stilled. His eyes narrowed upon Eglantine's blade. She hoped he observed she knew how to handle it. She did, after nearly a month of weapons training. But she had never thought to use it like this, to kill a defenseless woman.

Sir Garit was about to capitulate, she could see. They had beaten the English knight. Someone would die in this room if he did not surrender to Raf. Perhaps Garit was unconcerned about an attempt on his own life, but on the woman's? Unaccountably, the knife at Zhila's throat seemed to give him pause.

They had won. Garit would surrender, and she would get Con back. She would demand the English leave La Roque. The siege was over.

Then there were noises at the outer door and everything went to hell.

Men burst into the house. There were shouts. Raf whirled and slammed the chamber door shut. He flung the bolt across. Not that it would hold them back for long.

And when Raf turned to face his enemy again, it was to see that Garit too held a sword.

The knight had not wasted Raf's moment of distraction, and there was nothing Eglantine could do about it.

Heaven preserve them. The flicker of hope had been extinguished. What now?

Chapter Thirty-Three

"PUT UP YOUR blades," Garit barked. "My men see you thus, and they will not stop to ask questions."

The dagger was shivering in Eglantine's hand. He was right. But surely…?

"I challenge you to a duel, knight," Raf said. "The victor wins the right to the lady's hand."

Eglantine and the woman she threatened erupted simultaneously.

"No, I am not a *thing* to be fought over!"

Zhila just laughed. "Pity you'd not live to sing the tale, minstrel. Ah, it's the stuff legends are made of—the naked knight and the minstrel."

"Oh, I'll let him put his clothes on. I don't fancy the distraction should he go arse up," Raf retorted.

Garit made no response to that magnanimous offer. He cast Eglantine a considering look. "Your hand is unsteady, my lady. Pray do not mar my assassin. You will not like the consequences."

"I'll slit her throat if you do not guarantee Raf's safety," Eglantine snarled, hoping to God she sounded like she meant it.

"Ah, I see my wife-to-be will brook no rivals." Garit shifted his grip on his sword. "Perhaps I ought not to either."

The door to the chamber was shuddering under repeated blows. There was shouting on the other side. The voices of many men.

"A duel, Garit. Fair conditions. Your men must stay out of it," Raf said.

There was a tense edge to his voice. Time was running out, and he knew it.

"And why would I agree to that? A belted knight fight a mere minstrel for a noble lady's hand? She will never marry you, man. She would be a fool to do so. Lay down your sword and I may spare you. My men will be through the door any moment now."

"He is no mere minstrel! He is—"

"No, Eglantine. It does not matter." Raf's voice overrode hers.

Garit eyed Raf speculatively. "So. Are you worth a ransom, not-minstrel? Should I capture you rather than eviscerate you?"

"You are honor-bound to fight me," Raf snapped. "Else you are no true knight. I have offered you a challenge. Answer it!"

Garit stirred. He glanced at the door. It was shuddering convulsively. He glanced at the woman on the bed. There seemed to be a question in his eyes. What it asked, Eglantine had no idea.

"You question my honor," he said slowly, as if he had all the time in the world. "That would be reason enough to meet you in combat. Minstrel, or whatever you are." Then at last the cold blue eyes looked at Eglantine. "But there is no point. I have no wish to win this duel you propose. My honor is engaged elsewhere."

Before Eglantine could demand to know what he meant, the door burst open. Raf sprang aside as men with swords poured through.

"Stop!" Garit bellowed. "Put up your arms! I will have no bloodshed in my bedchamber. Christ, can none of you wait till I put my clothes on?"

A scattering of laughter. Some of it came from the woman beneath Eglantine's knife. She glanced at Zhila. Did a blade at her throat bother her not at all?

But at least the horde paused. All the same, there were far too many naked swords in the room now. The place was more of a smithy than a bedchamber.

"Be silent, all of you!" Garit barked.

As an order, it was mostly redundant. Everyone was eyeing each other warily, silently.

"An attempt has been made on my life tonight," Garit said. He did not look at anyone in particular when he said it. "A fresh burden has been placed upon my honor. Our plans have changed."

Raf stood beside her now, close to the bed's head. Cornered, with a company of men between them and the door. Eglantine still held the dagger over the bound woman's throat.

"Ain't just you who's had an attempt on his life," called one of the men. "You seen the mess in the street? Reckon this kaynard stuck Donal through the thigh, and Tommo's stone dead."

"Ah." Garit glanced at Raf. "So the minstrel can fight. I hope you are worth a ransom after all. I would have compensation for those men."

"I will pay your damned compensation. In fact, I will pay you to leave altogether, knight," Raf ground out. "Leave the lady. Return her son safely, and I give my word I will pay you royally for it."

Garit raised a blond brow. "A minstrel with money, then. A rare beast. What, do you carry around the worth of a chateau in your lute case?" He shook his head. "Even if you did, I would not take it. I have wealth enough, minstrel. What I need is a fortress to keep it and my men safe. I offered the lady honorable marriage. I am not a thief. I do not steal castles from unprotected women."

"No, you force them to marry you instead," Eglantine said.

Garit looked at her in evident surprise. "Of course. Noble-women do not choose their husbands, my lady. If they want love, they avail themselves of, say, a handy minstrel…but discreetly, so as not to bring dishonor upon their husband."

She could not look at Raf. Yes, she had acted much as Garit

said—she *had* availed herself of a handy minstrel. At the outset. Until he had turned into so much more. It wasn't that he was a vicomte, he was simply more.

He was everything.

And she had to make sure he came out of this alive, even if it meant she never saw him again.

"You want a castle?" she snapped. "Marry me, then. Take La Roque. But you must swear that Raf goes free and unharmed. And my son…my son will inherit. You will keep him safe."

Raf made an inarticulate noise by her side. She did not look at him.

Garit's icy eyes traveled from her, to Raf, and finally lingered on the woman on the bed.

The silence stretched. Something touched Eglantine's hand—the one that didn't hold the dagger to Zhila's throat. Raf's fingers twined with hers, long, strong fingers, warm and reassuring. They gave a gentle squeeze.

The reassurance was in vain. She would never feel his hands upon her again. This was the end.

"No," said Garit. He was looking at the dark-haired woman. "My plans have changed." Then he deigned to look at Eglantine. "Much as I appreciate your proposal of marriage, my lady, I must decline. I find there are other things I need more than a castle now."

Eglantine gasped in outrage. *She* propose to *him*? Did the bastard think she *wanted* to marry him?

Then the outrage evaporated in a flare of hope.

Mad hope, unwarranted hope. He didn't need her castle; he didn't want her. What, then?

"Now, if you will remove your dagger from my prisoner's throat, I will see to it that your son is returned to you." Garit glanced up at one of the goggling men. "Dickon, fetch the boy."

The man left, but Eglantine did not remove the dagger.

"What do you want?" she whispered.

"I want to put my clothes on without an audience, and I want an unmarred assassin. But apart from that, I want nothing from you, my lady."

Raf stepped forward. "What is your intention, knight? Be plain."

Again, Garit looked to the woman on the bed. "My intention is to leave La Roque. Tomorrow. Or is that today? All my men—and this charming creature—will accompany me. I do not believe we will return. We have business elsewhere." Then he looked directly at Raf. "You, minstrel, owe my men compensation. The two you carved up have families."

"You, Sir Garit, owe *my* people compensation," Eglantine retorted. "You have thrown my villagers out of their homes. You have devoured their substance. What of that?"

The knight regarded her passionlessly. "True enough. Though that is the way of war."

"As is the killing of men in self-defense," she retorted.

"Perhaps we should call ourselves even, then. Nothing owed on either side."

She stared at him. He was coolly bargaining over a month of siege as if it were simply a matter of balancing some merchant's scales.

"But be warned, my lady." Garit's voice took on a steely edge, and his gaze dropped to her hand. "If you damage my prisoner, I will consider all negotiation void."

Ah. Eglantine's dagger had drooped nearer the bound woman's throat in her distraction.

Raf's hand closed over the one gripping the dagger, steadying it, but not steering it away. *We do this together*, his hand said. *But it is your choice.*

Then his lips spoke too.

"Look, my lady. Con is here."

He was. A soldier shepherded him through the crowd of men at the door. Con looked bewildered, a little scared, but entirely whole.

Then he saw her.

Eglantine let the dagger clatter to the floor and held out her arms.

THEY REMAINED IN the village for the rest of the night. Garit said they were free to go, but there was no way in hell that Raf was going to risk walking back up that hill in the dark with a company of English soldiers infesting La Roque. Not with Eglantine and Con by his side. Even if Garit were as good as his word and no English longbow shot at them, Raf couldn't guarantee the reactions of those on the battlements. No, there had been enough dancing about in the dark for one night.

So they stayed in a small house in the village, one of the few that Englishmen had not overrun. It was a one-room affair with a curtained bed at one end. Raf had Con help him kindle a fire in the cold hearth. Small boys and fire, an irresistible combination. Con was effectively distracted, his mind diverted from the events of the last day. So Raf hoped.

Eglantine was on the bed, knees drawn up against her torso, arms wrapped around them. Her dress was a pool of green and gold on the rough, undyed coverlet. Her dagger lay beside her.

"If I may, my lady?"

She looked up at him, uncomprehending. Raf's gut twisted. Too much—she'd had to endure far too much tonight.

He did not explain further. He simply climbed onto the bed, settled beside her, and wrapped an arm about her rigid shoulders.

She stayed stiff a moment longer, her gaze fixed on Con. The boy was prodding the fire, making sparks whirl into the darkness. Then Eglantine subsided with a shiver and leaned her head against his shoulder, still holding her knees tight.

"That's a pretty dress," he said, aiming for light conversation.

"No, it isn't," she told his shoulder. "It's hideous. I'm never going to wear it again. I'll give it to whomever owns this house.

As compensation." A pause. "If they ever come back."

"You wore it when you wed Ferrand, didn't you?" he said softly, hoping Con was too preoccupied to overhear. "I remember. You were glorious in it. No, *you* are glorious, whatever your clothing."

"I was going to wear it to wed a second husband tonight," she said. "I thought it appropriate."

He stroked her long, loose hair. "You do not have to wear it ever again."

He hoped she'd understand the message beneath the words.

"My father arranged the marriage, you know," she went on. "He let me meet Ferrand before the wedding. He did not want me to marry a stranger. If I detested Ferrand, he said, he'd reconsider the marriage. I did not. Not immediately." A sigh. He felt her shoulders rise and fall. "He was a good father."

"Was?"

"He died in the war. Stupid, really. He brokered my marriage to make peace. A joining of French and English on the edges of French-English territory. And all I wanted was to return to England. I hated France, and what it had done to me."

Ah. He knew that, but it still scraped its unsheathed claws across his skin.

Con looked up. "You don't hate France. I'm half French and Raf is all French. You like Raf, don't you?" He waved a glowing stick about for emphasis.

Eglantine made a little choking noise, and Raf held her closer.

"Shove that stick back in the fire before you set the whole place alight, Your Grace. Your mother doesn't have to decide what she does and doesn't like tonight. You've caused her enough trouble already."

Con immediately looked contrite and shoved as required. Then he clambered onto the bed and nestled up to his mother on the other side to Raf. Eglantine released her knees and wrapped her arms about Con instead.

"Sorry, Mother," came the muffled words. "I wanted to see

Sir Garit, so I hid on the battlements. I wanted to look at my enemy, but Zhila saw *me*. That lady with black hair. She came and talked to me. She can do amazing things, you know. She's so good at climbing. She showed me how to climb the walls. She made it look so easy, but…I fell. I tore my tunic, and then she picked me up and took me to Sir Garit."

"Were you hurt?" Eglantine said quickly.

She'd already inspected Con pretty thoroughly when she first got her hands on him, in front of everyone. She'd yanked up his shirt in the time-honored way of mothers who give not a hen's tooth for the dignity of their children and only care that they are unharmed.

"Only a bit. Just a scratch," Con said airily. "Don't fuss, Mother. But…I *am* sorry. I shouldn't have left the chateau, I know. You came looking for me, didn't you? You and Raf."

Rafèu felt Eglantine breathe deep. *Yes, she came looking for you. She was willing to do anything to get you back in one piece. She would marry against her will just to spare you and your inheritance.*

But now was not the time to say all that. Later, Con would know. Recriminations could come later. Raf was simply glad to be here, holding the woman he loved. The woman he'd almost lost. And her pestilential but endearing son.

Con nattered on for a bit, snuggled against his mother. He talked of a man who'd sung Robin Hood songs outside his prison window, how it was just like something Robin himself would do, just before he attempted a daring rescue. Eglantine turned to look at him then.

Ah, he longed to drop a kiss on those questioning lips. But not in front of the boy. And not tonight, when men had already tried to twist her to their will under threat of violence.

Including him.

Eventually Con's words slurred and slowed and eventually ceased.

"Is he asleep?" Raf murmured.

He could see by the firelight that Eglantine was not. Even

without light, he would know. There was still a tension in her shoulders as she leaned against him.

"Yes," she breathed. "Are we safe? Will he really let us go?"

It was the same question that had been battering his brain ever since their audience with Sir Garit. Would a man truly lay siege to a castle for near on a month and then, just when he had its chatelaine and her son in his power, abandon the whole exercise? It made no sense. Unless, as Sir Garit said, something else had occurred to change the Englishman's mind. Some*one* else?

If it had not, Vicomte Rafèu would have fought him, whether Garit agreed to a duel or not. He would have fought him then and there, before Eglantine, before Garit's men.

And Raf would have died, even if he'd killed the knight first. Garit's men would have cut him down in front of Eglantine. At least she'd been spared that.

"He seems like a man of his word," Raf said slowly. "Even his notion of marriage seems to have arisen from a warped sense of honor. He couldn't just steal a castle from a noble lady—he had to marry it."

She gave a little laugh, barely audible. "Well, he can marry La Roque, then. And bed it too, if it takes his fancy. Better it than me. Ferrand wanted my money, Garit wanted my castle. For heaven's sake, it makes a woman feel entirely superfluous."

I only want you. You could come to me in rags—naked, preferably—and without a single stone to your name, and I would only ever want you.

It was what he wanted to say, but now was not the time or place. No more pressure on her tonight.

Besides, she had asked about safety.

He laid his cheek on her soft, loose hair and prayed he spoke the truth.

"He will let us go. Listen. I can hear his men gathering their things even now. They will leave at first light."

That, or the company was preparing for a final assault on La

Roque, now it had its lady and heir captive.

"Hmm."

She was right not to be convinced. Raf could do nothing but hold her close and watch the door as the night stretched on.

He could not tell her he loved her, that he would never leave her, or that a month of the most delightful dallying had done nothing to change his mind. Precisely the opposite, in fact. She was too vulnerable right now. She needed no more coercion by men. She should determine her own future.

Chapter Thirty-Four

E GLANTINE NUDGED HER palfrey along the track between the river lands. Raf rode behind her, still watchful, even with Sir Garit definitively gone from the region. Yet it was as if her minstrel-knight was not there at all, for the path was too narrow for him to ride alongside her. The soil here was too valuable to waste in wide tracks. There wasn't much flat, rich land around La Roque. The fertile river flats were divided into strips, each maintained by different peasants—or they had been before the English had arrived. Most of the grain had been harvested before the peasants fled. Not that it had done the peasant harvesters any good. Garit and company had simply helped themselves to the plentiful stores.

But her people were coming back. A few were at work in the strips even now, repairing the damage to their land incurred by a company's worth of horses roaming at will over them. Eglantine had stopped and spoken to them. Raf, too, had asked questions. It was evident he knew about the working of a chateau's land.

Of course he did. He was the Vicomte of Bruniquel, a sizable chateau to the north. She tended to forget he was anything but her minstrel…her Raf. But he would be returning to his vicomtely duties soon. He was no longer trapped in a castle under siege. He was no longer engaged in a lover's quest.

Raf had not mentioned marriage in the days since Sir Garit

had left.

He had not mentioned love. He had barely even touched her.

Not that he'd had much chance, Eglantine reflected. She had been occupied from dawn to dusk these last three days, furiously setting things to rights around La Roque. She'd even admitted a serving man to her garden to see to the watering and other basic tasks. She'd simply had too many other things to do.

But it meant that her garden was no longer a private haven. Raf could not meet her there to assist her…among other things.

Anyway, their month's trial was up.

Her minstrel-knight's quest was over—and what had it achieved?

Let us indulge this lust, she had said. *Let us wear the glamour of love out and see what emerges at its end. I contend you will be heartily glad to leave me and La Roque at its conclusion.*

The conclusion was upon them, and Eglantine barely saw the fields around her, for the truth was so blindingly clear. Raf might be heartily glad to leave her, but when he did so, he would take her heart with him. They had indulged their desire, and it had been utterly delightful, and what was the result?

She knew him.

She had learned who he was by his actions, the way he made love to her, and the consideration with which he treated her. And others. Raf was a romantic, an idealist who revered beauty and music and hated war, but there was a steely core to him. He was an artist with the sword, and he would use it if he had to. He would train others to defend themselves. He would have laid down his life to protect Eglantine and Con. Yet he would never hurt her—not knowingly.

But he *would* hurt her when he left. There was no more reason for him to stay. Just as Ferrand before him, Raf had conflated lust with love, and now his interest was worn out. Only Raf was too chivalrous, too essentially caring to let her know it.

There had been no more words of love, no more *canzos* in the evening hall. Robin Hood, however, had been given quite a going-over in the last few days. It turned out Osbert knew a ballad concerning the outlaw and a potter, of all things. He had decided that Raf was worthy of bestowing this gem of English culture upon, and Con had demanded reiterations, *con gusto*.

Yet Raf had slung his lute over his back when they set out this afternoon. Hardly a practical accessory for surveying the fields.

They had nearly reached the end of the flat lands. The hills closed in upon the river here, forested and rocky. Her people used the lands for foraging their pigs, for hunting, for gathering firewood and wild foods too. Paths wound up into the hills. One opened before them now.

"I came this way when I rode to La Roque," Raf said from behind her. "It was hotter then. I stopped in a grove when my nag threatened to expire. It was a pretty place. Come, I will show you."

RAF LED THE way now. Eglantine had ridden here before, sometimes with Con. But it felt different now. The cool green shadows closed about them, and Eglantine followed a dream into the woods. A dream with long, dark hair and a lute slung over his back.

And it was a tenuous, magical dream, for this was likely the last time. Her last moments alone with Raf. She had better make the most of them.

She hadn't seen the grove before. It lay at the end of a little side path in a dip between the hills. A trickle of water emerged from a rocky cleft, besides which had been created a shrine. A weathered wooden cross was propped there, and little offerings hung around, carvings, scraps of material, prayers for a better future. The air was hushed. There was no sound but trickling water and the twitter of birds.

"This is a holy place," she whispered.

Raf smiled up at her and lifted his arms. He had already dismounted. His horse was lipping at tufts of grass.

That smile. It still melted her. Dark eyes gazing into hers with all the depth and desire in the world. And kindness.

He was too kind to tell her that it was over.

All the same, she freed her feet from the stirrups and slipped into his arms. Just to feel his hands about her one more time.

"And beautiful, don't you think?"

The way he looked at her when he said that, she could almost think…

No.

"Yes," she murmured, and turned to the little cascade to cool her hands beneath its trickle.

The soft resonance of lute strings made her turn. Raf had seated himself on the ground, his back to a gnarled tree, and was cradling his lute. He was tuning it.

"What are you doing?"

Silly question, given the context, but Raf answered with a smile. Strange, there was something hesitant about that smile.

"I have composed a *canzo*, my lady. No ears but mine have heard it thus far. A minstrel sings of the beauties of nature, among other things. I thought I would give it its first airing here, amidst the forest. For an audience of one. Do you object?"

"A *canzo*—a love song in the *langue d'oc*. I'm sure you find it a relief to revert to French after abusing your tongue for so long with English."

Her tone was meant to be light and teasing, but the effect sounded barbed.

"It is not in the *langue d'oc*, my lady. Perhaps then I should simply call it a love song. But I have said enough. I will let the music speak for itself."

Eglantine nodded, and settled herself close by on a smooth stone. It would not do to dirty her skirts on the grass and leaves. She no longer wore plain russet gowns. She'd chosen a more elegant overdress today—fine green wool in a surcoat style, cut away at the sides. It was a more revealing design than she'd worn for years. No more primly confined widowhood for her. She would no longer define herself by Ferrand's life or death. She had even discarded her wimple for a simple floating veil.

Whatever the future, Eglantine would shut herself away no longer. The garden door was open—no more *hortus conclusus*. She would explore more delightful groves like this one. Con would like that, she knew.

But now there was the rippling music. And Raf's velvet-deep tones, singing in English:

I thought I knew so much about love
But how little I really knew…

Eglantine shrank inside. Her heart clenched into a tight fist. He had composed these words for a reason. He was telling her that he had been wrong. He had thought he was in love, but now he knew better.

He sang on. He wove a garden with his words. There was a weeping tamarisk tree, there were tender green seedlings, and there were roses. Especially roses. Raf seemed to have a fascination with them. But he sang of the sweetbrier, the wild eglantine. That plant did not grow in her garden. It was too thorny and hard to tame. Then again, Raf probably didn't know one rose from the next.

Its thorns have pierced my heart
Its sweet apple scent haunts my dreams

Oh. Maybe Raf did know what a brier rose was. Its leaves did smell like apple. She'd make a gardener out of him yet.

No, she wouldn't. He was leaving. And now he was singing of a rose that should not be pruned, or captured within garden walls, or trained to any man's whim. The wild eglantine should twine untrammeled. It did not belong to anyone.

She barely heard the music anymore. The words seeped into

her, and their meaning entered her blood.

Now she knew why he had uttered no words of love for days, why he had barely touched her, and why there was no hint of a mention of marriage.

The song told her. She was the wild rose that Raf refused to capture and constrain. And now she knew what she had to do.

THE LOVE SONG ended. The lute notes died in the leafy air.

Eglantine stood. She walked over to her minstrel-knight and took the lute from his hands. Gently, she laid it to one side.

Raf said nothing. He had sung all he needed to say. He simply watched her.

She crouched down. She lifted her skirts and, kneeling, straddled his outstretched legs. She settled herself on his lap and took his face in her hands.

"May I?" she asked, gazing into those bottomless black eyes, feeling the tingle of stubble beneath her palm, the strength of his jaw.

A flicker of a smile. "You may."

Eglantine kissed him.

She lowered her lips to his and held nothing back. He was hers for the taking, and she gave all of herself. Mouths united, tongues entwined, arms cradling.

By the time she withdrew, she was trembling. The force of want was shivering her apart. But it wasn't just physical need. She wanted him, *all* of him.

"I have a proposition for you, Rafèu of Bruniquel," she said.

He smiled. "Another quest?"

"Perhaps. Yet this will be no light digging of manure, so consider carefully. But first, listen. Be my priest, for I must confess to you in this holy place."

"I don't want to be your priest," he said huskily. "Priests

should not contemplate the sort of things I am contemplating right now."

He slipped his fingers through her hair, dislodged the circlet that secured her veil and flipped it into the leaves. The veil followed.

"Well then, just listen. For I must confess." She looked at him steadily.

It was hard, so hard to peel back the protected layers of her soul. But it had to be done, whatever the outcome.

"I have put you to the test. I declared love was an illusion born of lust. Perhaps it is at times. My experience would certainly suggest so." She felt him still beneath her. "But not *this* experience. That is what I must confess. And know that I put you under no obligation when I do so."

She paused, drew in a quick breath, and then said it. "I love you, Rafèu. Absolutely. No illusions, no fleeting fancy—I love all of you. I offer myself to you without reserve. Now, you may leave me and never return if that is what you wish."

She was definitely trembling now, her voice as well as her limbs. No defenses left. Utterly vulnerable.

She could say no more. She waited.

His voice, soft, dark velvet, slipped over her senses:

"You are the rose that has twined itself about my heart. I fell in love with a dream from a distance, years ago. I came to woo a dream, but I have discovered more. So much more." He smiled then, and cupped her face. "Reality. My sometimes-prickly reality. Yes, I find I prefer a rose with thorns rather than a soft and pampered bloom."

She arched her brows. "A well-manured rose?"

His smile widened. "Only if I get to wash it."

She kissed his smiling lips again, and found hers were smiling too.

But there was more to say:

"Will you marry me, Vicomte Rafèu? Will you take me and my son back to Bruniquel?"

"No, my love." He shook his head. "I will marry you and live with you wherever you want. Even in England, if that's what you wish."

The light glimmered down between the leaves, green and gold. Beautiful beyond a dream. He was her reality.

Eglantine paused, trying to grasp his words, the enormity of what he offered.

"Thank you," she said at last. "But you know, I realize now I hated France because I felt trapped here. I was trapped into marriage by a love that proved false. Even after Ferrand's death, I had to stay here to safeguard what was Con's. But I was also trapped inside. I hid myself away. I put myself under siege. I will not do so anymore. I think I'll give Osbert command of La Roque and put more men-at-arms at his disposal than before. He can safeguard the place. I do not need to live here, so long as I can return every few months. Besides, I am curious to see Bruniquel. Does it have a flower garden?"

Raf made a face. "None to speak of. Can't say I thought about plants much before." Then he grinned. "But now I find myself strangely intrigued by them. Not just roses, either. I am charmed by the way you create beauty from manure and buckets of water, my love. It even inspires me to song."

"Liar." She shoved at his chest. Of course he did not budge. He was leaning against a tree.

"No lie at all, my sweet, prickly rose. I am inspired to help you create a garden at Bruniquel, if you will guide my blundering fingers."

His fingers seemed not to need any guidance, so far as Eglantine was concerned. They had trailed through her hair and were now tracing her neck, her collarbone, and dipping ever lower. A shiver took her. His fingers slipped beneath her neckline.

"Will you make an immodest woman of me, Rafèu of Bruniquel, here in the hills? *Ah!*"

His fingers had brushed over one aching nipple.

"I'm afraid so. It's been too long, my love. Three whole days.

I pray no peasant comes to make an inconvenient offering to the shrine." Her minstrel-knight loosened her bodice and dipped his mouth to the tantalized breast.

Eglantine gasped and arched her back.

Inconvenient it would be, but she really didn't care. She wanted all of him, *now*. They would make their own offering of love in the grove. They were no longer besieged and confined, trapped by the past or by stone walls. She would dare to love her minstrel-vicomte, come what may.

Even if it was a curious peasant.

About the Author

Cara Hogarth writes historical romances set in a medieval past full of castles, knights, and damsels who definitely don't need rescuing. Her stories sparkle with passion, adventure, and a touch of humour. Cara studied medieval history at university before realising she much preferred writing fiction to research papers. Now she puts her historical training to good use by underpinning her romances with plenty of research. Her stories are usually set in fourteenth-century England and France.

Cara was born in Salisbury, England. She grew up on a sheep farm, but has since worked as a cake cook, in a fun fair, in a library, and as an academic tutor and editor. She now lives in the wilds of Western Australia with a book-eating ragdoll cat.

Website: www.carahogarth.net
email: cara@carahogarth.net
Facebook: facebook.com/carahogarth

9 781961 275195